Out of the Darkness

Edited by
Carol Hightshoe

WolfSinger Publications ⌇ Security, Colorado

Acknowledgements

The Beast of Primordial Fire © 2022 by Jennifer Lee Rossman
A Good Day Gone Bad © 2022 by Steven Lente
The Perfect Life © 2022 by db mcneill
Eclipse © 2022 by Andrew Gates
Broken Ones © 2022 by Natasha Morningstarr
DNF © 2022 by Stetson Ray
Finding Wonder © 2022 by Demi Utley
First Published in *The Green Shoe Sanctuary* – Sep 2022
The Ladies from the Outside © 2022 by Marianne Xenos
Izzy Tells no Lies © 2018 by P. James Norris
First Published in Fantasia Divinity Magazine – Feb 2018
Love Takes Wing © 2022 by Corinna Underwood
School © 2022 by Justin Zipprich
Strawberries © 2022 by LCW Allingham
There was Never Enough Time © 2022 by H. N. Hunt
First Published in MARY – 2022
Tatters © 2022 by Leanbh Pearson
Fifty Matches © 2022 by Gregory J. Wolos
The Dark © 2022 by Brian Rothstein
Angel of Death © 2017 by P. James Norris
First Published in Moon Magazine – Dec 2017
In a Sea of Night © 2022 by J. T. Seate
The Slipping Away © 2019 by Lee Conrad
First Published on StoryStar – 2019
Suppressed Shadows, Silver Scars © 2022 by Malina Douglas
Unborn © 2022 by Katie Kent
This Man Paul © 2022 by RF Thomas
First Published in Scars – 2020

Cover Art copyright 2022 © Lee Ann Barlow

ISBN 978-1-944637-21-7
Printed and bound in the United States of America

Table of Contents

The Beast of Primordial Fire – Jennifer Lee Rossman   1

A Good Day Gone Bad – Steven Lente   9

The Perfect Life – db mcneill   22

Eclipse – Andrew Gates   29

Broken Ones – Natasha Morningstarr   51

DNF – Stetson Ray   61

Finding Wonder – Demi Utley   76

The Ladies from the Outside – Marianne Xenos   86

Izzy Tells No Lies – P. James Norris   89

Love Takes Wing – Corinna Underwood   103

School – Justin Zipprich   106

Strawberries – LCW Allingham   113

There was Never Enough Time – HN Hunt   133

Tatters – Leanbh Pearson   135

Fifty Matches – Gregory J. Wolos   139

The Dark – Brian Rothstein   157

Angel of Death – P. James Norris   164

In a Sea of Night – J. T. Seate   177

The Slipping Away – Lee Conrad   186

Suppressed Shadows, Silver Scars – Malina Douglas   193

Unborn – Katie Kent   205

This Man Paul – RF Thomas   213

The Beast of Primordial Fire

Jennifer Lee Rossman

Samu jerked awake, staring at the blackness of the cave wall as she strained to hear anything over the heartbeat in her ears. She didn't dare move a single muscle, even as her lungs begged for oxygen. Something had woken her, something—

There it was again.

Beyond the shallow breaths of her family around her, under the rustle of grass in the wind and insects singing in the night. Footsteps, so deliberately quiet they existed only as the sound of gravel rubbing together under massive paws.

Samu's family slept lightly, conditioned by nature to wake at any sign of danger, each with their back to the cave entrance. They must have been scared, but they still had to breathe, and Samu cautiously matched their breaths as she watched the wall in front of her.

No shadows leapt and danced. She heard no snap of flames, smelled no smoke.

It was not the Beast.

Did her family know this? The children in her generation had to know; they were better at thinking abstractly than their parents. A necessity, to outwit the predators in their new home.

But no one said a word. Night was when the Beast roamed, listening for prey.

Samu thought she recognized the growl. It was only dogs. With their spears, Father and the uncles could fend them off easily.

But they didn't. To do so would mean facing the outside, where they might catch a fleeting glimpse of the Beast, and to see her was to die.

And so the family closed their eyes and ignored the struggle as one of their own who slept near the entrance was killed by the wild dogs.

Samu did not know if the others cried themselves to sleep that night, or if the echoes of the death forever rang in their ears like they did in hers.

~ * ~

The next night, Mother was gone.

Samu reached out until she touched the cool cave wall, swinging her arms in a frantic attempt to find her. Surely Mother had just rolled over, or snuggled up with an auntie to stave off the chill, but her hand found only floor and wall.

She couldn't have been eaten. No animal was that quiet, and the uncles and elders slept at the front to protect the mothers and children.

Samu's shadow grew before her as a faint orange glow flickered on the wall.

The Beast.

Samu contracted every muscle, making herself small, and held her breath as footsteps crunched in the grass outside. She fought the urge to turn and look until long after the glow faded. Her heart leapt at the silhouette of her mother standing unharmed at the mouth of the cave, beautifully brown and hairy like Samu, her stomach round with the pregnancy that made her need to go out with increasing frequency. Dirtying the cave made people sick; they knew that now.

But something was wrong; she walked with heavy steps, her eyes haunted and unfocused.

No.

No, no, no.

She had seen the Beast.

Samu let out a cry of anguish before she could stop herself, and woke the others as Mother tried to sneak back in. She watched, helpless, as they cast her out.

To see the Beast was to die, not by her teeth and claws but by the inevitable disasters she brought with her.

Once your eyes had graced her crackling mane of flames, the stories warned, you were marked. The Beast would find you, and she would bring death and devastation to the entire village.

The stories told of how she burned down the trees where they lived, back when humans were small apes. How she brought the fires that separated families, driving them to migrate further from home. How she scorched the plants they ate, starving them into inventing tools to hunt and kill.

It was only right for Mother to leave. It was the way. A tradition passed down from the elders before the elders. The Beast would find her, so let her find a single person alone in the wild, no family around to suffer for Mother's indiscretion.

It was the right thing.

So why did it hurt so much?

Mother didn't fight to stay, or even to say goodbye. Samu watched her disappear into the tall grass, not caring if she caught a glimpse of the Beast in the vast, thick darkness.

Samu *wanted* to see the Beast, to look into the flames and see her fate in the dancing tongues. And she knew, somewhere in the depths of the furious storm inside her heart, her fate would show her killing the Beast.

~ * ~

The next night, Samu donned the thickest fur cloak she could find and armed herself with a spear.

Both were new, made with skills unfathomable in the elders' youth. Stone sharpening, to make spearheads and to cut the flesh from carcasses. Knot tying, to make fur into clothes and to secure the spear.

The elders, and the elders before them, hadn't needed such skills in the trees, but the beast had burned them down, forced humans to face new dangers on the ground. Those who learned to adapt survived.

Samu knew this because someone, ages and ages back, had turned grunts into words and words into stories. But she couldn't use verbal language to explain where she was going; her voice would attract predators and her family would try to stop her anyway. But she still wanted them to know, when they woke up and found her missing, why she had left.

So she found some berries, crushed them in her hand. She dipped a finger in the juice and dragged it along the wall, leaving a streak on the rock just visible in the moonlight. More streaks, and the crude image of a person formed before her eyes. She added a line for her spear, being thrown through the air.

The Beast proved more difficult to draw, as no one alive had seen it. She knew it had a flaming mane, but made up the rest. The lean body of an antelope. A snake's tail. She gave it an extra head, because the stories always grew more fearsome with each telling, and now it was her story to tell.

Below it all, she pressed a handprint.

It was a story in pictures, and it said, "This is me, Samu. I am a brave warrior. I will kill the Beast."

She licked the tart berries from her hand and stepped out into the night.

She did not feel like a brave warrior.

~ * ~

The cool night prickled her skin, seeping through the fur to chill her in a way she'd never experienced. She had never known a night without the warmth of sleeping bodies around her.

Stars and the sounds of crickets filled the air, lights and music that were dulled by the cave but flourished in the open savannah.

No walls, no roof. No safety.

She gripped her spear tighter, whipping her head at every sound. She felt eyes on her back, but the blanketing night refused to give up the Beast's location.

A lifetime of stories swirled in Samu's mind, growing into monstrous fears that gnawed at her gut and whispered in her ear.

Turn around. Run, fast as you can.

But Mother might still be alive; if the Beast hadn't gotten her. She had to keep going.

Prints and scratches marked the ground, but Samu was not a hunter like Father, and didn't know how to read the signs. So she did something she had been told never to do, something dangerous. Deadly.

She called out into the night.

She *taunted* the Beast.

"Come and get me!" she shouted, shattering the stillness and sending hidden birds squawking through the sky. "I will fight you, Beast, and I will wear your skin! You don't scare me!"

In the silence that followed, her heart drummed in her ears.

Then she heard it, the snapping roar of fire.

She turned, every instinct screaming inside her, and she locked eyes with the Beast.

The creature stood on an outcropping, gazing down at her domain, a bright spot in a darkness that stretched into eternity.

And she was beautiful.

The face of a lioness melded seamlessly into a sleek, long body like nothing Samu had ever seen. She stood tall on four spindly, hoofed legs, and her many tails whipped back and forth.

But her *flames*.

Her flames were more than a mere mane. They enveloped her, dancing down her body and reaching high into the air, glowering orange and yellow tongues hungering for death and destruction. She was fire itself.

She crackled, roared. The sounds of her power filled the valley, made the dry grass quiver.

It would only take a single burning ember. It had happened before, and had driven the family from their homes, chasing them as they spread across the continent.

The Beast looked down at Samu. Their eyes met.

Neither moved, but in her mind Samu saw the Beast growing closer, larger, until nothing existed but the inferno. It swirled around her, its heat more stifling and choking than the sun. Brighter, too, but in the searing light dark shapes flickered and resolved themselves into an image of Samu's family, safe at home in their cave.

They slept, unaware of an encroaching pack of dogs, driven to the cave by wildfires. Not just dogs. Leopards, hyenas. All starved to the point of desperation. There would be no survivors.

Another image. The same cave, but no predators. Mother was safe, holding her new baby.

Though neither the Beast nor her flames spoke, Samu understood. This was a negotiation.

The Beast did not hunt. The Beast simply waited for people to sacrifice themselves. If Samu went with her, no harm would come to her family. Mother would be returned.

As quick as it had sprung into existence, the whirlwind of flames died down. The Beast stared at her, gaze unwavering, waiting for an answer.

Indecision struck Samu, left her breathless and immobile. Mother hadn't been harmed yet. She could *save* her, bring her and the baby home.

But what of the rest of the family, and the families that would follow? Her new baby sibling, and the children they would have one day. They would still be hunted, afraid to make a sound or let their line-of-sight wander into the night for fear of seeing the Beast.

Samu tightened her hand around the spear's wooden shaft and looked the Beast square in the eye.

"No," she said. "This ends now."

~ * ~

The Beast had been a hunter since the dawn of time, and she did not like being hunted.

Her hooves thudded against the ground, leaving scorch marks on the earth. She glanced over her shoulder, panic in her eyes as Samu pursued. She was fast, but Samu was faster, a trait the Beast herself had bred into humans by forcing them from their trees and into a world of new predators.

Sometimes Samu fell behind, but her eyes were sharp and excellent at spotting the movement of parting grass. She marveled at the way the Beast dampened her flames to avoid setting the field ablaze.

Her legs ached, her lungs protesting every breath that propelled her onwards. An awful thought crossed her mind: she couldn't run forever.

A shape appeared on the horizon, the silhouette of a large rock. No, not a rock.

The cave.

This time, when the Beast looked back, Samu swore she was grinning. She'd brought her home to witness the destruction firsthand.

With the last of her energy, Samu sent the spear flying and dropped to her knees. There was a yelp. Samu smiled, panting.

But the Beast did not fall.

She struggled to her feet, plumes of light flaring as she fought, howling against the pain. Samu heard the spear snap off, and the Beast staggered towards the cave.

Why not just set the whole field ablaze? she wondered, hauling herself up and following her. She stumbled; her flames dimmed to a faint smolder. Ah. She was too tired.

Another stumble, and this time she stayed down.

This was Samu's chance. She summoned all her strength and charged forward, grabbing the broken spear along the way.

The Beast lay on her side, spearhead embedded in her shoulder. It shouldn't have been a fatal wound. She glanced up as Samu approached and let out a labored growl. Her body gave only the faintest glow, but Samu felt the emanating heat as she stood over her, spear poised to end the Beast.

She had terrorized her people long enough, forcing them from the safety of their trees into the dangerous grasses where they had to stand upright to see predators. Making them learn to make weapons and tools to survive, develop language to pass on the warnings.

She had changed them at their most basic level, shaped them from mere apes to something different. Ugly, gangly animals capable of cruelty, who waged wars with their neighbors over food supplies and hunted animals that had no natural enemies.

They could never go back to what they were.

What right did she have to change them? To take away their place in the order of things?

To...give them songs. Art. Family that meant more than another ape you mated with and never saw again.

Samu's hands shook as the realization chilled her.

The Beast did not bring death or destruction. That was the nature of life, for all things to end and be destroyed so new things could take their place. The Beast merely gave them a choice in the matter, an opportunity to change and survive.

If not the Beast, disease or drought would have killed their trees, perhaps so slowly the apes would have stayed, stubbornly clinging to dying branches instead of learning to walk upright and hunt for food. The Beast was merely the catalyst, nudging them towards survival.

Samu knelt beside her, pressed her forehead to the Beast's and felt the heat that radiated like a sunbaked stone.

She was dying not because of Samu's spear, but what it represented: her purpose, completed. She had given them so much, but could take them no further.

Samu kissed the Beast. "Thank you."

A shriek cut through their quiet moment.

Samu stood, spear in hand, and turned towards the sound of rustling grass. It was Mother, a pack of dogs on her heels.

Samu looked to the Beast for help, but the life had gone from her. Only a few burning embers remained, dripping like blood from her wound. Samu touched it with the end of her spear and the wood caught fire.

Without a second thought, she brandished her torch and ran at the dogs. The sight of a fearless human was a new one to the dogs. They could have changed their hunting strategy, evolved and learned to take down a human who fought back, but their species had not had a Beast. They ran away.

Samu returned home, where she and her family slept under the stars. Small fires burned at the edge of their land, the Beast's final gift warding off all dangers.

The safety would not last. There would be floods, plagues, new dangers all the time. But they would survive; the Beast taught them how.

~ * ~ * ~

Jennifer Lee Rossman (they/them) is a queer, disabled, and autistic author and editor from the land of carousels and Rod Serling.

Find more of their work at jenniferleerossman.blogspot.com and follow them on Twitter @JenLRossman

A Good Day Gone Bad

Steven Lente

After touring in Vietnam in 1971, Johnny Cash said (and I paraphrase), "servicemen and prisoners have much in common… loneliness, separation from standard society, and camaraderie with others who share the same fate." One year later, President Richard Nixon called Cash to perform at the White House, and Johnny's two encore songs were "The Man in Black" and "The Ballad of Ira Hayes." Nixon was not impressed.

Nixon resigned from the presidency in August three years later, but my friend John Hanscom had killed himself by then. John's death affected me more than the President's departure, and in some sense, I still blame Nixon. John might be alive today if Tricky Dick had focused on ending the war during his first term rather than scamming his way into a second.

Some people believe if you are not in direct combat you cannot develop PTSD, and to be clinically diagnosed with it you must experience *shell shock*. Medically, I suppose that's true, as the "T" in PTSD is *traumatic* and the daily tensions of non-combat duty certainly aren't that. Perhaps the correct phrase is *acute stress disorder,* but this doesn't mean the accumulated pressures caused by being deployed or standing watch over nuclear weapons are no less critical nor less fatal.

I got only two tattoos in my life, one on my right upper arm, and the other on the left. I had the one on my right done shortly after John died, and it is a red, white, and blue star surrounded by a wreath made with olive branches. Above the star are two crossed arrows, and tying the arrows together is a yellow-ribboned bow. The symbolism of the star is my pledge of allegiance to the United States of America. The olive branch stands for peace, and the arrows represent the preparations needed to defend that peace. The yellow ribbon is for those who did not make it back home, and for me this means John Hanscom.

Hanscom and I grew up with Cash's music, as well as Merle Haggard's "Okie From Muskogee" and "The Fightin' Side Of Me."

John and I were born in the fifties, grew up in the sixties, and joined the Air Force ten years later. I was from a small town in Colorado, and he was from a smaller one in Nebraska.

Neither of us had ever seen the Pacific Ocean until we deployed to Anderson AFB Guam, almost sixteen hours west by air from the California coastline. During B-52 bombing operations supporting the war in Vietnam, almost twelve thousand airmen were assigned to Anderson for six months at a time, then they would rotate back to home bases in the States until needed again in SE Asia.

Typically, though, we had open-ended orders for Anderson, and Kadena Airbase in Okinawa Japan, and U-Tapao Airbase in Thailand, and we could go to any of these three. Anderson was where the Air Force needed us this time. With respect to Johnny Cash's earlier observation, to recognize the camaraderie between OUR aircraft crews, cooks, medics, cops, and others who shared the same fate, we called ourselves *Prisoners of Guam* or *POGs*.

~ * ~

There are other actors important to this American tragedy, and I'll get to them, but know their stories will be different seen through the eyes of another.

One night in September of 1973, after our time as *POGs*, Tom Pendleton and I were working law enforcement at the main gate for Mountain Home AFB in Idaho, and we were completely caught by surprise when John Hanscom pulled up to it.

"Hey guys, what's up?" John yelled out of his car window. He acted as if we had just seen him yesterday, but it had been over a month since we left him on Guam.

"John, what're you doing here?" Tom asked.

"They're rebounding me to Thailand, our bombers aren't coming home until next spring. I'm shipping out of California in a week and wanted to see you again before I left."

Hanscom drove away two days later and three weeks after that while on his jungle post outside of U-Tapao Airbase, he shot himself in the head with his government issued .38 cal. Smith and Wesson combat masterpiece.

There were plenty of signs and I should have seen it coming, but in the 1970's there were no awareness programs and no help, unless you wanted to talk with a chaplain, who typically worried more about your soul than your mental health. Oh, and there was one other Catch-22, the Air Force Personnel Reliability Program, or PRP. The PRP said in order to work around nukes, which our bombers normally carried, you had to be in stable mental health, BUT, if you felt stressed out and went to a counselor to discuss it you were decertified under the PRP. AND, if relieved under the PRP, you could no longer carry a weapon, thus you could not be a cop. A vicious circle few of us ventured to take on. Go figure.

~ * ~

Now stay with me for a minute, and I'll explain how John plays into this and why I got my second tattoo.

~ * ~

When we joined the Air Force in 1972, basic training was at Lackland AFB in San Antonio and after basic we would stay at Lackland because the Security Police (SP) Academy was on the other side of the base. This is where I met John, and in six weeks, we learned guarding airplanes and people, arresting and handcuffing, using self-defense techniques, qualifying with our primary weapons, working the radio, and more.

About four weeks into the training, we marched to the base theater where a map of the United States was projected on the screen showing options for our initial base assignments. John picked Dyess AFB near Abilene, Texas and I chose Mountain Home. I arrived there in December where I became partners with Tom Pendleton and Greg Rust, both destined to be my friends for the rest of their lives.

Mountain Home was technically a Tactical Air Command (TAC) base with jet fighters, but Tom, Greg, and I were assigned way out at the edge of the runway to a Strategic Air Command (SAC) detachment with B-52 bombers and air refueling tankers. The only problem was that most of SACs aircraft were in SE Asia, and ours were on Guam. So, not to waste our SP training, we were loaned to the TAC cop squadron to work law enforcement (LE) before we went to Anderson and then again after our return to the States until our bombers would come back months later.

Our home on Guam was a large canvas tent which, with plywood cabinets for closets and storage, held six POGs. Tom, Greg, and I got the same tent with three other SPs, one of whom went back to the States early, leaving the bunk open for the eventual arrival of John Hanscom who came to Guam when the Dyess AFB bombers rotated over.

Try to imagine the movie or the TV series *M*A*S*H*. This is what our area looked like, only with hundreds of tents set up to house more POGs. Conversely, all the officers, and the senior sergeants had concrete barracks rooms, with two people per room and their own bathrooms. But we were grunts, and our bathrooms were plywood buildings with open stalls and common showers.

Now, among SPs, there were two types of grunts. Flightline cops were *security* with green fatigues, baseball caps, and M-16s, and they guarded the one hundred or so deployed bombers and other aircraft. Then there were the grunts like Tom, Greg, John, and me who patrolled the base and other areas. We were *LE* and wore khakis, white bus driver's hats, and carried .38 revolvers.

Although our attitude then was SPs are SPs, it took me a couple of years to recognize how easy Security cops had it. For them, there were red lines, fences, and ropes marking where people were authorized to go. Additionally, we had a variety of ID cards and badges that made it easy to ensure the good guys got in and the bad guys didn't. The rules for the use of deadly force were well established and reinforced by those red lines, ropes, and fences.

On the other hand, LE officers had to make split-second judgments on the correct use of force while dealing with the public, responding to alarms and traffic accidents, and juggling varying jurisdictions with different rules. John was the first of us to go down because of these differences.

One of our patrol stations was Marbo, a small military housing area surrounded by jungle and named after the nearby public beach. It was about ten miles from the main base and had five cops assigned. Three of us were gate guards controlling base access and the other two SPs were a mobile patrol in a government-blue Chevy pickup. Supporting Marbo's residents was a small convenience store with gas pumps, a fire station, a bank branch, and an entertainment club, which was really just a large bar that served food. We called the club, *The Flip Club*, because most of the workers were Filipinos who stayed in barracks in Marbo and sent money home to support their families.

John and I had patrol one day. Normally the patrol leader was a sergeant, but our regular one was on sick call, and so John drove while I had shotgun. Early in our morning shift, a burglary alarm sounded from the Flip Club. John dropped me off at the front entrance, and he drove around to the back. I went in towards the bar with revolver raised (yes, back then during a response we carried them near our heads). I saw movement to my left, and just caught a glimpse of someone running through the kitchen door.

I heard John shout, "Stop or I'll shoot!" Then I heard two shots.

I worked my way to the back and saw John standing over the prone body of a Filipino man. Blood pumped from the man's chest for a few seconds, then stopped. John's right foot was on a machete, and he was still pointing his revolver at the fallen man.

"John, holster your weapon." John didn't move. "HOLSTER YOUR WEAPON!" I shouted, and John did.

The alarm also activated a response from the main base. Calling on my radio, I told dispatch what happened and within fifteen minutes, our senior officers and the first sergeant arrived and took over the scene. The Office of Special Investigation sent their agents as well. John and I were relieved of duty, our weapons confiscated, and we were separated and confined to the commander's and first sergeant's offices until the agents could interview us.

We were in limbo for two weeks and not allowed to leave the base, but soon enough the investigation showed the shooting was justified. It was also a perfect textbook two-shot, range-trained, center mass kill on a madman with a big knife, although the report could not say it that way. That night at the airman's lounge we celebrated our return to service with the others, but John kept mumbling something between his drinks. I finally got it out of him, and he said, "Steve, I could only think about who he was sending the money to. I barely saw the machete."

We carried a passed-out John back to the tent and turned him on his side so he would not vomit in his cot.

~ * ~

During the time we were suspended, John learned to cut hair. He bought a clipper set at the base exchange, practiced on me, and went into business for himself. Several of the guys had side hustles to make extra spending cash, including playing poker, doing laundry for other airmen, or getting paid to clean the showers and bathrooms when it was someone else's turn (No maid service in our tent city…nope, nope, nope).

John got to be a pretty good barber, although it was not difficult to cut our hair high and tight. He charged us a dollar and a half.

~ * ~

As if the shooting wasn't enough, the next month, Hanscom got a dear-John letter (ironic isn't it) from his girlfriend, Sylvia. With even more irony, just like in the Dr. Hook song, Sylvia's mother actually wrote the letter because her daughter had already married another man. The mother always liked John and thought it only proper to let him know why there would be no more letters from Sylvia. The mother was truly sorry, she wrote. We headed back to the lounge again with John.

The airman's lounge was not a classic bar. The area was not much bigger than a typical living room, the exterior walls were wooden poles faked to look like a jungle village hut, and palm trees with coconuts surrounded it. The bar itself was made from old bomb and shipping crates salvaged from the supply POGs. There was no roof, and we airmen mostly stood under the stars at makeshift tables, but there was a jukebox.

John burned the letter from Sylvia's mother in an ashtray, then he slammed down Black Russians most of the night, while the rest of us sipped on Singapore Slings or straight whiskey. Now, guys who are barely out of high school can be cruel to each other because we played the Dr. Hook song over and over and teased John about now being free to get back in the saddle with some Guamanian hottie. John was not amused and again we carried him back to the tent to sleep it off.

~ * ~

The next test for John the Barber was just before Tom, Greg, and I returned to the States. Downtown Agana Guam hosted a row of tourist hotels on the beach. Anderson offered a free shuttle bus from the base airport terminal to each hotel in sequence, then when it reached the end of the line, the shuttle turned around and hit the hotels again before returning to the base. Our favorite hotel lounge was at the Tokyu, and we were jamming to a rock group from Australia. The lead singer was a knockout, short-skirted and long-legged Amazon named Julie. We were all in love and some of us even got our Polaroids taken with her.

Anyway, Greg and I had to work the next day, so we had our two Singapore Slings and caught the shuttle on its inward leg. Tom, John, and two of the other guys, Webb and Riley, stayed behind. The bus went on to the remaining four hotels, turned around and when we got back to the Tokyu, Webb and Riley got on.

"Where's Tom and John?" I asked.

Riley responded quickly then turned to look out the window. "They're back at the lobby about to get their asses kicked."

"You left them, you sons of bitches?"

"Well, the Guamanians have knives!"

"Cowards," I yelled. "Stop the bus!" Greg and I jumped off before the shuttle came to a full rest. We ran back to the hotel and found Tom standing over the limp body of our Barber. Eight or nine natives circled them, and like Riley said, they all had switch-blades out and pointed at Tom. Being loud enough not to sneak up on the Guamanians, I stepped through their ring and up next to Tom.

"This isn't your fight," one of the men said.

"These guys are my friends, so it is."

"Mine too," Greg said as he joined Tom and me.

"What's this about?" I asked.

The brown man pointed with his knife to John passed out between Tom's feet. "That drunk guy said some nasty things to Julie. He can't get away with that."

"We agree. Let us take care of him ourselves. He can be stupid sometimes. And his girl left him hanging."

"You got this?" the native asked.

"I promise you'll never see us again."

They disappeared into the jungle. Greg, Tom, and I cursed Riley and Webb, took deep breaths, and relaxed a bit.

"What happened?" I asked.

Tom told us the band started playing "Sylvia's Mother," and Julie came down off the stage crooning straight at John as if she knew. John was drinking doubles, and the rest was history.

A few minutes later another base shuttle pulled into the parking area, and we hauled John onto the bus. Back at the base, we continued to drag John's dead-weighted and passed out body back to the tent for the third time.

~ * ~

What happened next was our final clue to John's mental state. Tom, Greg, and I were going home, our kit bags were already at the base airport terminal. I know this is a cheap defense, but we knew if we reported what I'm telling you now, we'd be grounded during an investigation.

Weeks earlier, Tom fashioned a hangman's noose of about six wraps of clothesline rope and tied it from a rafter in our tent near the exposed light bulb. (Yes, I know these things are not acceptable today, but remember this was 1973, and about six thousand miles away from the US, so try not to judge.)

Launch time was eleven that morning, and we were making the rounds through the tents to say goodbye. John was on duty, but he was waiting in our tent with his patrol vehicle parked outside. When we came in, John was standing on a chair with his neck in the noose, and just that fast, kicked himself off the chair.

I rushed over, grabbed his legs, and lifted him up to release the pressure from the noose. John kept grabbing for his revolver, and Tom had to take control of his gun hand while Greg climbed on the chair and untied the rope from the rafters. We lowered John back to the floor, took the noose from his neck, and made sure he was breathing. We got him awake and back on his feet, gave him back his handgun, patted him on the butt, and left to get to the terminal for our flight home.

The next and last time we saw him was when he pulled up to the gate in Mountain Home that September. A few weeks after we got the news of his suicide, I wrote a poem.

For John, My Barber

One song kept repeating on the broken-down jukebox,
Ninety-nine bottles of unopened beer.
Two olives sink gently into black Russian vodka
But the records stopped playing and the song disappeared.
We were far from familiar places,

I try to remember the traces,
But the night that he died
Isn't clear in my mind
And I can't remember the faces.
No one can find them, they're deep in my mind, and
I can't understand why it happened this way.
But a man's just a man, and a song's just a song
So, tell Sylvia's mother he won't be coming this way
Just tell her John won't be coming today.
Today is a time spent in yesterday's songs.
Today is a mind spent in yesterday's wrongs.
Tomorrow is a time that tells us when yesterday is gone.
Yet the answers are hidden deep in my mind
And a life is merely a measure of time.
Time can be short, or time can be long
Just like the verses of this broken-down song.
So put your dime in the jukebox and open the beer
Sing along with the music till the song disappears.
Tell Sylvia's mother he won't be coming to stay,
Just tell her John won't be coming today.

~ * ~

I stayed in the Air Force for twenty years, and for some of that time was on a deployable SWAT team with classified missions in the US and in jungles further south. I spent a lot of hours at a couple of those locations looking through a sniper scope, and I got shot at and had a few close calls as well, but I was never in any real firefights.

After John's passing, my personal losses began to add up. Next was Rich, who was one of my non-cop friends, a C-130 load master who deployed with me on many of those missions. I was the best man at his wedding in 1985. Two years later, in front of a hundred spectators at an airshow at Fort Bragg, NC, Rich was killed during a demonstration of a low-level airdrop of supplies when his cargo plane came in too fast and hit the dirt landing strip hard. It slid for almost a thousand yards before it exploded.

Appropriately, I gave the eulogy at his closed-casket memorial service, and in the circle of life, death, and rebirth, Rich left behind two sons, now grown and with their own children. Damned CNN

Headline news kept playing that crash sequence on the TV for a week, and you can still find the video today if you do an internet search, but I don't watch it anymore.

Later in about a two-year period, I lost my maternal grandmother, an aunt who helped raise me, and both my fraternal grandparents. My mother passed a year after my grandparents. Oh, and my marriage started to break up just before I left the service, probably because of too many nights apart, and it didn't help that I could not share my experiences with my wife. You've heard the line before…*we just grew apart.*

Then there were Greg and Tom who took different paths from mine. Greg did not re-enlist after his tour and moved to Anchorage where he started his own private security business. He survived getting assaulted during various attempts to serve court papers and bragged that only kryptonite could kill him.

Pancreatic cancer took Greg down when he was forty-two. Go figure.

Tom left the military after seven years and signed on with Metro PD in Las Vegas. During a domestic call in Rancho Charleston, Tom was trying to save a common-law wife from being beaten by a druggie husband, and when he tried to handcuff the man, the woman jumped on Tom's back and stabbed him in the throat with a pair of scissors. Despite efforts from his partner, Tom bled out before medics could get there. Tom was fifty-one.

Metro really lost two good cops with this incident. The after-action report said the wife should have been hand-cuffed first, and this judgment made by someone who wasn't there was the tipping point for Tom's partner to resign a month later. No good deed goes unpunished.

~ * ~

Once I finally retired from the Air Force, I went through that divorce (and half my retirement pay) and a new job about every eighteen months. I even went through counseling once, but not by choice. I applied for a position with the County Sheriff's Office that required a psychiatric eval, and I made it through two sessions. I didn't get the job, but the County did pay for the meetings.

During the first session, the shrink asked me about my childhood. My answers were short. Dad left us when I was six, and mom had three more marriages, thus three stepdads (my father had four more wives before he died). The last one of these *dads* beat mom regularly and once tried to kill me with a butcher knife. I got away and ran to the police station (no cell phones in the sixties) and rode in the car with the responding officer back to my house. Mom was barely conscious, stepdad was arrested. Mom was treated at the scene but refused to go to the ER, and stepdad spent two days drying out only to be released because mom wouldn't press charges. During another beating a couple of years later I did aim a rifle at stepdad, although one of my brothers quickly got to the police who arrived before I pulled the trigger. I was fifteen, still a minor, and besides, things were different back then. By the time I graduated from high school three years later, I was on a first-name basis with the chief of police, who suggested I join the military to learn some discipline.

Counseling session two had a lot of give and take, and we decided my association with law enforcement during my formative years is what drove me to become an SP in the military and then to later apply for the County position. Regardless, by the end of the second hour the psychiatrist told me, "Steve, you are the source of, and the cure for, your own unhappiness." He was a behaviorist by profession, and philosophically a Stoic, and he believed we all have control over how we respond to the things that haunt us.

He continued, "According to Epictetus, a man is responsible for his own judgments, even in dreams, in drunkenness, and in melancholy madness. You can only be a victim of yourself. Some things are up to us, some things are not. Knowing the difference results in peace and control."

If I bought into his analysis, this guy just took away all my excuses for how I behaved, but, on the positive side it also meant I wouldn't need chemicals to maintain any balance. None the less, I failed the eval because the shrink noted I *tended to be over-reactive in situations* and *without continual supervision could present a liability to the County.* In English, he meant I could not control my anger. I eventually understood his line of thinking, but I was slow to respond to it back then, thus the lost marriage and frequency of job changes.

Fast forward to present times. When I get in a mood, my second wife, who works with the VA, knows enough to leave me alone until I am through it, although she does lock up the guns. My volatility doesn't happen because of a particular anniversary, and it often catches me by surprise, but I've learned the signs well enough to head into my cave where I will be safe.

This time, though, will be different!

It's December 29, and my last day at work with the big box hardware store where I've worked part-time to supplement my social security. I'm done, and I am not ever working another hour for someone else starting New Year's Day. But my celebration starts now!

Fifty-two years ago, a fifth of Seagrams VO had a yellow and black striped ribbon wrapped around its neck. The unofficial military edict was that once you had less than one hundred days on an assignment (a two-digit-midget), you could wear this ribbon on your uniform. It was unauthorized, of course.

On Guam, we SPs modified that rule to make it harder to get the ribbon. Our change was IF you opened a bottle AND you finished it <u>in one sitting</u>, you *earned* that damned ribbon and could tie it to your gun belt. Now, a sitting could be an all-nighter or longer, we didn't mean you had to down the whole fifth in one gulp. C'mon, we were crazy, not stupid.

Anyway, tonight I'm in my cave with its wide-screen TV on the wall and a dry bar in one corner, and off to the side, a spare bedroom with its own bath. This works well because in my twilight years, I don't recover from hangovers as well as I used to, and the downstairs den is a nice place to hole up for a couple of days once I break that ribboned seal. I typically pass out before I finish a bottle, but I still collect the ribbons, and I have over thirty in a desk drawer somewhere.

I turn on the TV to one of the classic movie channels and start drinking straight whiskey. My wife manages to sneak down chips and pretzels to me, but no food of real substance as my hangovers can be ugly, and I'm down for two full days.

It's still dark the early morning of January First, and I sort of stumble into the bathroom. My mouth tastes like the bottom of a birdcage, so I brush and rinse my teeth first. Then I shower, and in the hot steam of it, I scrape the bristle from my face with a safety razor. After that and very carefully, I remove gauze wrappings from my left upper arm. I wash the antiseptic cream and dried blood away, and gently rub my fingers over the colored and still welted skin.

This is the tattoo I said earlier I would tell you about, and I got it just a few days before I quit my job. It's a Bird of Paradise, a beauty of a Phoenix, mainly in blue and purple ink. The creature is flying into an immense yellow sun with red flames shooting from its edges, because according to legend, it must die in the fire during bad times before it can be reborn in the good.

I dry off, dress in comfortable jeans and a black tee, and comb what's left of my gray hair. I go upstairs to greet my wife and the new year. She hands me a fresh cup of coffee and I go out on the front deck to watch the daybreak through the eastern tree line, and as it does, I pull up my left shirt sleeve to let the sun shine on my new Phoenix.

Am I truly the cure for my own unhappiness? Am I totally responsible for my own melancholy madness? Is it acute stress or PTSD, and does the difference make a difference? Can I ever get over my guilt for what happened with John my barber? I don't know, but I am done with the man I used to be, and I aim to welcome this seventy-one-year-old with his new tattoo. Go figure.

~ * ~ * ~

Steven Lente is a USAF veteran whose credentials include an MA in Organizational Management, a BA in Business Management, and an ASIS International certified protection professional lifetime rating. *A Good Day Gone Bad* is Steve's third published short story in various anthologies; he also received Honorable Mention for an unpublished short story submitted to the L. Ron Hubbard *Writers of the Future* 2022 anthology.

Fully retired, he and wife Brenda travel regularly with and without an RV. Their home is in Colorado Springs, CO.

The Perfect Life

db mcneill

"CONGRATULATIONS!" AutoDoc™ boomed. "You have Alzheimer-Adjacent Dementia-Two-Nineteen. You may know it as AAD-Two-Nineteen!"

"Great," Laura said, rubbing her head, "fucking great."

"I'm sorry," AutoDoc intoned. "I didn't get that. Please rephrase your response as a question."

Laura sighed. "What are my treatment options?"

"Congratulations—you're *so* smart for asking!"

She pressed her lips together. The more she asked, the more she'd be inundated with "affirmations".

"You have several options. Please wait while I print to the nurse's station."

Laura sang the alphabet song before walking to the nurse's station. The song took 26 seconds. The print-out would be ready in 26 seconds. She'd spent lots of time at AutoDoc. *At least I have a diagnosis now*, she thought. *Whatever that's worth.*

"Laura Ingram treatment options" she said to the robo-nurse.

An image of a bland, smiling face scrolled across its surface as it spooled out a stunningly short plati-cel. "A co-pay of two hundred and fifty Euros has been removed from your account," it said. "Congratulations!"

Like other forms of dementia, AAD-219 was treated with neuroplasticity-nanites, through synaptic-pathway restoration, or with magnetic or electronic applications that diminished cell death. Scientific research groups could still do meaningful work but were limited to uploading data to AutoDoc. They couldn't provide treatment. Not legally. They were techs, not doctors, and actual human doctors were rare—and exclusively encelled to the highest GovCorp[LLC] officials. Everyone else had to use AutoDoc. And AutoDoc wasn't cheap.

Laura glanced at her print-out of "several" options, a menu complete with pictures and prices. She supposed four options technically qualified as several, but it didn't matter. She couldn't afford any of them.

~ * ~

Laura was waiting for her home-tram (brought to you by LetsGo™) when a man in a lime-green business suit sidled up to her. She didn't look at him, but he waved a plati-cel bizcard in her face until she snatched it from him. "Do you wait outside AutoDoc for everyone? Or just old ladies?" she snapped. "What the hell's wrong with you?" She turned to tell the man exactly what she thought was wrong with him, but he was gone. She blinked and flipped the card. It read:

> Momentify!
> Choose Your Past
> Call 1-800-555-9278

"Huh, a phone number," Laura said, crumpling the card. She looked around for a pneuma-tube to toss the card into. Finding none, she stuck the card in her pocket and forgot it.

~ * ~

Laura stood in the door of her unit, taking in the watercolor tin she'd left open on the table, the brush she'd left, bristle down, in her coffee-faux cup. The cup she used for painting sat empty beside the stale faux with a sheet of paper underneath. There were broad swaths of paint across the paper, the *real* paper, the colors muddy, coffee-dark. This was the beginnings of a painting, but a painting of what? She angrily shoved everything aside, dropped into her ReadyBeddy™ bed-chair and let her face fall into her hands. She laughed. And then, she wept.

She called Theo up on the VidWall. "Hi Theo!" she said as the VidWall colors unpixellated, resolving into her son's face. She opened her mouth to tell him her diagnosis, to ask him to come help, as something fell, clattering, behind him. Children streamed around him, laughing. It looked like a party.

"Mom," he said, sounding amused and exasperated, "it's the big birthday celebration today—you know how it is. We'll call you back tomorrow!" The VidWall went dark, and Laura was alone.

Theo had expatriated during COVID-37. He'd told her, "I'm going somewhere that got this shit under control during CO-thirty-two. I'm going somewhere less stupid." She couldn't blame him. Now Theo had his own family, a husband and little girl, a bright child who cheerfully said, "hello gammy!" on VidCalls before crashing off to play. She couldn't remember the child's name. She couldn't remember how old she was. *It's the big the birthday celebration today.* She hadn't remembered her granddaughter's birthday. She tried to recall Theo's husband's name but could only picture his kind, angular face.

She shook her head. She couldn't ask Theo to come, to risk illness, just to watch her memories of him disintegrate. Worse, he'd watch her forget everything important about everyone who mattered to him, and if he got sick, if he took a virus home to his family, they'd have to go to AutoDoc too, just like she did. She wouldn't wish that on anyone.

"Congratulations," she murmured, darkly. No wonder no one travelled anymore.

~ * ~

Laura found the bizcard in her pocket days later while walking in the park that looped her complex. She found her phone under a pile of empty NutriReadyFood™ wrappers. Tears welled in her eyes. She punched the code into the phone and listened to the burring ring at the other end, waiting for the auto-response. Laura took a shaky breath, surprised, when a human voice chirped, "Momentify! May I help you?"

"Um, yes" Laura said, "I have AAD-Two-Nineteen?" It came out as a question.

"Okay!" the perky voice replied. "Did you want to contract our services?"

"Uh, I think so. What do your services, uh, do?" Vocabulary failed her.

"We offer decorative memories," the voice said, "We codify a random series of your memories as art—wall-hangings, paintings, sculpture—and you'll never forget your favorite things!" A second voice said something unintelligible, and the bright voice continued more slowly. "Or" the voice said, "we offer a customizable package which allows you to, uh, *extract* and customize memories before they're codified as art."

"Can I use my own art?" Laura asked, her eyes scanning the wall where she tacked her finished work.

There was a muffled conversation on the other end, and the voice returned. "Sure, we can do that," it said, "but it won't reduce the cost."

"That's okay," Laura said. "I want the customizable package."

"Uh…" the voice faltered. "You know how this works? You understand memory extraction must be *very* thorough for that option?"

"Yes" Laura lied. She shook a food wrapper. "I have a catalogue right here".

There was a long pause before the voice said, "I'd like to go over it with you anyway," in a tone that meant *you're farther gone than you think or you're a liar.*

"You have a day to adjust memories and stabilize them. After that, they may leave an echo, an empty feeling, but they'll only exist as art. You won't be able to access them without the art, even on your best days. If you choose not to keep the art for any reason, you forfeit your memories to us."

"I plan to keep the art," Laura murmured. "I understand."

~ * ~

Laura wasn't sure, but it seemed like The Momentify technician arrived minutes later, accompanied by the man in the lime-green suit.

"Hello Miss Ingram," he said, "May I call you Laura? My name is Lu McLughpherson, Laura," he continued without pausing for a response "Call me Lu. This is my colleague, Fia." He waved toward the technician, who hurried around the unit, placing delicate machinery in each corner. "Just Fia, no last name" Lu continued as if Laura had asked. "Don't mind them," Lu said and bumped elbows with Laura.

Lu pulled out a sheet of *real* paper and flourished a pen. A *real* pen.

I bet, right now, this unit has the most real paper in the complex Laura thought. *And the only real pen.*

"Let's discuss details," Lu said. "How much can you spend?"

"How much can you cost?" Laura replied.

Lu laughed, pulled out more papers and set them down in front of Laura. He showed her options for one memory, several memories. There were no prices listed and he didn't tell her any. He flipped over a paper and said, "This one's is my favorite, but it costs."

Laura tried and failed to read the contract. "Tell me," she said.

"You get five memories, and I slow the progress of your disease."

"You can do that?"

"Yes, but like I said, it costs." Lu hesitated. "I can't heal you. I can only slow things down, but your memories will be *forever* safe. You pay nothing now, and in six months—give or take—we take proprietary ownership of your memories to ensure their sanctity." He enunciated the t's in "sanctity" like "d's".

Sank-diddy, Laura thought, amused.

"Of course," Lu continued, "we also take ownership of your material possessions, along with your memories, and we inherit your payment accounts." The words tumbled rapidly from his mouth.

Word bullets, Laura thought. She grew distracted. Didn't Theo say he'd call tomorrow? Was this tomorrow? Maybe he'd call soon.

"The last part is a special service to your next-of-kin, should you have any, because we'll take responsibility for your debts, not that you have any. I checked. You don't have any."

"I—," Laura began, thinking of Theo. Had she asked him what he thought? She couldn't remember.

"What happens to me?" Laura asked. She took the pen and thumped it against the table.

"You die," Lu replied. "Of natural causes, quite painlessly," he hurried to add.

"How is that possible?" Laura asked.

"It just is," Lu said, spreading his hands.

Laura fidgeted with the pen and signed shakily, once again trying and failing to read the words crawling across the page. "Six months of my life," she said, "rather than years of God knows what."

"Yes," Lu whispered.

"What?" Laura asked.

Lu didn't reply but smiled as Laura leaned out to bump elbows again. He pulled her into a gentle hug before quietly leaving the unit. He closed the door behind him. Laura smiled. It had been a long time since she'd been hugged.

Fia gave Laura a small metal rod, smooth except for a button and dial. The dial was labeled *customization*, the button *stabilize*. Simple enough. Fia showed Laura how to use the rod and left.

~ * ~

The first memory Laura chose was of the most beautiful boy she'd ever seen. She used a small landscape for this one. It was the first day of UpperSchool and as the boy passed back a bookdisc, he'd said "The road goes ever on and on." She'd taken the disc and responded, "Over rock and under tree." His eyes had widened, and they'd been instant friends. She wished they'd stayed in touch. She wished they'd been more than friends. Did she want to change this memory? Yes. She decided to remember herself as bold, bold enough to lean forward and whisper an inspired modification from the same ancient discs. "I wish to go and see the great mountains, and hear the pine-trees and the waterfalls, and *I want to do it with you.*" She nodded and stabilized the memory before she could change her mind. She tapped the landscape with the tube, checking the memory. She wondered what ever happened to that boy.

She chose a painting of Theo as a baby for the day he was born. Not imaginative but it didn't matter. She made the birth less painful. She quieted Theo's wailing and gave him a beatific smile. *Yes, that's it* she thought and pressed the button. *Stabilized.*

She made the afternoon of Theo's graduation a little cooler and removed the scent of marijuana from his hair. She changed the memory so when she hugged him, he hugged her back a little harder and said, "I love you, Mom." *Like that* she decided. This painting looked abstract, but she knew it was the sky that day. *Stabilized.*

She saved the day she and Huxley returned from their honey-moon. She hoped to forget most of their short marriage but wanted something good from it too. When they'd opened the door to their unit, her cat had jumped onto the counter and meowed. Hux had slapped the cat and Laura, shocked, had watched the animal sail across the room.

"Don't hit my cat," she'd said flatly.

"I didn't hit your cat," Hux responded matter-of-factly, as if it were true.

She worried at the customization dial and tapped the rod against her forehead. Should she wipe this? Choose something else? She turned the rod, looking for a trademark symbol, but there was only the dial, the button, and the labels. The rod was, otherwise, quite smooth

She adjusted the dial and made Hux pick up the cat and kiss it on the nose. She made him say "Hello Miss Kitty" then snorted. Even Kitty wouldn't have liked that. She dialed back the counter and made Hux scoop the cat gently into his arms and deposit her on the floor. *Better*, she thought and hit the button, gazing at a painting of Hux and Theo she'd done when Theo was little, and she still thought they'd be a family.

Finally, she chose the memory of meeting her granddaughter. It wasn't much, a memory from a vid-call, but she'd painted the girl's wide-eyed face. She tapped the rod and adjusted the dial, but it wasn't enough. She decided to hold the baby, snuggling. She smelled the baby's head and marveled at her little fingers. Now she could hold her granddaughter until the world went dark. She stabilized that too.

Laura looked around the room, satisfied, then went for a walk knowing by the time she came home, she would have lived a perfect life. "Congratulations," she said and shut the door.

db mcneill lives in the shadows of the Rocky Mountains with her family, which includes a spouse, three sons and a cast of critters. She has always loved fiction—both reading and writing it—so after years of penning environmental chemistry documents in semi-darkened rooms, she decided to walk into the sun and write as much fiction as life allowed. Her fiction has been published in various literary magazines, most recently Bright Flash Literary Review and Corner Bar. She's a neurodivergent woman with a brain injury and this story, her first anthology publication, was inspired by that experience. You can find out more at dbmcneill.com.

Eclipse

Andrew Gates

Signe stared at the daylight outside, knowing she would not see the sun again for two weeks. She hated this part of the year, as did everyone at the hospital. Days from now, she would practically forget what the sun looked like; she would lose all sense of time; she would wish anything to return to the light. She dreaded that.

Everyone knew the eclipse was coming. It seemed like it was *always* coming. As usual, those who could evacuate did, but Signe was not one of them. She never was. Not everyone was so lucky.

"Signe," a familiar voice greeted.

Signe turned from the window to face the speaker. "Doctor Hrothgar," she responded, tapping her chest to greet the grey-haired man before her, "heill ok sæll."

Hrothgar, tall and imposing, nodded back to her. "Heil ok sæl. Catching one last glimpse?"

"Aye," she replied as she turned back to the window.

As faraway asteroids drifted into view across the sun like a slow tide creeping up the sand, Signe sighed. On one hand, she was relieved her family was safe somewhere up there in orbit. That would soon be the safest place of all, shy of another planet entirely. She wondered what it looked like up there. She had completely forgotten. Perhaps she would see it for herself again one day. But if that day ever came, it was certainly not today.

Family aside, there was little else to feel relieved about. Soon the planet Tromsø would be a deathtrap and all residing on its surface would endure the cold, dark, black of night.

"How many be this for you?" Hrothgar asked.

"Nine. My family evacuated every year when I was young. I was twenty-one for my first eclipse. That was my first year working in the hospital. I am twenty-nine now."

Hrothgar chuckled and tapped his chest. "For me, thirty-seven. I have yet to miss one since I was eighteen."

"Does it get any easier?"

"Easier?"

"I mean…less scary?"

"One can take solace in modern security. Oseberg Colony Memorial Sjukhus, and Tromsø for that matter, are equipped to handle the eclipse. We have seen countless eclipses before and have endured, each time growing and learning. We cannot be so easily vanquished by the dark. You must know this, having endured nine yourself."

Of course, Hrothgar was right. The hospital was well-equipped, as was the rest of the planet. Signe knew this. But alas, it was still the eclipse. People died every year, no matter what.

The nurse sighed as she slid her fingers through her loose chestnut brown dreadlocks. She nodded her head and said, "I know this, but still…"

Hrothgar placed his right hand on her shoulder, comfortingly. "It is right to be nervous. Nerves and caution keep us alive. But keep your nerves within reason. Recall that you are safe here. This facility has shields, lights—"

"—and a security chief who knows what he's doing," added another, deeper voice.

Further down the hall came Security Chief Bjørn, the broad-shouldered, shaved-headed man who stomped around like a bear, moving as if he had the hall to himself. Unlike the rest of the staff who wore their standard woven coats adorned with the runes of healing, Bjørn wore heavy lamellar armor.

Bjørn tapped his armored chest with gusto as he stopped beside Signe and Hrothgar. Signe rolled her eyes.

"Doctor Hrothgar, you fail to give me enough credit," the man said in a tone of sarcastic offense. "Shields and lights are one thing, but what happens when the old batties learn to stop fearing the light, eh? Or they want to test the integrity of the shields? What happens then, huh? We all know if the security was foolproof, I'd be out of a job." The arrogant strongman winked at Signe. "Rest easy, lass, but not because of some shields that rise up around the hospital, nor because of some elaborate system of lights that wards off killer bats. No, rest easy because Bjørn here will keep you safe."

"That's enough, Bjørn. Don't you have something better to do? Like raise the shields?"

"The shields are automatic. They don't need me there to watch 'em come up. But for some reason, the hospital insists I be there."

"I'm sure they have their reasons."

"Well, for your information, yes, I was just on me way anyway. Catch your last look, you two. There won't be a sun in a few minutes." With those words, he shuffled off, not bothering to stop for the sick and weary patients navigating the hall.

"Sorry about him," the doctor said. "He's…well…you know how he is."

"Unfortunately, yes." Signe paused for a moment before continuing, "is he right though?"

"Right?"

"About the bats?"

The eclipse was deadly for sure. The darkness brought plunging temperatures that destroyed crops, hardened the ground, burst exposed pipes, and turned the fjords to ice. But the real danger did not come from the darkness; rather from what the darkness brought with it.

"The bats…" Hrothgar muttered. "What can I say that you don't already know? What horror stories have you yet to hear? It's your ninth eclipse, after all."

Signe inched closer to the doctor. "Have you ever seen one?"

"Seen one? An eclipse bat? Not an illustration you mean? Of course not! If the shields do the job, I'll never see one. But heard them? Aye, I've heard enough to never forget the sound."

Signe knew that sound too. As soon as the sun disappeared, the bats rose from their underground tunnels. In an instant, they covered the sky like a wave overtaking a beach. A perpetual cacophony of shrieks, fluttering wings, and thuds that occurred whenever a bat flew face-first into the shield filled the air. Anyone caught outside when the bats appeared would be dead in minutes, if not seconds, as the predators who emerged for two weeks out of every year proved to be Tromsø's true chieftains.

"I'm sorry for asking you about it. I suppose your knowledge of the matter is just as mine. I guess I hoped for anything reassuring you might know that I didn't," Signe said.

"See it this way. With my tenure in the hospital, I could have left long ago, and I still can. I could decide today this career is not for me. I could find a profession which allows me to escape for the eclipse. But yet, I am still here. Do you know why?"

Signe shook her head. In fact, she had often asked herself the same question.

"I serve Oseberg because what I do—what *we* do—is more important than escaping the night. These people for whom we care cannot leave. They do not have that luxury, so neither should we. Do I fear the night? The cold? The dark? The bats? Of course—the bats most of all. But as I said before, keep your nerves within reason. I have seen thirty-seven eclipses…and I am still here."

Not knowing whether that helped her or not, Signe looked to the sky once more. The asteroids were well over halfway across the sun now.

The sound of hydraulics filled the air. In the distance, a wing of the massive metal shield slowly ascended. It would only be a matter of seconds before all light disappeared. In a nearby room, Signe heard patients enthusiastically counting down the seconds. Their excitement, she knew, was misplaced. Surely, they had never experienced an eclipse before.

Signe and Hrothgar simply remained in place, quiet and unmoving as the seconds dropped.

When at last the counting patients reached 10, Signe felt her heart race powerfully. Only a small sliver of light shone now as the various wings of the shield came together. When the counting reached five, she held her breath. And when the counting reached zero, only the dim bulbs of the hospital provided any illumination.

The nurse let out a deep breath, trying to calm herself.

It was two minutes before faint bat shrieks filled the air, slowly crescendoing.

It was only another two until the nightmarish cacophony was all she could hear.

~ * ~

Signe smiled as she read the runes. She wanted one last look before seeing the patient. Once satisfied, she lowered the tablet, knocked on the door, and entered.

"Ms. Vilulf?" Signe greeted.

The patient shifted in the sheets and looked up at Signe. Though it was dimly lit, Signe saw every essence of the anticipation in the young woman's glance as she said, "Heil ok sæl."

"Heil ok sæl."

The pale-skinned, frizzy-haired, blonde patient, no more than 20-years-old eyed Signe curiously and straightened her back. "You're smiling," she noted as a smile formed on her own face.

"I have good news, Ms. Viluf. By Odin's beard, you pulled through. The tests show a full recovery!"

The woman's eyes widened. "You're certain?"

"Aye. No signs of typhus. The treatment worked. Congratulations, Ms. Viluf, you shall live a long and fruitful life!"

The woman cheered, shaking her hands in the air. "My goodness! Praise be to you, nurse."

"Thank you, but I just do as I am trained. True praise belongs to the doctors…and to Eir and Odin."

"Nay, I will not hear it! You have been by my side. My recovery is your doing, so says I."

Signe blushed. "Well, that is kind. I am, of course, overjoyed you are well, regardless of who may claim the credit." She spun the screen in her hands to show the patient. "Wish you to see the results for yourself?"

The woman shook her head. "You know I cannot read that. I am not versed in medicine. I take it at your word that I am healed and, as I said, I thank you."

"You are too kind." Signe placed the tablet in her jacket pocket and took a step nearer to the patient. "Your family will be overjoyed to learn you are well."

"They will!"

"Are they here?"

The woman shook her head. "They evacuated when they could. They were the lucky ones."

"I understand."

There was more Signe could have said on the subject, but it was not worth saying. Everyone knew the eclipse was awful; even those who didn't know it before sure knew it now. It had been two days since darkness consumed the planet…or so the clocks said. To her, two days seemed like one long meandering night stretched on forever. And the noise…that dreadful noise.

"Do I need to wait, or can I share the news with my family?"

"Please, share the news! Where is your communicator?"

"Hardwired into the wall," she said, pointing. "The internal battery is broken. It only runs when plugged in, I'm afraid."

Signe walked to the communicator, when suddenly the lights went out. To say it was dark was an understatement. Signe had never experienced such darkness in all her life. She stopped in place, her heart racing, when suddenly the lights flicked back on. She sighed in relief.

"What was that?"

"I…I don't know," Signe replied. "But the power is back now."

Signe reached for the communicator, but noticed the screen was dark. She scanned the room, noticing now that not everything was back online. While the lights and a few vital machines were on, clocks, fans, and most monitors remained out.

"I'm sorry to say, Ms. Viluf, it appears your communicator is not getting any power. I'm not sure what to do."

"Please, I have to tell my family. This is too important. Surely there must be some way."

Signe unwired the communicator from the wall and nodded back to the woman. "I know someone who might know what to do. I'll return shortly."

Exiting the room, Signe noticed the hall was only half lit. She walked a few seconds until she came to the nearby control room. She knocked.

"Who is it?" a male voice asked.

"Nurse Signe."

"Nurse? What do you want?"

"May I enter?"

"Sure."

As soon as Signe opened the door, she realized at once it was a bad idea. Two men attentively studied their screens, the look on their faces showing signs of immense worry. It was clear there were greater issues at hand.

"Oh…I have this communicator here. It's not running." She paused before continuing, "if this is not a good time, I can come back."

"There's a breach," Ragnar, the hospital wing's IT manager explained. He strode from one monitor to another as if on a hunt. He was full of energy, like someone 20 years younger. "We're running on backup power, but it won't last long."

"A breach? What do you mean?" Signe asked, realizing it may not have been her place, but she was here, so she might as well ask.

"The bats. They cut through the shield somewhere and chewed on a power cable," answered the other man, Frode, a technician about her age. His tone was stern. This was serious.

For years, there was something about Frode that caught Signe's eye. Although she knew little about him, she respected the attention he seemed to give to his work, to the patients, to life. He was engaged when it counted, celebratory when he could be, and always respectful. Though she rarely spoke to the attractive, brown-haired man, she sometimes found herself thinking about him. But today, Frode's relaxed attitude and attractive demeanor were gone. Here was a man engulfed in the seriousness of the situation. This jarring change in him was enough to send Signe's heart racing.

"What did you want again, nurse?" Ragnar asked.

"I..." Signe could not even remember. "I don't know."

"I found it," Frode said, quickly pointing to a monitor. "It's about a kilometer away. The breach point is on a surface cable running from the hydroelectric plant to the hospital."

"Our end?" Ragnar asked.

"Aye. We're the closest team. It's a kilometer from us, two for the other wing's team, and four for the team at the hydroelectric plant."

"Then that leaves us to fix it," Ragnar accepted with a reluctant exhale.

"How is there a breach? Aren't the shields supposed to protect all of those things? The dam? The cables? All of it? All of Tromsø's infrastructure?" Signe asked, basically now part of the team.

"It is, but as I said, somehow the bats got through," Frode answered.

"I...I don't understand. How can the bats get through a thick metal shield?"

"The batties only fly two weeks out of the year. They're not exactly experts. They basically just fly wherever the bat in front of them flies, and that bat in front has no idea where it's going either. So they swarm like mindless waves and crash into shit. One bat hitting a shield is not enough to do damage, but thousands repeated over and over? That can cause some problems," Ragnar explained.

The thudding noises. Signe knew that horrible sound all too well, but she never quite understood the visual associated with it.

"But...I thought there was a ring of floodlights around the

premises. Don't the lights scare them off?"

"Lights scare some of them, not all," Ragnar explained.

"Studies show the sustained lights tend to ward off only about sixty percent of bats. Quick flashes like flashbang grenades or flamethrowers have better results," Frode added. As he spoke, he turned away from the monitor and took off his jacket. He let out a deep breath, then looked to Ragnar and said, "Alright. Here I go."

"Go?" Signe asked. "What do you mean?"

"What do you think he means, lass? That cable's not going to fix itself. You want power, Frode here must fix it," Ragnar explained, motioning to the young man.

Signe gasped. She could hardly believe it. Was Frode actually going *outside* to repair something a kilometer away?

"I'll notify Bjørn," Ragnar continued, picking up his communicator. He sighed. "He's going to love this."

~ * ~

Minutes passed since Frode left the control room to bravely repair the damaged cable. Those mere minutes felt like long, tense hours. The entire hospital practically held its collective breath beneath the flickering lights as news spread about the breach.

Signe did not know why she came back to the control room after returning the inoperable communicator to Ms. Viluf. Perhaps she returned out of a yearning for the adventure, perhaps out of her desire to know what happened next, or perhaps because she feared for Frode. Nonetheless, she was there, standing beside Ragnar as he stared at the monitors.

"Confirm the armor is secure," Ragnar said into his headset.

"Affirmative," Frode's voice replied, echoing through speakers.

"Don't you worry, lad. Bjørn here won't let your boy walk into the darkness unprotected," the arrogant voice of Bjørn added. "Lookie, we'll make a quick walk, blast some bats while we're at it, then repair your thingy in time for supper."

Signe recalled what Hrothgar said about keeping nerves within reason. From the sound of his voice, Bjørn had no nerves at all. That seemed unreasonable. What did that say about his chance of success?

"Putting you on screen now," Ragnar narrated as a monitor displayed an ariel map of the hospital grounds. Two green dots appeared near each other on the edge of the building and a red dot appeared farther away in what looked like an empty part of the grounds.

"What is this?" Signe asked, stepping closer.

Ragnar glanced at her, his expression questioning what she was still doing here. He exhaled, then looked to the monitor again and answered. "The green dots are our boys. Red is the breach."

"They need to walk that far?"

"Aye. One kilometer."

Signe thought she knew what a kilometer was, but seeing it on the map, it seemed so much farther.

"Pressure readings inside the suit look good," Frode continued. "Syncing them to your screens now."

Two sets of vital readings appeared on another screen displaying information like heartrate, oxygen levels, and more.

"I see it," Ragnar answered.

"Permission to proceed to airlock?" Bjørn asked.

Ragnar paused for a few seconds before saying, "Granted."

A red line pinged on the screen, along with the runes, "Airlock Opening." This was it. Soon they would be in the open air beyond the shields. Signe held her breath in anticipation.

At first, there was no change on the comm. It was as if nothing happened.

Only seconds later, a cacophony of shrieks and heavy breathing erupted. Both men's heartrates spiked.

"Shit! They're everywhere!" Frode called out. "Fuck, fuck, fuck!"

The sound of a loud blast filled the comms, followed by a momentary quiet. Once again, the quiet was short as the sound of the bats returned.

"I got the lad," Bjørn said. "A quick flashbang cleared the batties for a second or two. We're moving now."

"Good. Proceed to target. You should see the location on your HUD."

"I have it. Heading there," Bjørn confirmed before yelling, "Fuck you, flying vermin! You miss old Bjørn?"

The green dots on screen slowly began to move. When it seemed like there was a brief lull, Signe stepped closer to Ragnar. "How are they alive out there?"

"Armored suits," Ragnar explained. "They're pressurized to maintain a livable oxygen temperature inside, resistant from cold, got their own built-in night vision, and armored all around."

"Sure, but the power cable is armored too, yet bats got to that."

"True, but standing shields are a motionless target. Not to mention, that blast you heard was a flashbang grenade. Bjørn has grenades and a flamethrower to keep the bats off 'em for a few seconds. Frode and Bjørn'll be pelted, clawed at, and bitten for sure, but not like the walls."

"Is the armor strong enough to withstand that?"

"You could shoot the suit from an arm's length away and whoever's inside would hardly feel it. It's like they're walking in their own personal tanks."

Signe gulped. "So…they have nothing to worry about, right?"

Ragnar turned to look at her again. His facial expression told her the answer; no. Yet his voice said, "Yes. Nothing to worry about."

Getting a lie was worse than getting the truth. Signe felt a lump form in her throat. Despite all the technology they had at their disposal, it seemed this would not be easy. Not at all.

"How's it going, you two?" Ragnar asked, returning his attention to the screens.

"Fifty meters in," Bjørn answered. His voice was followed by what sounded like the blast of a flamethrower, then another grenade. "Got some good news. It looks like the floodlights are still working. Can see 'em above us."

The floodlights, Signe remembered. She recalled what Frode said about them. So long as they were operational, it meant they only had to deal with 40 percent of the bats. That thought was, at least, relieving.

"Roger that. How about you, Frode? Talk to me."

"I'm…I'm here…" Frode's voice was strained. Each word came through heaving breaths.

"You're doing fine, Frode. I'm checking your vitals. Just stay with Bjørn."

"Roger."

As the green dots moved across the screen, part of Signe wondered what they were seeing out there, but another part was glad she didn't know. She supposed it couldn't be anything good.

Several minutes passed as Signe watched in anticipation, waiting for something to go awry as the dots progressed across the map. Part of her knew *something* was bound to happen. And yet…all seemed fine…for now.

Beep, beep, beep! A warning blared over the speakers as a grey mass like an amorphous blob appeared on the screen. It came from the north.

"Odin's beard," Ragnar muttered, tapping away at his keyboard. "Bjørn, watch out! I've got a swarm coming in from the north."

"Repeat, Ragnar. Did you say 'swarm?'"

"I did."

"How big?"

"The hundred meters wide by the looks of it."

"Shit," Bjørn said in an exhale. "Let's get a move on, boy!"

Signe turned to Ragnar and asked, "What's a swarm?"

"A cluster of bats, like a densely-packed group."

"I thought they always flew in a densely packed group. They take up the entire sky! How is this any different?"

"Yes, they pack together, but not normally like this. They're basically a solid mass when they swarm."

"How can they move like that?"

"Poorly. In a swarm, bats have basically no space between them. They crash into each other as they fly. It's madness. This… this is where our shields will struggle the most."

Signe hated that she was right, but she *knew* something was bound to go wrong. This was it. This was when the mission would go awry.

A loud crashing sound emanated over the speakers.

"Shit!" Bjørn hollered.

"What is it? What do you see, Bjørn?" Ragnar asked.

"The swarm! It hit a light tower. The tower is coming down! I repeat: the tower is coming down! Oh shit! It's right on top of us!" In an instant, Bjørn's vitals dropped from the screen as the swarm proceeded south, closer to the hospital.

"Bjørn!" Ragnar shouted. "Come in!"

Thud, thud, thud! From the control room, Signe heard the pelting of the swarm against the hospital shields.

"Aah!" a voice called out.

"Bjørn?"

"No, it's me! It's Frode!"

"Frode, what's going on?"

"My legs! Aah!"

"What's going on? Where is Bjørn?"

"He's…oh, Odin! He's dead!"

At the word "dead," Signe gasped and nearly lost her footing.

"Oh no! He's dead!" Frode repeated.

"How? Was it the swarm?"

"The swarm smashed into a light tower. The tower collapsed. Debris fell right on top of him. He's crushed. The debris got me too, but just my legs. Aah, my legs!"

Signe examined the map. The swarm passed over the hospital and continued south. Meanwhile, the two green dots were so close to the red dot: just a bit over 100 meters by the looks of it.

"Frode, stay with me. You're close to the target. Can you free yourself?"

"I…I don't know. I need medical help. Then, maybe I can move."

Ragnar sighed and slowly bobbed his head. "Understood." He glanced at Signe as he continued, "I'll send someone to help you."

Signe pointed to herself as she gasped, "Me?"

Ragnar pulled the headset off his head and stared straight into her eyes. "You've been watching this entire mission. It will take too long to brief anyone else, and time is one thing we don't have." He stood up from his chair and took a step toward her. "You need to rescue Frode."

~ * ~

"I'm getting in *that*?" Signe said as she stared at the armor. The suit was large, shiny, and bulky. The sleeves alone were as wide as a moderate-sized tree trunk. The helmet, adorned with two horns that produced small beams of light at their tips, looked equally bulky.

The red-haired technician walked around it and nodded, unphased by Signe's concern. The young man smacked the chest plate. "It's an older suit, but it'll hold. It passed all the diagnostics. You shall be safe within."

"An older suit?" Signe repeated.

"Worry not about the age. Forget I said anything."

"You think so? Truly? Can you not tell I am worried?"

"You are right to worry, but because of the danger outside, not because of the suit. I would not bring you to harm in a suit I deemed unworthy. I assure you this suit shall sustain the journey, plus you will be armed. That counts for much."

Armed. That word brought little solace. Signe was still to venture into a world consumed by darkness, cold, and killer bats. Whether she was armed was among the least of her concerns.

"*Leaving in the field his arms, let no man go a foot's length forward, for it is hard to know when on the way, a man may need his weapon.*"

"Or woman," Signe retorted.

"Aye, or woman."

"Do you recite scripture whenever you suit someone up?"

The technician chuckled. "No, not normally, but I thought it might help you."

Signe smiled. She supposed a bit of levity was good for her. After all, she needed a clear head. There was too much at stake to quit. The entire hospital would lose power if Frode did not make his repairs…not to mention Frode himself. He would die if Signe could not save him.

Despite her reservations, the choice was simple. She *had* to do this.

"Come, I'll suit you up."

Signe trembled nervously but followed the man's direction. To enter the suit, she first stepped into the legs, then into the boots. After the boots were thoroughly screwed in, then came the torso, then the oxygen tank, then the sleeves, then the gloves, and finally, the helmet. As soon as the helmet was on, a monitor filled her vision. She saw the airlock around her, along with vitals, a map, two green arrows, and one red arrow.

The nurse-turned-rescue-operative took in a deep breath of filtered oxygen, then coughed it up.

"It can take a while to get used to the filtered air," the technician said. Signe was surprised how clearly his voice came through the speakers. "Unfortunately, we don't *have* awhile. Ragnar says he needs you moving."

Signe cleared her throat. "Yes."

"Did I just hear you, Signe?" Ragnar's voice asked, echoing

through the helmet.

"Ragnar? I hear you."

"I hear you too. I'm guessing that means you're all suited up."

"Aye, it looks that way, sir."

"Good. I'll prime the airlock on my end. Make sure the technician goes over everything with you, alright?"

"Alright," Signe said.

"I heard that," the technician said. "I'll make it brief. On your screen, you'll see your vitals. That tells you your heart rate, oxygen levels, suit temperature, internal body temperature, VO2 max, and time spent in the suit. Any questions?"

Signe shook her head but realized the technician would not be able to see her movement from outside the bulky suit. Instead, she replied, "Understood."

"Good. The green arrows on your HUD show the other two suits: that's Frode and Bjørn…or…Bjørn's suit. The red arrow leads to the breach. Beneath the arrows, a number displays the distance between you and that target. Questions?"

"Understood."

"Good. The last thing on your screen is the view itself. Right now, you are looking through normal light, but when I switch this mode in a moment, you will see in night vision. Everything will appear green, but you shall see outside. Questions?"

"Understood."

"Good." The young man lifted a pack of cannisters in the air and attached the pack to the suit's left arm. The cannisters stuck magnetically. "These are your flashbang grenades. Remember when I said you'd be armed? This is it. Separate the top piece and throw. The grenades are non-lethal. They emit a blinding light, so don't look at it, especially with night vision. They'll scare the bats away for a second or two. They are temporary fixes to clear an area, not long-term solutions. Questions?"

"Bjørn had a flamethrower."

"That he did. He was trained to use a flamethrower. It's a good weapon, but you don't have the training. Remember when I said I didn't want you to go out there unprepared? You are unprepared for a flamethrower. You must go without it."

"Won't I need it?"

"You can make do with the grenades. Trust me. The flamethrower is good to have, but not essential."

The young man held up a woven bag with two magnetic rods on the outside. "This is your splint pack. This is what you will use to get Frode moving. I hear you're a good nurse, so you must know how to apply splints. Everything you need is here. The difference is, when applying splints, Frode's suit must remain intact. If his suit is breached, either the cold will kill him, or a bat will find a way in to finish the job. Therefore, you must apply the splints *over* his suit. Any questions?"

"Understood."

"Good. I'll magnetize that to your right arm," he said as he stuck it to her other arm. "Right arm, splints. Left arm, grenades. They remain stuck like so. There are also flare guns on either of your shins."

Signe practiced moving her arms around in the bulky suit. Hydraulics helped carry the weight of the suit her muscles could not. It was clunky, but it worked.

She nodded, forgetting again the technician would not see it, then said, "I'm ready."

"Good."

"I heard that," Ragnar added over the speaker. "Good timing. I've got the airlock ready when you are. Get that technician out of there and I can send you out."

The young man nodded and moved to the exit. Before he left, he stopped and said, "May Odin watch over you." With those words, the technician exited the room.

Seconds later, the lights went out. Seconds after that, the suit's display switched to the green of night vision.

Signe watched as her heartrate spiked on the HUD. She clenched her fists nervously. She felt sweat form everywhere.

"Alright, it looks like it's just you in there," Ragnar said.

"Aye."

"Confirm the armor is secure."

"Aye."

"Putting you on screen now. And…there you are. I see you. Verify pressure readings."

"Pressure readings nominal."

"Great. I'm syncing your vitals to my screen now. Ah, there it is. Looking good, Signe. You're doing great." He paused before continuing, "Alright. This is where you ask for permission."

Signe gulped. She closed her eyes for a moment, then reopened them. She trembled as she asked, "Permission to proceed to airlock?"

Ragnar paused before replying, "Granted."

Signe held her breath as the doors parted before her. As the sliver of the outside world revealed itself in the night vision, she saw her first real view of the bats. They appeared like a spinning swirl of dots moving beyond the threshold. It was unlike anything she had seen before, like a living tornado that filled the entire sky. In a weird way, it was beautiful.

And then…the bats entered the airlock.

Immediately, Signe felt the force of hundreds of bats collide into her. She spun around and fell to her knees. She struggled to stand, the force of the bats keeping her down. She screamed, not knowing what to do.

She was on her own. No one could save her here.

Then she remembered Frode. He was alone too, only he was far from the hospital. He needed help more than she did. She was his only hope.

This was bigger than her. Frode depended on her; the whole station depended on her.

Signe collected herself, then, in one quick motion, rose to her feet, pushing the bats from her back. She turned, bracing her body against the onslaught like bracing for a fierce ocean wave. She stepped forward, then again, then again, redistributing her balance through each powerful collision that tried to knock her off her feet.

"I see you moving. Keep going," said Ragnar.

Crossing the threshold, Signe entered a nightmarish hellscape unlike anything she ever imagined. Only two days into the eclipse and it seemed all vegetation had withered and died long ago. The world was dark and desolate, like the Realm of Hel. She wished she could stop and examine it further, but bats pelted her from every corner. It was difficult to look anywhere.

With each step, Signe tried to keep the green arrows ahead of her. Occasionally a powerful collision sent her spinning, but time after time, she managed to reorient herself.

Minutes passed and her muscles ached. She exerted so much and yet, looking at the distance on screen, she only moved less than 100 meters.

"Shit. This is going to take all day!"

"Calm down, Signe. You're doing great. The others moved just as slowly."

"Really?"

"Really. You're doing fine. Remember to use a flashbang if you need."

The flashbangs. Signe had forgotten all about them. She grabbed a grenade, pulled the pin, and tossed it forward. She averted her eyes to the right, but despite looking the other way, a powerful white light filled her screen. The flashbang combined with the night vision was the brightest thing she had ever seen—like standing inside the sun itself. She shouted, closed her eyes, and dropped to her knees, blinded.

"Signe, are you alright?"

"No! The grenade must have bounced off the bats mid-throw. It blew in front of my eyes. Dammit! I'm blind!"

"Take a breather. Close your eyes. Your vision should return."

Signe did exactly that. Eventually she opened her eyes again, but they stung. She blinked heavily. Her vision was blurry, but she could at least see the green arrows. That was enough.

"How do you feel?"

"Odin, my eyes feel terrible, but…dammit…I'll manage."

The bats dissipated, at least for now. Signe quickly got to her feet with little issue and pressed forward while she had the opportunity. She made it about 50 meters before the bats filled the area again.

After a few more rigorous meters, Signe grabbed one of her two flare guns this time, got down low, diverted her gaze, and fired directly forward. This time, nothing blasted in front of her eyes. When she faced forward again, the bats diverted along the flare's flightpath, leading a clear path for her, albeit a temporary one.

This was her best opportunity yet. Taking full advantage of it, she dashed forward. She made terrific progress and even passed the flare itself with little trouble before the bats finally returned. By that time, she had 500 meters left.

In the distance, Signe spotted the line of light towers. Just as Frode warned, one of them had collapsed. Sure enough, not too far ahead, the area by the collapsed tower was flooded with bats; far more than she had encountered thus far. She gulped nervously, knowing she had not even faced anything close to the worst of it yet.

Pressing forward, Signe withstood the barrage of bats, blasting grenades when she could, and moving at what felt like a crawling pace. Finally, with less than 100 meters to go, she saw Frode struggling in the rubble. She smiled.

"Ragnar, I see him!"

"Patching you through now. You can talk to him."

"Signe?" Frode gasped. "Is that you?"

"It is me. I'm here. I see you."

"I can't feel my legs, Signe."

"I'm almost there."

Another step forward and Signe entered the densest part of the journey. Here, the absence of light meant there was nothing to thin out the bats. The force of their chaotic movements was enough to toss her backwards a full two meters. She fell on her butt and cursed as she stood back up. This would be difficult.

Acting on instinct, Signe popped another grenade, averted her eyes, and dove forward as the bats temporarily cleared out. Sprinting as she came to her feet, she made it about halfway into the depth of the darkness when the bats returned. This time, not wanting to use another valuable grenade, she got down on all fours and dug into the dirt, clawing forward. Pain reverberated through every muscle in her body. She shouted, crawling and crawling until …her glove touched something metal.

Signe was right on top of a green arrow. She looked down, then gasped in horror as a pale, bludgeoned, mangled face looked back at her. Only a breath away, a bloodied helmet rested in the dirt; its horns covered in pale bat shit.

"Oh my…I'm too late," she muttered, feeling tears in her eyes. "Odin's beard…no…no!"

"Signe!" Frode's voice called out.

"Frode?" She looked around in confusion.

"That's Bjørn's body, not mine! I'm here! To the right!"

Signe turned. She let out a powerful sigh of relief as the man waved to her, then motioned to his injured legs.

"Frode! I thought you were dead!"

"Not yet. Help!"

Signe crouched next to Frode and held onto him. "I have you.

How are you feeling?"

"Terrible."

"Likewise."

"What do you need me to do?"

With a patient in her arms, it felt like Signe was back in the hospital. In a strange way, this was the most comfortable she felt since exiting the airlock.

"We need to get you standing," she said as she lifted the debris and tossed it aside, effectively freeing Frode's legs.

Withstanding the bat barrage as best she could, Signe removed the kit from her right arm and pulled out the pieces, holding onto everything tightly, knowing the pieces could be knocked away any second. Inside the kit, she found two metal rods and sticky gauze. She straightened out Frode's bent suit pants and attached a metal rod to each one, then wrapped the rods thoroughly in gauze. All the while, bats darted in and out of her line of vision and tossed her around as she worked.

"Your legs are likely broken, but you'll need to move whatever you can to get you upright. The debris is gone, so it's just you now. The splints will keep your legs straight. I'll hold onto you and pull you up, but I'm going to need you to help me."

"I think I can do that."

"On three. Ready? One…two…three!"

Frode moaned as he struggled to stand. He was heavy and the sound in his voice proved that he was in immense pain. It took nearly 30 seconds, but together, they got him to his feet.

Panting, Frode managed to utter the words, "Thank you."

Signe smiled. "Glad to have you upright."

Frode motioned to the red arrow. "Not done yet. The breach. Get me there!" He grabbed a tool bag from the ground. A large metal sheet was magnetically attached to it.

Signe wrapped her left arm around Frode's shoulder, propping him up. Walking was already difficult, but it was all the more challenging with an injured man. Each step felt more strained than the last. Her muscles ached, her vision was blurry, her balance was impossible to maintain. And yet, somehow, she pressed forward.

Frode moaned again, the sound of his voice proving he would not make it. Signe looked down at the last flare gun and reached for it with her free hand.

"I'll clear a path."

"Is that the last one?"

"It is."

"We still have to get back to the airlock after this," Frode reminded her.

"We'll deal with the breach first. Right now, it's all that matters," she returned as she fired the flare forward. Like last time, the light produced a straight path through the bats. This was their opportunity. They took it.

Hobbling, they reached the target. The red arrow hovered above a gaping hole about a hand's width wide along a half-meter-tall metal tube-like shield that ran along the ground.

Frode dropped to the icy dirt and looked into the hole. "There're bats everywhere! Give me a grenade!"

Signe handed him a grenade and realized it was one of two remaining. She chose to withhold that detail.

Frode popped the grenade into the hole. When the flash of light appeared, a wave of bats evacuated, clearing it at least somewhat.

The technician pulled out his toolkit and got to work. "Cover me!"

Not knowing what that meant, Signe spread her arms and legs out and did her best to literally cover Frode and the breach as if she were a human shield. Bats pounded into her relentlessly. Everything ached. Her vision went in and out.

After what felt like five grueling minutes, Frode yelled, "I've done it! Power should be back soon!"

The man grabbed the sheet of metal and held it to the hole. "I'm going to weld this. Switch your vision settings or you're going to go blind!"

"What? I wasn't taught how to do that!"

"Then look the other way!"

Still pounded by relentless onslaught, Signe looked away as the sound of the torch filled the air. They were so close now...so close...

After another few minutes, Frode yelled, "Done!"

"Done?" Signe repeated as she turned to view the breach. Sure enough, the hole was sealed.

"Aye, done. We did it, Signe! *You* did it! Now let's get the hell out of here!"

Signe reached for her final grenade and sighed. "This it is. This is all I have. It's not enough to get us to the airlock."

"Shit," Frode muttered. "Well, use what we have. Do it!"

Pulling the pin, Signe tossed her last flashbang. She lifted Frode up and the two ran as best as they could. They only got a few meters before the bats overwhelmed them again and knocked them to their butts.

They were back in the dark section now. This time, the force of the bats was too strong. She could not get up. If she couldn't stand, there was no way injured Frode could stand.

Was this it? Where they to die here?

And then…all at once, a string of LEDs lit up around the hospital grounds. Bats shrieked and diverted, moving to higher altitude.

"The power!" Frode cheered. "The power is back! Quick! While we have a chance!"

Not wanting to waste a second, Signe got to her feet and helped Frode stand. Once up, they darted to the airlock, taking full advantage of the clearing. Even with the heavy, bulky suit, Signe never ran so fast in her life.

When they finally entered the airlock, the two dropped to the floor. Ragnar's voice echoed in their helmets, "Door closing!"

The door closed, but a few bats remained inside. As soon as it was shut, Signe felt the instinct to remove her helmet, but Frode placed his hand on hers, prompting her to remain suited.

"Get down and close your eyes! It's going to get hot and bright!" Ragnar warned.

A second later, the chamber filled with fire as the remaining bats inside were burned to death.

It felt like an oven. Signe gasped and felt her head drop to the ground.

That was the last thing she remembered.

~ * ~

Singe awoke in a hospital bed. She was dizzy. The room was blurry and bright.

"Wh-where am I?" the nurse muttered in strained words. The last thing she remembered; she was in the airlock. Bats caught fire above her head. Everything was hot.

A familiar voice responded, "You're awake!"

"Doctor Hrothgar?" Signe made out the familiar sight of her colleague. She smiled.

"It's me, yes. And you have a visitor," he said, motioning to the door.

As soon as he said that another man entered in a wheelchair. It was Frode. Despite her blurry vision, Signe knew it was him right away. The man tapped his chest and looked right at Signe as he said, "Heil ok sæl."

~ * ~ * ~

Formerly an on-site educator at the Smithsonian National Air and Space Museum in Washington, DC, **Andrew Gates** is now a Delaware-based science-fiction writer, editor, and magazine contributor. He is best known as the author of the epic four-part series, *Color of Water and Sky*.

When Andrew is not writing, he enjoys running, playing with animals, and playing Xbox.

Broken Ones

Natasha Morningstarr

Carmen and Javi watched in horror as the car sped down the street, its tires screeching against the pavement. They were only 10 years old, but they had already seen so much violence in their short lives.

As they stood on the corner, watching warily, a dark sedan slowly drove past them. They knew it was too late to run—they could already hear the telltale sounds of gunshots ringing out through the air.

As the car sped away, Carmen and Javi saw the bodies littering the ground. Their home was no longer a safe place—not for them, or anyone else.

That was when it hit them—*this* is what their lives had become. Having to constantly run from bullets, trying to dodge the gangs and the drugs. This was their reality.

"That was terrifying," Carmen said to Javi as they walked home from the store. "I can't believe we saw that."

"I know," Javi replied. "It's like this is our reality now. So we have to be careful all the time."

"Do you think our parents will ever get better?" Carmen asked.

"I don't know," Javi said. "But we have each other, and we'll never let go, no matter what happens."

"Sounds cool, cuz," Carmen smiled at Javi as the sirens of the ambulance and cops drew closer. They couldn't wait to return to Javi's to tell his mom what they had just witnessed. As they climbed the steps, they could smell the liquor and cigarette smoke from inside. Pulling open the screen door, Javi called out for his mom, Bridgett.

"She's in the kitchen with her friends," one of the men said. "Go on back."

As they walked through the living room, Carmen and Javi were shocked to see how many people were inside their home. Men filled the living room and kitchen, all surrounding Javi's mom, Bridgett. They played cards, smoked cigarettes, and laughed.

"Mom?" Javi said, walking up to her. "What's going on?"

"Oh, nothing, honey," Bridgett said, leaning over to kiss him. "Just having some friends over."

But these didn't look like regular friends. Bandanas that were all the same color were draped from their pockets and wrapped around their heads. It was no secret Bridgett was a gangsta. This intrigued Carmen, who was used to only seeing men belonging to gangs in her neighborhood. *There was something empowering about seeing a woman do the same.*

"Carmen, come meet my friends," Bridgett said, motioning her over.

"Hi," Carmen said shyly.

"These are my homegirls," Bridgett said. "The Eastside Sistaz." The Eastside Sistaz was the all-female chapter of the notorious Eastsiders gang, known for their fierce dedication and unwavering loyalty to one another.

Carmen had never seen anything like this before. She was used to the women in her neighborhood being afraid of the gang members; not being friends with them. But here they were, laughing and joking like they were family.

"Do you want to play cards with us?" one of the women asked.

"Sure," Carmen replied, pulling up a chair. Then, she turned to look over her shoulder, noticing Javi frowning at what he was witnessing.

Carmen didn't know it then, but they were sizing her up. Seeing if she was tough enough to be a part of their gang. And from that day forward, Carmen was no longer just a witness to the violence in her neighborhood—she was a part of it. Hustling her cousins and the kids on the block for their lunch money and weekly allowances became a way for Carmen to keep money in her pocket. Her mother's heavy drug use left the pantry empty on most days. So, if Carmen wanted to eat, she had to provide for herself.

~ * ~

A few weeks had passed since Carmen had last seen her cousin Javi. Excitement to catch up consumed her. Arriving at his house, she could hear laughter coming from inside.

"Javi, is that you?" Carmen called out as she walked in. Silence followed as she walked into the bedroom where he was watching tv, his eyes telling Carmen she was not welcome.

"You're one of them now," Javi said to Carmen, his voice laced with disgust. "I can't believe you would do something like that."

"What's wrong with it?" Carmen asked. "They're my friends."

"They're not your friends," Javi spat. "They're a gang. And you're nothing but a thug now."

Hurt by her cousin's words, Carmen had thought he would understand why she did it. But Javi was always the good one. He never got into trouble. He always did what his mother asked, even when Bridgett terrorized him. Carmen knew Javi was just trying to protect her. But this was something that had to be done.

Carmen grew tired of being a good girl. She wanted to be bad for once. And if that meant joining a gang, then so be it.

"You're never going to amount to anything," Javi said, walking towards her. "You're a broken girl who will end up like your mom."

The Eastside Sistaz became her family. They protected her and taught her how to survive in an often brutal and unforgiving world. And Carmen would need all the strength and courage they could give her to stay.

Carmen tried to reach out to Javi, but he refused to see her. This upset Carmen, leading her to turn to her gang members for support. Quickly Carmen climbed up the ranks within the gang and became one of the most respected members. Carmen was no longer a scared little girl—she was a tough, badass woman who would do whatever it took to protect herself. Carmen had finally found a place where she belonged.

But as the years went by, Carmen began to see the reality of her situation. The gang was involved in drugs, violence, and crime. It wasn't the happy family she thought it would be. They only looked out for themselves and didn't care about anyone else. Carmen became increasingly disillusioned with the gang. But she was in too deep to turn back now.

As she swaggered into the dimly lit alleyway, Carmen knew tonight was going to be one hell of a ride. High on drugs and looking for a fight, she and her gang were out to make some trouble.

But instead of finding their usual rivals, they came across a group of thugs from another gang. A brutal brawl ensued, with punches flying and knives flashing in the moonlight. And then suddenly, amid the chaos, someone pulled out a gun and started shooting.

Carmen gasped as a bullet tore through her side, leaving her bleeding profusely on the cold concrete. She felt her strength fading fast as she slipped into unconsciousness, wondering if this was how she would die—in the gutters of some seedy back alley with her blood staining the ground.

Carmen saw her life flash before her eyes. She thought about Javi and how he warned her about this lifestyle. *About how he tried to protect her.* She wondered if he would ever talk to her again.

~ * ~

Javi refused to answer any of Carmen's calls or texts. It was difficult for him to wrap his head around how, after all they had seen and experienced at the hands of drugs and violence, she would choose to become a gang member. It made no sense to him. Not even when he was high could he make logical conclusions about it.

Carmen had always been his rock, the one person he knew would never leave him no matter what happened. But Carmen did leave by choosing a life of crime and violence over him.

It hurt more than anything else ever had.

Javi tried to forget about Carmen by throwing himself into work, but it was impossible. In the back of his mind, she was always there, haunting him with her betrayal.

One Saturday, as he was hanging out in the living room, his mom approached him with an opportunity.

Smacking her lips together, Bridgett clapped her hands to get Javi's attention. "Why are you sitting there looking like that?" his mother asked. "I have an idea."

"What is it?" Javi asked, not interested.

"You should come and work for me," his mom said. "It would help you take your mind off of things."

"I don't know," Javi said, shaking his head. "I don't think me getting involved with what you do, mom, would help. It'll make me just like Carmen."

"It's not what you think," his mom said. "I know you're still mad at her but give her a chance to explain herself. You might be surprised by what you hear."

Javi thought about it for a moment and shook his head. "Mom, why would you ask me, your son, to get into the life?"

His mom looked at him with a sincere expression. "Javi, I love you," she said. "You're all I have left in this world. I just want to make sure you're taken care of."

Javi knew his mom was only trying to help, but he didn't want anything to do with her or the life she adopted. Yet deep in his heart, Javi knew all his mother knew how to do was scheme, cheat and steal. That's how Bridgett was raised and learned to survive in the hoods of the northside. He knew if he ever lost her, he would lose the will to stay.

The only thing Javi's mother had ever showed him was how to be a criminal. As much as he didn't want to admit it, he was just like Carmen. He was a broken one.

"Okay, mom. I'll do it!" Javi had nothing else going on for him. He needed a distraction and working for his mom would provide him with one.

Javi's mom smiled at him, her eyes twinkling with excitement. "This is just a one-time thing, Javi," she said slowly. "You don't have to do this forever if you don't want to."

Javi nodded eagerly, already starting to get excited about the prospect of working for his mom's gang. He hated his day job, with its long hours and low pay, and he couldn't help but feel a thrill at the thought of doing something more exciting and meaningful.

Soon, Javi was completely immersed in his new job, turning the gang into a sophisticated criminal organization that operated with precision and efficiency. He was good at business management, and it showed as he quickly rose through the ranks to become one of his mom's most trusted lieutenants.

For Javi, working for his mom's gang was the best decision he had ever made. He felt alive and fulfilled in a way he never had before, and he knew without a doubt this was where he truly belonged.

~ * ~

Javi smiled to himself as he looked around the crowded room, knowing just a few months earlier, he never would have dreamed of being in charge of the Eastsiders. But thanks to Carmen's near-fatal shooting months ago, he had been given the opportunity to run the gang and take them to new heights.

None of the other members believed in Carmen's ability to keep them moving forward after she was shot, so they had chosen to replace her with Javi. And although it hadn't been an easy transition at first, Javi was determined to prove his worth and lead the gang to even greater success.

Determined to make his mark on the organization, Javi threw himself into his work, hustling day and night to move up through the ranks and build his reputation as a ruthless leader. Slowly but surely, he rose through the ranks and took control of every aspect of operations.

With each passing day, Javi grew more confident in his abilities, knowing he made the right decision by staying with The Eastsiders. And as he looked around at all those gathered before him, he knew this was only just the beginning—he was destined for great things as long as he kept working hard and pushing forward.

Looking over at her, he saw her laughing and joking with some of the other members. Carmen had changed since joining the gang. She was more brutal and colder. But Javi knew underneath all that, she was still the same girl he had trauma bonded with all those years ago.

"Carmen," he called out as he walked over to her. "I need to talk to you."

"What is it?" she asked, a smile still on her face.

Javi pulled her aside so they could talk in private. "I met this girl, and I want you to meet her," he said. "I think you guys will hit it off."

"What girl?" Carmen asked, her brow furrowed in confusion.

"Her name is Teresa," Javi said. "She's different than anyone I've ever met. She's not like us, Carmen. She's special."

Carmen looked at him, her eyes softening. "Javi, I think you're falling for this girl."

"Maybe, I am," he said, not denying it. "But there's something else. Teresa introduced me to something that had me feeling so good last night. I mean, it was *really* good, Carmen. I can't even explain it."

"What are you talking about?" Carmen asked, her confusion turning into concern.

"Teresa had me try ecstasy for the first time last night," Javi said, his eyes wide with excitement. "It was unlike anything I've ever experienced before. I felt so good, Carmen. It was like my soul was opening up."

Carmen looked at him skeptically. "Javi, that stuff is dangerous. You don't know what you're getting yourself into."

"I know, but it felt so good," he said pleadingly. "Please, just meet her. I think you guys will hit it off."

Carmen sighed and relented. "*Fine*, I'll meet her."

Carmen was hesitant to meet Teresa at first but was quickly won over by the girl's bubbly personality. Soon she could tell Teresa was different than anyone else Javi had ever brought around.

However, Carmen grew worried when she overheard Javi telling Teresa they should do ecstasy again. Selling it herself, Carmen knew the drug was dangerous and didn't want Javi to get addicted like the ones who lined her trap house daily.

"Javi, we need to talk," Carmen said, pulling him aside.

"What's up?" he asked, a smile on his face.

"I overheard you talking to Teresa about doing ecstasy again," Carmen's eyes filled with concern. "Javi, that stuff is dangerous. I don't want you to get hurt."

"I know, Carmen," he said, his smile fading. "But it makes me feel so good. I can't explain it. It's like I am finally connecting to something like never before."

Carmen looked at him sympathetically. "I know, but you have to be careful. They put all kinds of stuff in that drug, so you don't even know if what you are taking is pure ecstasy."

Javi nodded his head in agreement. "I'll be careful, I promise."

Despite her warning, Javi soon became addicted and couldn't function without popping pills daily. Carmen watched helplessly as he became a shell of his former self. The handsome, charismatic man Carmen once knew was replaced by someone always chasing that high.

His once-perfect skin was marred by acne, and his eyes were sunken from lack of sleep. His breath always smelled of alcohol, and he was constantly sweating. Carmen begged him to stop, but it was like he couldn't even hear her anymore.

Javi's addiction led him down a dark path, and eventually, he started stealing from friends and family to make money. Finally, on a Saturday afternoon, the Eastsiders gathered to vote Javi down from his leadership role, leaving him to stand on corners begging for money from passing strangers.

Javi's addiction led him to desperate measures, and he eventually tried robbing a local bank. However, he was quickly apprehended by the police and was sentenced to jail time.

Carmen was devastated after learning what Javi had done. He had hit rock bottom, and there was no coming back from this.

~ * ~

Javi was sentenced to ten years in prison for robbing that bank. Carmen will never forget his mother's cries in the courtroom that day. She also shed a few tears but seeing Bridgett cry upset her. This was the same woman who led him down this path. The same woman who never cared for him. His mother only cried that day, realizing she would no longer have anyone to leech off of.

Carmen tried to keep in touch with Javi while he was away, but it was hard. She would visit him sometimes, but it wasn't the same. He was different. The Javi she knew was gone. He had been replaced by a cold, heartless man who only cared about himself.

~ * ~

Weeks turned into months; eventually, they lost touch, and Carmen moved on with her life. The Eastside Sistaz fell apart, making it easy for Carmen to move away and start over. She graduated high school with honors and went to college and then to law school. She built a new life far away from the hood and her old toxic friends and family.

But Carmen never forgot her cousin. On the contrary, she often thought about Javi, especially after reading one of his angry letters.

"You think you're much better than me, don't you?" Javi's letter started. "You've always looked down on me, thinking you're better than me because you went to school and got good grades. Let me tell you something, cousin: I'm smarter than you'll ever be. I may not have your fancy degrees, but I can survive. You're a *spoiled little girl* who's never had to work for anything."

Carmen was hurt by Javi's words, but she didn't reply. She knew he was just angry, and he didn't mean what he said. They both grew up poor, so his letter made no sense. Carmen had worked hard for everything she had. Javi, however, had always taken the easy way out. Even when he was robbing that bank, he could have just walked away, and no one would have been hurt.

But he didn't. He chose to take the money and ended up getting caught. And now he was paying the price.

Carmen would never forget her cousin, but she had moved on with her life. She knew Javi was where he belonged and there was nothing she could do to change that.

~ * ~

Carmen clutched the phone tightly, her knuckles turning white. Carmen couldn't believe what she was hearing. Javi had overdosed while in prison and didn't make it. Carmen felt like the ground had been pulled out from under her. All she could think about was the last hug they had shared.

With only two weeks left to go on his prison sentence, Javi had been so close to coming home. Now he was gone.

Carmen couldn't help but feel guilty. She had been the one who had made it out. She was the one who had escaped the grip of poverty and being a kid of an addict. But Javi hadn't been so lucky. Carmen knew if it hadn't been for a few positive role models in her life, she might have ended up just like him.

Javi's death hit Carmen hard. But it also made her realize she needed to make the most of her life. She needed to live for those who didn't have the chance to. Javi would always be in her heart, and she would never forget him.

Carmen had always been driven to make a difference in the world. And when her beloved cousin, Javi, fell victim to addiction and mental health issues, she knew she had to do something.

So she started *Healing the Broken Ones*, a nonprofit organization dedicated to raising awareness about mental health and helping struggling teens in the urban community. Through her tireless efforts, Carmen was able to reach countless young people and help them get back on their feet.

With her unwavering dedication and relentless spirit, Carmen truly made a difference in the lives of so many. Her efforts illuminated hope for those who felt lost in their struggles, giving them strength when they needed it most.

Carmen stared at the photo of Javi she kept on her nightstand. It was taken just a few weeks before she joined the Eastside Sistaz. Carmen remembered how happy and innocent they looked at that moment, making her heart ache.

But Carmen knew Javi was at peace now. And she also knew he would want her to keep fighting. So that's what she would do. She would keep fighting for all the *broken* ones who needed help.

~ * ~ * ~

Natasha MorningStarr is a creative writer with a proclivity for all things horror. She is a member of the Horror Writers Association, enjoys glasses of white wine, rituals with her husband during the new moon, and speaking to the dead with her family of Wanderers. Her first short story publication is Miss Fortune—Anastasia in the Wasatch Witches: A Collection of Utah Horror anthology available now on Amazon.

DNF

Stetson Ray

I'm going to be honest. When I first saw the cover of *"Mommy is My Friend,"* I could feel myself internally recoiling. Great, I thought, here's another writer who takes themselves too seriously, another novel that examines the volatile and complex dynamics of mother/daughter relationships.

But despite my first impressions, I am thrilled to report I was wrong to judge this book by its cover.

Never during my career as a literary critic have I been floored by a debut novel until now. Most writers' freshman attempts are mediocre at best, but not this one from Valerie Stone. The language is simple, but beautiful. The pacing is perfect. The dialogue sings. The world contained within the pages of this novel is as rich as any ever created. And the characters...where do I start? I can't stop thinking about the protagonist's mother, wondering if a version of this woman is really out there somewhere.

Some will say Ms. Stone's style is gimmicky or relies too heavily on inciting an emotional response from the reader, and that's okay, because not every book is for everyone. Besides, I doubt a few negative reviews will bother the author once the royalty money starts to roll in (and I'm certain it will—this novel has *bestseller* written all over it).

I gladly give *"Mommy is My Friend"* five out of five stars, and I have already chosen it as my featured book of the month for February.

—Paul Bernard,
Literary reviewer for Lines and Spaces Magazine

~ * ~

Valerie Stone didn't cry when her mother died. Or the day after. Or the day after that. Not at the funeral, or at the cemetery when they put her mother's body in the ground. Relatives and friends offered to keep Valerie company, but she refused. Valerie wanted to be alone, so she went back to her mother's house by herself.

It was odd to be back after being gone for so many years.

Valerie waited in the foyer, half expecting her mother to come gliding down the stairs to admonish her for having the nerve to set foot inside the door.

She waited.

The house was quiet.

Her mother wasn't coming.

Valerie felt like a little girl again. She had the feeling her mother was watching her, just waiting for her to make a mistake. She went to her mother's bedroom and opened the door, breaking the number one rule.

"Mommy, I'm home."

The smell of the room brought back memories, mostly bad ones. She shut the door and walked through the house slowly, moving as though she were touring a museum. The home was packed with antique decor—all of which now belonged to Valerie. Every mahogany wardrobe and every oak table, every grandfather clock and every handmade chair. For reasons she did not understand, she had inherited everything.

Eleven years prior when Valerie had escaped, her mother had been furious her only daughter had no interest in following the correct life path: college, career, marriage, reproduction—in that order. But Valerie had to get out. Her mother ran her household like a military academy and eighteen years of being the only cadet was all Valerie could handle.

Those first few months of living in the city had been difficult for Valerie. Even though she was glad to be free from her mother, she missed her. On the advice of a friend, Valerie started writing. She had never written for fun; it turned out she had a knack for it. Her roommates actually enjoyed reading her stories and would ask her what she was working on regularly, without prompting. Better than the encouraging comments from her friends was the feeling writing gave her: afterwards she felt empty, and the voices inside her head weren't so loud.

No one had ever told her writing was like free therapy

Valerie went to bars on the weekends and worked temporary jobs and dated temporary boys, all the while writing to self-medicate the symptoms of her past trauma and mental issues. She decided to submit her scribblings to a few magazines and was shocked when one of her stories was accepted. An editor sent a note with a referral to a literary agent—a friend of the editor—and Valerie sent the agent an email along with her story.

The first thing the agent asked in her reply was, "Have you written a novel yet?"

Valerie had not, but she decided to give it a try.

She went upstairs, her head spinning from the funeral, wondering what she was supposed to do with all the things she had inherited from her mother. She didn't know what the antiques were worth, or who to contact about selling them, but she didn't plan on keeping a thing, not even the house. It wasn't that she needed the money; the estate felt like more of a burden than a gift. She went into her childhood bedroom and lay down on the bed and kicked off her shoes. She took a bottle of whiskey out of her bag and lay there drinking until she was drunk enough to sleep.

~ * ~

When Valerie woke up the next morning, she didn't know where she was. She tried to go back to sleep, but it was no use. Her head was pounding, and her thoughts were racing. Memories of everything that happened when she had moved out were pulsing through her mind, playing back like a movie.

Writing that first novel nearly took Valerie over the edge. And once it was done it wasn't *really done*. Working through draft after draft made Valerie doubt everything, and the process threw her world into chaos. Her boyfriend left, and she was one mistake away from getting canned at work, but she couldn't make herself care. Completing the book was all that mattered, even if it ruined her life.

Eventually she finished (had to make herself stop) and sent the manuscript to her agent and waited. For days she expected her phone to ring, her agent to be on the other end of the line laughing so hard she couldn't speak, all of it an elaborate prank to trick a fool into writing a book just so the whole world could have a laugh.

That's not what happened.

Her agent loved it. The book sold after a bidding war. Not to an independent publisher, but to one of the big ones. The editors loved it more than Valerie's agent. They kept saying it had "cross-over appeal" and was "commercial." After her book was put into the publishing schedule, there was nothing for Valerie to do but wait for the release date. Those eighteen months felt like eighteen years.

Doubt crept in slowly until she believed it was all a prank again.

So when the book was released and sales doubled each month until the first printing sold out, Valerie could hardly believe it. People said that reading *"Mommy is My Friend"* was like having their minds read, that the characters were like real people. Even the critics couldn't find many negative things to say. One of them said Valerie's novel was the perfect mixture of literary and genre, and another called it the single most compelling piece of American pop-literature released in the last twenty years.

None of the praise seemed real until the fan letters began to arrive. Valerie tried to respond to each one, but it was an impossible task; the letters never stopped, and she couldn't keep up.

She went on a book signing tour. She was interviewed on TV and radio. She received a fat check when the movie rights sold.

Emboldened by her success, Valerie tried to call her mother, but she hung up the moment she recognized Valerie's voice. Valerie sent letters but never received a response. She tried not to think about it. It was easy. She had big things going on.

Everyone wanted a piece of her, and watching her name rise through the ranks on The New York Times bestseller list until it reached number one was the biggest thrill of her life. Unbelievable: her first novel was a certified hit. The whole country loved what Valerie had thought was a simple story, the tale of a timid girl and her emotionally volatile mother. Sure, Valerie knew her book was good, but she never thought it would be number one on any list. But over the next few months, she found out all the royalty money and good reviews in the world felt like nothing without her mother's approval. It was a cliche, but it was also true.

Writing suddenly didn't clear her mind like it had before; it didn't matter how many words she wrote. Valerie felt like she was living under a concrete block, like the whole world was waiting to see what words she put down in what order. The pressure was too much. She started drinking more.

Each of Valerie's next three novels sold better than the last, and the critics were kind to her work. Each of her books had that special touch, that realer than real dialogue and those relatable characters her fans (at some point they started calling themselves "Stoners") couldn't get enough of. It all seemed too good to be true.

~ * ~

Valerie stared at the patterns on the ceiling above her bed. The warped face that had been there since she was a child looked the same as it always had. The face grinned at her, sad and happy at the same time.

Valerie finally did what she hadn't been able to do at the funeral.

She cried.

Sometime later she rolled out of bed and went downstairs. She needed to be rid of the house and its contents. She needed to get back to her own life. She called the estate lawyer. He said it would be a while before the house could legally be sold, but there was a company that cleared out the houses of the recently deceased and sold the contents at auction for commission. Valerie called the company and later that day a box truck arrived. The truck driver—a burly man with hairy arms—knocked on the front door and she opened it.

"Valerie Stone?"

"Yes."

He stood back and gave her a look she was familiar with.

"Do you write books?"

"Yes."

"That's what I thought. My daughter loves your stuff." The man nodded as he talked, starstruck. "You know, I read one once, just to see what all the fuss was about."

He waited for Valerie to comment, but she had nothing to say to him. She wanted him to close his mouth, take the furniture, and leave.

"It was pretty good," he said, nodding again.

"I'm glad you liked it."

Valerie waited upstairs while a few men took everything of value from the ground level of the house. Then she waited in the mostly barren living room while they pillaged the second floor.

Even though she wanted the furniture gone, seeing her childhood home empty brought tears again. The burly man came into the living room and saw Valerie before she could fix her face. He looked away and they both apologized while Valerie sniffled.

"I think we're all done, but if you find anything else, you give us a call." The man fished a card out of his pocket.

Valerie went to him and forced herself to smile.

"Thank you," she said, and took the card.

The man stood there, staring.

"I'm sorry, but is there any way I could get your autograph? It's for my girl."

Valerie wanted to scream. "Sure," she said instead.

He handed Valerie a piece of paper and a pen and she signed it, feeling empty inside. She had learned to sign her name the way it appeared on the cover of her books—thin, loopy letters; it looked great, especially in red.

By the time the movers were gone, it was almost dark. Valerie decided to stay one more night and leave first thing in the morning. She was already getting the shakes and didn't want to drive drunk if she didn't have to. Being rich and famous only goes so far, and only works with some cops; her fans might not forgive a second DUI.

Valerie was digging in a closet for a blanket when the doorbell rang. She went to the door, hoping it wasn't one of her distant relatives come to tell her how sorry they were. Looking through the glass paneled door, she could see someone on the porch, but couldn't tell who it was.

Valerie opened the door and an unfamiliar woman said, "Hello."

She was thin, and her hair was dark and short and scraggly. She was wearing professional looking clothes, business casual more or less, but her outfit had a sideways look about it. It was hard to discern how old the woman was. She wasn't old, but she wasn't young.

"I really hate to come by so late, but I didn't want to miss you," the woman said.

Then Valerie knew who the woman was.

A fan.

Somehow, a Stoner had found her.

This one had the look: she wanted something, probably an autograph. Valerie wanted to slam the door in the woman's face, but so far in her short career as a famous writer, she hadn't been rude to a single fan who wasn't first rude to her.

"I'll need a pen," Valerie said.

It only takes a few seconds to sign an autograph—a small

price to pay to get someone to leave you alone.

Seemingly confused, the woman said, "I'm sorry. I'm forgetting myself. My name is Cynthia. The company I work for saw your mother's obituary in the paper, so they sent me to see if there's anything you would like to get rid of."

Valerie's head was starting to hurt, and she struggled to process the information.

"You mean, you don't know who I am?"

"Should I?"

"No, I guess not. You said you saw my mother's obituary?"

"Yes, ma'am. Well, my company did. They sent me right over."

"What exactly can I help you with?" Valerie asked, crossing her arms.

"Like I said, I'm so sorry to bother you, but I wanted to see if there's anything you needed to get rid of. Anything you don't want to carry anymore."

The thought crossed Valerie's mind that she might be dreaming—possibly blacked out and hallucinating. She looked past the woman. The neighborhood was quiet. No one else was around. The wind blew gently through the trees. Everything seemed real enough.

"I'm sorry, but I've already had an auction company take care of that. Thank you."

Valerie took a step back and started to close the door.

"Wait," Cynthia said. There was a desperate tone in her voice that made Valerie pause.

"I already told you, I—"

"I don't want your silverware or your antiques. I'm talking about you. I can take anything you don't want anymore. *Anything.*"

Valerie stared at the woman. Her eyes were big and far apart. Her face was not quite gaunt, but her features were oddly defined. She kind of looked like…*an addict.*

"I have no idea what you're talking about," Valerie said.

The woman who claimed her name was Cynthia stepped forward and said, "I can help you get rid of whatever you're carrying. You don't have to live with it anymore. The bad memories. The trauma. The sadness. All that baggage, I can take it from you."

A memory flashed to life in Valerie's mind: the time when she was eight and her mother made her eat an entire loaf of stale bread in one sitting because Valerie forgot to put the bread tie back on. Sure, Valerie had plenty of stuff she'd like to get rid of, but who doesn't?

"Can I touch your hand, just for a moment?" the strange woman asked.

Valerie was reluctant, afraid the woman would notice her hand was shaking, but she held it out anyways and their hands met.

"*Oh yes!*" the woman cried in absolute ecstasy, her eyes closed, her eyebrows furrowed.

Valerie yanked her hand back.

Breathing hard, the woman said, "All that stuff—I can take it from you if you let me. Please let me. *Please.*"

Valerie said, "I don't know what this is," and slammed the door.

She watched the woman through the glass, wondering what would happen next. The woman didn't knock or ring the doorbell. She crouched down and slid a card through the bottom of the door and left.

Valerie waited, looking at the card. She picked it up. On one side was a handwritten phone number; the other side was blank. She thought about calling the police, but what would she tell them? A woman touched my hand then gave me a card?

She made sure all the doors and windows were locked and found a pillow and a blanket. She curled up on an old sofa (one of the only things the auction company didn't want, old but not an antique) and sucked down what was left of her bottle, which was just enough to help her sleep.

Valerie dreamed she was small again and her mother was standing over her yelling, mad as a devil Valerie had sold all her things. Valerie tried to explain herself but couldn't stop crying. Her mother wouldn't stop screaming, fire in her eyes.

Valerie woke up crying, sure her mother was back somehow, sure the dream was real. Eventually she slept and dreamt again, this time of her father. He looked how he looked the week before he died. He was sitting in his recliner watching a ballgame. She could only see the back of his head but knew it was him. She wanted him. He was busy watching the game, muttering under his breath and sipping a beer. No matter how far Valerie walked, she could get no closer to him.

The next morning the house was so bright she could barely stand to open her eyes. It was cold; the instant Valerie moved she began to shiver. She leapt off the couch and hurried to gather her things, feeling like a trespasser. She could feel her mother's ghost gliding on her heels, urging her to get out.

It was cold enough to have frosted during the night; the windows of her car were covered in ice. She threw her bags into her car and stuck the key in the ignition and turned it over, but nothing happened. She tried again.

Nothing.

Dead battery.

Valerie laid her head on the steering wheel and cried. When she was finished, she used her cell phone to call someone to bring her a new battery. They said it would take at least an hour. She offered to pay double—still an hour—so there was no choice but to wait.

She leaned her seat back and closed her eyes. The last few days flashed in her mind in blurry snippets: the call, the drive, meeting with the funeral home, picking her mother's casket, having to stand by it as people she hardly knew filed past and shook her hand, all saying the same things. Then Valerie remembered the woman from the day before. The card the woman had slipped under the door was still in her pocket. The encounter still didn't make sense, but since there was nothing else to do, Valerie called the number.

It only rang once.

"How can I help you?" a man asked.

"Yes, I was, uh…who am I speaking with?"

A few seconds of silence.

"Would you like to schedule an appointment?"

"An appointment for what?"

"For pickup."

"No, I'm sorry. Everything I needed taken was picked up yesterday. I don't know why I even called."

Valerie faked a laugh.

"Are you sure they got everything?" the man asked.

"Uhm, yes. I'm sure."

"There's nothing else you would like to get rid of? Nothing weighing you down or holding you back? If you have anything at all, we can take it off your hands."

"For auction?" Valerie asked.

The man laughed then said, "Something like that."

Valerie had the feeling there was no use in asking the man what he meant.

She found herself saying, "Yes, I believe I'm holding on to some things I don't want anymore."

"Very good. What is your name and address?"

She told him.

Why, she wasn't sure.

"Ah, I see here you spoke with one of our associates yesterday, correct? I'll put you through to her. She'll guide you through the rest of the process."

Valerie mumbled, "Okay," telling herself she could hang up whenever she wanted.

Then the woman from the day before was on the other end of the phone.

"Did you change your mind?" Cynthia asked.

"It seems that way. So how does this work?"

"It's very simple, but I'm afraid I can't explain the specific details. I assure you the process is completely safe. My company has been doing this for a very long time and has a spotless track record."

"What did you say the name of your company is again?"

"I wouldn't worry about it."

"What exactly do they do?"

"They find people like me, then they find people like you, and they help us get connected."

"People like you? What does that mean?"

"Afraid I can't say."

"People like me?"

"That's right."

Valerie waited, hoping for elaboration.

It never came.

"Is it some kind of hypnosis?" Valerie asked. "Or some new form of therapy?"

"Sure."

"How much is this going to cost me?"

"It's free."

"Is it safe?"

"Perfectly," Cynthia said. "Would you like to move forward?"

Valerie could hear her heart pounding. There was acid in her throat.

For some reason, she said, "Yes."

"Great. Here's how it works: anything you wish never happened, write it down on paper, and when you're finished, I want you to put that paper under your head when you go to bed tonight."

"Whatever I write down won't bother me anymore?"

"More or less."

"And you'll take anything I write down?"

"Yes, we'll take anything on your list. Just don't write down anything you'll want back, because once it's gone, it's gone for good."

"Gone?"

"Gone forever."

None of it made sense. Valerie felt like she was dreaming again, like she had on the porch the day before.

"I'll come tonight," the woman said.

"Should I leave the door unlocked?"

"It doesn't matter."

Before she hung up, Cynthia asked a final question:

"I'm assuming you drink."

Valerie looked at the white, frosted windshield.

"Yeah, I drink."

"Drink a little extra tonight."

~ * ~

After someone came and replaced Valerie's battery, she drove across town to a package store and picked up a bottle of her favorite. Part of her couldn't believe she was going to stay another night inside her mother's house, but she had to see what would happen. And besides, it had been a few days since she had written anything, and she was excited to create her trauma-list. There were plenty of things to write down.

When Valerie made it back, she snuck inside the house as quietly as she could, determined not to wake the dead. With the gas fireplace up as high as it would go, and sitting on the sofa with her notebook, the one she never traveled without, Valerie thumbed past the idea page, past an unfinished outline, and stopped on the first blank page.

She closed her eyes.

It didn't take long for the first memory to come.

Valerie started with her fifth birthday—one of her strongest and earliest memories. Her mother had ended the party prematurely and made all the guests leave, thanking them and smiling as they left. When they were gone, she burned all the gifts Valerie had received in the backyard while Valerie cried and begged her to stop. Apparently, Valerie had forgotten to say "thank you" after she had opened one of her gifts, an honest mistake. Her mother explained she wasn't raising an unappreciative brat, and next time Valerie received a gift, she would remember to be thankful.

It felt good to write it down, and her mother's ghost didn't seem so close anymore. The house began to seem like a house, nothing more. Valerie wrote for hours, and by the time the sun had set, she had filled forty-eight pages. She re-read what she had written, just like always. Even if it was just a list, Valerie couldn't stand to let anyone read a first draft. Going over it, she decided it was actually pretty good, maybe even publishable after some serious work. It needed some kind of narrative—a solid framing device—but the bones were there: a story featuring every negative memory Valerie possessed of her mother.

By the time she was done with the second draft, her eyelids were so heavy she could barely hold them open. She probably didn't even need the liquor, but she reasoned she should follow Cynthia's instructions. She drank as much as she could stand to. Maybe she should've been, but Valerie wasn't worried about what would happen once she fell asleep.

She stuck the pages beneath her pillow and drifted away.

She did not dream.

She woke up the next morning feeling like she had closed her eyes only a moment before. The list was gone. There was an empty bottle lying on the floor. Her mouth tasted of acid and bile. Her head throbbed. She stumbled into the kitchen and poured herself a glass of water. Valerie couldn't recall ever having such a bad hangover, and she'd had a few. She could remember writing the day before but could not recall what she'd written about. Then she remembered the woman and the instructions. Valerie had done what Cynthia said, but why? What had she been thinking? Valerie had the distinct feeling something was missing, something she didn't need anymore, but she wanted to know what it was.

She decided to eat a can of soup, hoping it would ease her hangover. In the top of one of the cabinets she found the same bowl she had used as a little girl. It was bright blue with a pink smiley face inside, so that when you finished eating you saw the smile.

Valerie suddenly missed her mother very much.

She wept as she ate the soup, no longer drowning in misery and regret, but mourning.

Her phone rang.

It was the number from the card.

She pulled herself together and pushed the green button.

Cynthia asked, "How are you feeling?"

"Good," Valerie answered. "Hungover, but good."

"That's great."

Neither of them said anything for a moment.

Cynthia said, "I just wanted to say I've never seen someone with so much they needed to get rid of."

"Really?"

"Yes, and your list was written quite well. You could be a writer."

Valerie said, "Thanks," and remembered the question she had been wanting to ask all morning. "There is one thing I wanted to know: may I ask what you took exactly?"

"You may not."

Valerie didn't know what else to say, and only a moment later the phone call was over. She went and stood by the fireplace and thought about it some more, but no matter how hard she tried, she couldn't remember what she had forgotten.

~ * ~

Later that day, Valerie drove back to her apartment in the city and resumed working on her novel outline, but she couldn't get the ball rolling. She failed for days, then decided to shift gears and write a short story, but that didn't work either. She couldn't stop thinking about her mother. Valerie thought of all the good times and missed her so much it hurt. It wasn't long until she began to feel like a stranger in her spacious apartment, the one she had bought for three times what her mother's house was worth.

She called the estate lawyer and told him she wanted to keep the house. Two weeks later Valerie and all her things were back where she had grown up and her apartment was on the market. Being where she knew she needed to be, Valerie started writing again. She abandoned the outline and started a new novel, no plan, no idea where the story might go. It felt different than it ever had, almost like she was having to re-learn things she had always known. The writing was slow, but after a few weeks she was routinely hitting her word count goal by lunchtime—and for the first time in years, Valerie didn't feel like drinking when she was done for the day.

When the manuscript was finished, Valerie's agent and editor had much more feedback to give than usual, and the revision stage lasted for months. When it was obvious the book wasn't getting any better, people in high places decided to publish the project anyway, saying her name would carry it. The book sold well, but public reaction was not positive.

Fans were angry, and critics eviscerated Valerie's newest mind-baby. Valerie stopped opening letters and stopped reading comments online. She wrote and published another book, but sales never took off.

Valerie went on a quest to get her creative juices flowing again. She quit drinking altogether, which was easier than she thought it would be. She went on spiritual retreats and prayed and traveled and even bought a few crystals, but nothing changed. One day she called the number from the card, but no one answered.

The phone rang and rang and rang.

Royalties from her early works kept her wealthy, so eventually Valerie quit writing altogether; it brought her no joy. She married but never had children. She spent the remainder of her life living in her mother's house, living what anyone would call a happy life.

But sometimes, even when she was old and well past the point of caring, she would catch herself trying to remember what she had lost.

~ * ~

There isn't much I can say about Valerie Stone's newest book that my fellow critics haven't already said. As a fan of Ms. Stone, my hopes were high, which only made reading *"Five Roses"* that much more disappointing.

There is nothing new here. No insights, no keen observations. The dialogue is stilted. The characters are flat. I liked the idea, but the potential was lost on the writer. It appears an advanced computer program was fed the entire works of Valerie Stone, only to pump out this stillborn imitation. Or maybe it went over my head. Maybe Ms. Stone set out to write a book that covers every cliche and trope imaginable in order to teach a lesson to aspiring writers everywhere. My point being: if you want to know the no-no's of great writing, read *"Five Roses"*. I had about a hundred pages to go when I threw in the towel, so technically this isn't a full review.

I hope *"Five Roses"* is a one off, a tragedy Ms. Stone can overcome, but something about this newest novel makes me think the magic is gone, that me and my fellow Stoners should be thankful for what we have.

One out of five stars.

Would not recommend.

Did Not Finish.

—Brenda Fowler, lit critic for The Sun Coast Observer

~ * ~ * ~

Stetson Ray lives in Tennessee. He enjoys watching movies, reading books, and using the Oxford comma whenever possible.

Finding Wonder

Demi Utley

The paper blanket on the metal bed crumpled under Silvia's weight. To distract herself, she focused on steadying her breathing until it silenced the "tick, tock, tick, tock" of the clock on the wall. Today was not the day for an overzealous heartbeat.

The nurse opened the door, "Fifteen more minutes. Sorry about the wait!"

Silvia smiled. She didn't mind.

Unlike most people, she loved her visits here. It was one of the few places where she could be a superstar. Silvia always left with top reviews and positive feedback.

"Ready, Silvia?" the doctor asked before stepping inside.

"Of course, Doctor." Silvia pushed her shoulders back and sat taller, ready for her annual assessment.

Dr. Neil covered his hands in sanitizer and sat on a spinning stool in front of her. "We got your results back, and as usual, everything looks perfect," he said, scrolling through his tablet without glancing at her. "I must say, you're one of our star patients. No medications, no ailments. We may have to study you further."

Silvia's cheeks burned at the compliment. "I'm happy to help however you need."

Dr. Neil laughed and started to stand but stopped, a look of concern spreading on his face. "Oh, I spoke too fast."

The warmth in Silvia's cheeks receded in the face of clamminess and a growing horror. "Is there something wrong?" she asked, trying to keep her voice level. Of course there was nothing wrong. This was the one area where she always succeeded. It must be a mistake.

Dr. Neil tapped on the screen and looked up at Silvia, his eyebrows wrinkled. "It says here that you're a bit low on wonder."

"Wonder?"

Dr. Neil nodded and flipped through the screen again. "Yes, it's not too bad though. Just add some wonder to your routine, and you should return to normal."

Silvia tried to maintain her usual confidence, but she felt her eyes burn at this new development. "But…how does one add wonder to their life?" She couldn't acknowledge that she was the "one" who needed to add wonder.

"It's fairly simple. Just do something a little different. Take a different route home, walk through a park, go see a sunset. Novelty is normally the best option."

Silvia's shoulders loosened. She could do that.

~ * ~

The sun warmed Silvia's scalp when she stepped out of the doctor's office. It was an unusually warm day for this time of year, but she forced herself to be grateful for the unexpected. Did that count as novelty? She sighed and started heading home.

Her feet led her of their own accord, and before she realized her actions, she found herself nearly halfway home following her standard route. Silvia forced her brain to overpower her feet and stopped at a crosswalk. Her usual path lay to the left as it was the fastest way home, but she recalled the doctor's comment. She took the right.

To her surprise, this path *was* filled with wonder. She passed beautiful homes with perfect gardens she had never seen before. Dogs of all sizes raced about a dog park, barking in delight and catching frisbees in the air. On one corner, a large mural of a man playing a saxophone dominated the building, adding a rainbow of colors to the scene. She could almost see the look on Dr. Neil's face when she improved her wonder deficit in a simple walk home.

One block from her building, she crossed the street to the park. She knew about this park but always avoided it because of its giant, ancient trees with gnarled trunks and droopy canopies. She feared getting lost in its darkness.

Today was not a day for fear, however, so she set her jaw, and crossed the street to walk beneath the trees. Silvia stuck to the less dense section by the main sidewalk, which filtered a bit of the sun as it streamed through branches. The shade muffled the brightness of the day to a pleasant level, and she arrived home in a better mood.

That evening, Silvia scheduled a follow-up with her doctor for one week later, the first available appointment. She fell asleep with all worries lifted, proud of herself for returning to her normal perfect health in such a short amount of time.

~ * ~

"Your wonder levels are higher, but they're not quite there. I recommend you keep exploring."

Silvia's heart dropped. This was not what she was expecting. Her pulse pounded in her ears as her mind raced through the activities of the last few days, searching for a flaw in her approach.

Then she saw Dr. Neil eyeing her for any sign of concern and rallied herself. "Of course. I wasn't sure how long it would take."

Dr. Neil tapped through the tablet. "It's different for everyone. You've made great progress."

Silvia thought of the block with the park and how much she had visited it the past week. That walk was no longer novel but familiar. She scolded herself for making this mistake. "Dr. Neil, can exploring a familiar place still bring novelty and increase wonder?"

He looked up from his tablet. "Sure, if it brings you joy. You just have to make sure you find the new parts to fill you with wonder."

"Thank you, Doctor."

~ * ~

On her walk home, Silvia rushed to the park. It had quickly become one of her favorite spots, and she didn't want to have to give it up in the name of wonder. Instead of walking along the sidewalk, she took a path that led deeper into the trees. The unfamiliar trunks would surely bring about a new level of wonder.

Silvia recognized the trees as ancient, but walking among them, she began to understand their power. The sun disappeared from view within ten paces, and the trunks pressed so close together she could barely see through them. Squirrels and other creatures bounded across the branches overhead. She marveled at the hidden, dark world of this forest.

A speck of light interrupted the darkness on a small trail to Silvia's right. She paused for a moment, wanting to find the source but hesitant to go too far into the forest at this time of day. The light bounced towards her, and a body became visible below it. The person wearing the headlamp carried hiking poles and a heavy backpack. Scruffy cheeks and a red hat signaled a seasoned explorer.

"Be careful back there. I almost didn't make it. Excellent hike though," the man said, giving Silvia a nod as he passed her and joined the main trail. She watched him go, the darkness returning as his light fell from view.

Silvia wanted to follow him back to safety, but she knew this might be the dose of wonder she lacked. *No risk, no reward*, she told herself. Besides, she wanted Dr. Neil's long overdue approval.

She stepped onto the narrow trail covered with dirt. As she walked, the path made sharp turns through the trees, and she could often see only a foot or two in front of her. The sound of her breathing overwhelmed her senses in the stillness, and she considered turning back to avoid getting lost. The thought of Dr. Neil's frown pushed her forward.

Thirty minutes in, Silvia discovered many new things but nothing so awe-inspiring as to push her squarely in the "full of wonder" category. She started to worry that maybe this was a mistake. After all, the sun had dipped beneath the trees. She could always come back tomorrow.

Not wanting to leave without making good progress, Silvia decided to take three more turns and then head home.

One.

This turn revealed a small mossy clearing where a deer drank from a spring. She paused for a moment to watch before it leaped into the trees.

Two.

A wall of trees. An unremarkable turn.

Three.

Darkness.

Darkness so thick Silvia reached out to see if a black curtain hung from the branches, but her hand passed through empty air. She lifted her foot for another step, eager to see what lay beyond.

Silvia put her foot down and fell through the empty space.

Down and down and down she tumbled. In the complete darkness, she lost her sense of direction, finding it momentarily every few seconds when her body hit the earth.

Then with a soft "smoosh" she stopped.

Silvia lay on the ground, willing her mind to stop spinning. She tried to orient herself to the new space and longed for her phone. At least then she'd have a light.

At that thought, a light ignited in front of her face. She scrunched her eyes from the glare and shielded her face with her hands.

"Oh, sorry. You're a human," a voice said, moving the light.

Silvia blinked a few times and watched the light stop moving about six feet away. She sat up and saw a man in his mid-thirties sitting cross-legged beside her.

"Of course I'm human. Aren't you?" she asked, scooting away from him a few more inches.

The man placed the light on the ground between them, which gave her a better view of this stranger. He wore a dark, zip-up hoodie and jeans. The light from the phone reflected off his glasses and created shadows in the curls of his beard.

"Yes, but not everything down here is. You never know what you might find."

Silvia looked around and saw a few shapes in the distance, none of them clear enough to identify.

"Where is 'here'?" she asked.

"Dunno if it has a name. I just call it the Darkness," the man said, leaning back against a dark wall and staring forward with a sigh.

Silvia waited for him to say more. When he didn't, she asked, "Do *you* have a name?"

"Robin," he said. "You?"

"Silvia."

She joined him in staring forward at the darkness. She knew she should be afraid of this lost place, but instead she felt…empty. Not a light, exuberant emptiness, but empty in a heavy, collapsing sort of way. Her arms pulled her shoulders down, and Silvia could feel her eyelids drooping as if sleep were long overdue, but she knew it must only be about 5pm. She blinked a few times to wake up, but then realized it didn't actually matter if she slept. It might be nice.

So she let sleep overtake her.

~ * ~

Silvia awoke to the darkness again. With no stars nor sun, she had no idea how long she napped, but Robin still sat next to her with his light. She waited for her stomach to rumble telling her it was time for dinner, which she always had at 6:30pm on the dot.

Her stomach stayed silent though. Everything was silent here.

"What time is it?" she asked Robin.

He shrugged. "Time doesn't matter down here."

Silvia sat back against the wall. He was probably right. She paid too close attention to time anyway. She watched Robin, waiting for him to engage her in conversation. When that didn't happen, she returned to staring forward, that empty sensation pushing thoughts of any activity from her mind.

A scream above interrupted Silvia's mindlessness. The suddenness of it forced her to her feet, searching to pinpoint the exact location. She looked around wildly. "What was that?"

Robin shrugged again. "Just someone trying to get out."

This comment chilled her veins. "Trying to get out? Why would they scream?"

"You can't leave here. It's impossible."

Silvia stood still. "What do you mean it's impossible? I'm stuck here?"

Robin nodded. "We all end up here eventually."

Silvia's heart fluttered in her chest. She wanted to try and climb out, but her heavy body forced her back to the ground. "As in…am I…dead?"

Robin laughed. "You should be so lucky. That only happens if you go in the Hole."

"The Hole?"

Robin sighed and stood up with his light, motioning for Silvia to follow. After walking for five minutes, Silvia noticed a few creatures run from the light. They fled before she could identify them, though she saw them observing her, their eyes reflecting in the distance.

Silvia ran into Robin when he stopped. "*That's* the Hole," he said, pointing with his finger and the light.

Silvia followed his direction and gasped. She grabbed his arm. "What is that?" she asked, her voice shaking.

In front of them swirled a massive black pit, like dark quicksand forming a whirlpool of black earth. It made no sound. If it weren't for Robin's light, Silvia knew they would walk right into it.

"I told you, it's the Hole," Robin said, annoyed. He turned with the light and started walking away. Silvia raced after him, afraid the Hole would swallow her up.

Back at the edge of the clearing, Robin sat down and leaned against the wall again. Silvia joined him.

"So what do you do?"

Robin stared forward and waved his hand in front of his face.

"That's it?"

"What more would you want to do?"

Silvia thought for a moment. She remembered doing things. She used to like dancing, reading, cooking, and even running. She loved calling her parents and watching holiday movies. She even liked her work; when it was going okay.

Right now though, none of those sounded fun. She wondered why she ever did them anyway. They were pointless activities with little benefit other than passing the time. Robin was right. Staring passed the time too, and it required so much less effort.

So Silvia joined him in staring.

She stared for a long time. So long that she stopped thinking of herself as Silvia or even as a human. She just was. Another thing in the darkness.

Then something heavy landed beside her.

"Ignore it," Robin grunted.

Silvia wanted to ignore it and continue staring, but it started to move. She stood and walked about five feet for a closer look. A long object wriggled on the ground, frayed strings poking out every few inches.

"It looks like a rope," she observed.

Robin sighed. "Yeah, they throw them down every so often. They want me to come back up."

"Who is 'they'?" Silvia asked.

His phone lit up his face as he picked it up. "You know, family, friends, doctors, my agent. None of them understand the Darkness."

Silvia nodded. Her family didn't understand the Darkness either. Even before she fell down here, she had felt the empty weight from time to time. Normally it went away on its own, but she had felt it coming on more and more often. That's why she looked forward to Dr. Neil's appointment. She needed a bit of light to keep the darkness away.

"Yeah, I understand." Silvia sat back down.

They stared more. One day (or night, impossible to tell in the darkness), a person fell not far from Silvia. Robin stood to shine the light on the person, but the minute the light touched their face, they screamed and ran straight for the Hole. The Hole made a happy gurgling sound for a moment, and silence returned.

"Yeah, it does that," Robin said.

Silvia didn't respond. She already knew what the Hole did.

~ * ~

"Silvia? I can help you."

A rope landed right beside Silvia, so close she could touch it without moving, which she did. This one was different than the others. It felt warm, familiar. Touching it reminded her of leaping in pools as a kid and eating cookies in front of a snowy window. She smiled.

"What are you doing?" Robin asked.

Silvia jumped. She found herself on her feet, and he stood beside her.

"Just checking out the rope," she answered.

Robin shook his head. "Don't do it. You won't like it. Trust me. I've tried."

"You've tried to leave?"

Robin nodded. "Many times. It never works for too long. I always end up back here. I think the Hole is my only option sometimes. It's the only way out."

"Why would you leave?" Silvia asked. He had never mentioned leaving before.

Robin scratched his head. "You know, sometimes I just wish I could feel something, even if it's bad. It's better than feeling nothing and failing up there again." He pointed above them, to the source of the rope.

Silvia looked up in the darkness. "You could try going one more time. I'll go with you."

Robin shook his head and sat down again. "I like it down here. I'll stay."

Silvia let go of the rope with one hand and sat down too. She held onto the rope in her other hand though. She liked feeling the memories.

~ * ~

After a while, Silvia stopped feeling heavy. She wanted to live those memories again. She missed her mom's laugh, her favorite falafel place, even her neighbor's cat. She tried to stare into the darkness but couldn't do it anymore. She gripped the rope.

"I'm going to try," she said to Robin.

He ignored her.

Hand over hand, Silvia climbed the rope, moving higher and higher up the cliff. Her feet struggled to find traction and ground gave way beneath each step. She knew it would be easier to let go and fall back to the ground beside Robin, but she didn't give up. She reached what she thought was a ledge and paused for a breath, placing the rope on the ground.

Dim light filled the space up here. She saw the outline of the Hole, swirling in its madness. Robin's light was a small insect below her. She could squash it with a step.

Without the memories of the rope in her hand, the emptiness came back. She sat down on the ledge, not remembering why she wanted to leave anyway. It was more comfortable to sit and stare. Maybe she'd even go back to be by Robin.

The rope disappeared before long, and she had no choice but to continue sitting. While she stared, she saw three more people fall into the Hole. Two landed beside Robin and ran when he shined the light. The third fell straight into the Hole, making a soft splash with the impact.

Silvia wondered what it would be like to jump in the Hole. She could probably do it from here.

She started calculating angles, thinking she could get it just right when another rope fell.

"Silvia!" it said, louder and more intense than the last time. She grabbed it with her left hand, and felt the warmth of the memories wash over her. She grinned, her face almost breaking from the change of expression. The Hole swirled, and her heart skipped a beat as she thought about how she almost jumped.

Silvia clung to the rope with both hands. She knew she needed wonder, but not like this. The Darkness was the opposite of wonder. It only allowed escape and indifference. She wanted to feel again. She wanted to laugh again. She used to love laughing. Most importantly, she wanted to do something just for her, not for meeting Dr. Neil's requirements, or her boss, or her mom. She wanted to find the opposite of the Hole and jump into that.

So she climbed again. This time it was harder. She felt the weight of the Hole pulling her down. Every few steps she fell backwards. But she kept going.

Eventually, she made it to real dirt. She smelled the earth that lay beneath the forest, not the black sand of the Darkness. She lay on it for a moment, breathing in the smell of life and decay, grateful to feel something.

Then she ran. She ran out of the trail, back to the path, and all the way to the main sidewalk. Daytime sun poured through the branches. She ignored the questioning glances from strangers as they noticed her bruises and mud. She didn't care. She finally understood.

It wasn't about her. Silvia didn't need wonder. She needed life. She needed to live and stop checking boxes.

Jumping in the Hole was one box she would never check off. She'd rather have no list than a list that ended with that.

Silvia raced home and found her to-do list sitting on her counter. Her plants had died, food spoiled, and her cell phone sat on its charger, full of countless messages.

She ignored all of them.

Instead, she picked up the to-do list, threw it in the trash, and took the trash outside. Then she did the one thing she never thought she would ever do again when sitting in the Darkness.

She laughed.

And she felt wonder at the beauty of that simple sensation.

~ * ~ * ~

Demi Utley is a speculative fiction writer who believes we all need a bit more magic in our day-to-day lives. A business writing consultant by day, she splits her time between writing corporate content and escaping the daily monotony through character-driven speculative stories. Her work recently won Honorable Mention in the 2022 First Quarter Writers of the Future Contest. Demi holds a Bachelor's Degree in English Literature from Roosevelt University and an MBA in Entrepreneurship from Loyola University Chicago.

Born and raised in the Midwest, Demi now resides in Washington, where she uses the misty winters (and constant darkness) as inspiration for her stories, shares insights on Instagram at @demiutleywrites, and writes her upcoming novel.

The Ladies From the Outside

Marianne Xenos

Rosa Benevento set the platter of cookies on the kitchen table. The buttery befaninis were dusted with sugar and dotted with marzipan leaves. At the center of each was a secret, an ingredient never written on an index card, but handed down from mother to daughter, or from Nonna to Nonna. But tonight Zia Rosa, as she was called, was sick of secrets. She was ninety-three years old and ready to tell the truth. She put out coffee, soda and sweet wine and waited for the Ladies to knock on her back door.

Every night since Christmas she had dreamed of her grand-mother, her own Nonna, telling her, "Your time is short. Pass on the secret of the cookies." Nonna had always been bossy, and even as a dream ghost, she tended to repeat herself.

For generations, before coming to America, one Benevento woman baked befaninis on Epiphany, with a recipe originally shared by the good witch Befana herself. In the old country, in Sicily, once the children were in bed, promised a present from the beautiful Befana, twelve women gathered in the eldest's kitchen for a ritual as old as baking. The Ladies from the Outside, as they called themselves, gathered together and told the truth. The magic of the befanini called them together, and empowered them to tell their stories.

Zia Rosa believed the truth was not a straight line, not a gush of words, or the purge of shame. The truth was a pattern like a dance or the beating of birds' wings. Truth was sometimes listening in silence, or it could be a song, a story, or a garden.

While she was thinking about pattern, a sharp rat-a-tat on the back window drew her attention. The first three Ladies had arrived, all elderly, and all born near the Mediterranean like Zia Rosa, but now living in a Boston suburb. One was Greek, one Syrian, and the oldest—by tradition Zia Rosa's heir—was a Sicilian cousin named Paloma whom she loved dearly, but who was—god help her—a bit of a bigot, and had trouble with change.

More taps at the back door, and the Ladies arrived in layers, like generations. Three of the Ladies had died during the year—

older women, but none had been as old as Zia Rosa—and three replacements were expected. Zia Rosa poured coffee, and reminded the group. "The cookies call the Ladies. Whoever comes to the door is ready to speak the truth."

Rat-a-tat at the door. Two young women arrived—one Black and one White—holding hands—obviously a couple. Zia Rosa watched without surprise as Paloma stiffened, but she gave her a stern frown, and showed the young women to their seats. When she opened the door for the final knock, there was a surprise. A teenager known to them as Tommy Dooley stood on the threshold and said, "I have a feeling I'm supposed to be here."

Paloma was on her feet. "No boys allowed!" she began.

But Zia Rosa was the keeper of the befaninis. She said, "Did you have a dream?"

"Yes, I dreamed of a beautiful witch, and she told me to come here for a cookie."

Zia Rosa pulled out a chair, patted the teenager's shoulder, and offered Paloma another stern look. After brewing more coffee, she brought out a platter of sandwiches and asked the group, "Who will begin?"

Paloma usually went first, but tonight she was sullen and simply shrugged. Some Ladies brought secrets about ambition, love, or failure. One sat embroidering her unspoken words on muslin, a detailed pattern of periwinkle and pink. One told of her abortion, and another, who lived in a one-room apartment, showed a design for an expansive herb garden.

A woman who Zia Rosa remembered having been a thin child with shadows in her eyes—secrets had clung to her like the smell of camphor—took her turn and sang. She never spoke her story out loud, but each year she sang an Irish ballad in which a woman smashes her abuser with a broken bottle. After she sang, she looked at the group and nodded, and the group sang again with her.

A long silence followed. The youngest member, who they'd known by a different name, the one who'd dreamed of the beautiful witch, took a third cookie and said, "My name is Abigail. But you can call me Abbie." Her words were met with respectful silence, and Paloma took a deep breath, then nodded and reached over to touch Abbie's hand. Zia Rosa smiled.

The elderly Greek Lady handed Zia Rosa a cassette tape, as

she did every year, and when the music began, she stood and danced. It was a Greek zeibekiko, a dance traditionally performed only by men or loose women. Alone, at the center of the kitchen, the respectable Lady in widow's black spread her arms like an eagle, circled and dipped, and then bent and slapped the floor. And then she slapped it again with meaning. When the music ended, and the group waited in respectful silence, the two younger women—the young couple—said, "Could we dance too?" Zia Rosa rewound the tape, and every Lady present took a turn in the center while the others clapped.

After they returned to the table, Paloma finally took a cookie and spoke. "I'm always afraid," she said without flourish. "I'm afraid of men, the past, the future, change. And, I'm afraid of losing my dear cousin, Rosa." This time Abbie reached out to take Paloma's hand, and the group sat in quiet for a moment.

Last to share was Zia Rosa. Each year she shared some small morsel of truth, but never the secret at the center. She reached in her apron pocket and took out twelve index cards, passing one card to each Lady.

"The truth is a pattern," she said, picking up a spoon before continuing. "You stir once to the right, then twice to the left. Tap the bowl like this: *rat-a-tat-tat*." Zia Rosa demonstrated the tapping. "That wakes up the sugar. Then you speak a one-word charm taught to us by Befana herself, but never written down."

Never written, not even here in this story.

~ * ~ * ~

Marianne Xenos is speculative fiction writer living in western Massachusetts. Along with short stories about shapeshifters and suburban witches, she is working on a fantasy novel set in Boston's queer community in 1983. Xenos grew up in a working-class community outside of Boston, in an enormous, close-knit Greek family, with beloved Sicilian cousins, and an Italian stepmother. The immigrants, rebels, mechanics, and visionaries of her childhood inspire her stories. After years of working as a visual artist, Marianne turned to writing fiction. She published her first short story last year in *The Future Fire*, and a second in *Not One of Us*.

Izzy Tells No Lies

P. James Norris

I step out of the air-conditioned quiet of the Basilica and into the cacophony of Colfax's incessant traffic and its attendant smell of auto exhaust. I do what I can to shut out this assault and cross myself. "Lord, grant me the strength to bring Your comfort to those who most need it."

Only then do I allow myself to look south across Colfax. To do otherwise is to invite a nearly paralyzing despair over the quiet desperation of the far, far too many lost souls who wander up and down the street looking for sex, drugs and, often times, oblivion.

I close my eyes again. "Lord, I am your servant. But the task you have set before me…I am beginning to doubt I am its equal." I cross myself again, and opening my eyes, see *her*, as though she has been waiting for me, knowing exactly when I would emerge from the nave and out into the hot, muggy August twilight. As she seems to every night, she comes to tell me of her latest vision.

For a moment, her eyes focus on mine, and I see *her*. Not what her brain's natural chemical imbalances have made of her. Not what the drugs, prescribed and not, have made of her. Not what her guilt has made of her. Not what her parents have made of her by throwing her out of their home like a Jezebel on her eighteenth birthday.

I see her—I see *Isabelle*.

Such sadness. Such compassion. Such thwarted strength.

As always, it is her cornflower blue eyes that first draw my gaze. But then I notice her dish-water blonde hair is even dirtier than normal—when was the last time she showered? Would it be a brighter, more lustrous blonde if she had the opportunity to wash it regularly? The slight Adam's apple. And good Lord, is that stubble or just dirt from living on the street, or wherever it is she sleeps at night?

But then the confusion takes grip, and *Izzy* starts lashing the air before her face, as though swatting at a cloud of gnats. She turns east and starts walking, almost stumbling, toward Pennsylvania

Street.

When she reaches it, she will turn around and pace down to Logan Street and back to Pennsylvania.

Over and over.

Until I approach her and she tells me of whatever vision it is that has brought her all but to the steps of the Cathedral Basilica of the Immaculate Conception. Steps I know she will never climb because she is convinced God can no longer love her—would no longer welcome her in His house. But God is infinitely forgiving, and He *would* welcome her in His house as readily as He once welcomed...Isaac.

I grit my teeth to push thoughts of that poor, tormented boy from my mind—they still have the power to push me to a despair worse than the contemplation of all those who choose, for whatever reason, to desecrate their bodies and souls on Colfax.

That her parents, "good Catholics," could not accept their son's inability to see himself as a boy.

That they would throw her out of their home on her eighteenth birthday for...

With the determination of a man who knows he's lost his way in the desert and yet must soldier on, I walk down the steps to let Isabelle tell me of her latest vision. But, of course, I'm forced to stop before I reach the sidewalk.

"Heypaaadre."

Benny manages to slur even just those two words. He's an elderly...gentleman. Every night he scoots up and down five blocks of Colfax on a wheeled walker with fluorescent orange tennis balls on the rear legs. He's not fat, but is portly. His legs are bowed, and the same quarter inch of grey stubble covers his liver-spotted head as his throat and jowly cheeks.

He wears a Marine baseball cap—claims to have served in Saigon during the war—claims to have saved more than twenty people during the evacuation. A cigarette dangles from his lips even as a portable oxygen tank pumps what he claims is "pure oxie" directly into his nose. If it were, indeed, pure oxygen, I suspect he would have blown his head off long ago while trying to light one of his ever-present cigarettes—I've seen him thumb his zippo a dozen times before managing to light a cigarette to his satisfaction.

Even from five feet away, I can't tell which odor is stronger, the stink of his nicotine saturated clothes or the whiskey on his breath.

Ignoring the man would be rude.

He comes to a stop just a foot from me.

I breathe through my mouth to avoid *some* of the stench. "Good evening, Benny. How are you tonight?"

"Same'ld, same'ld. Ya know-oww it is, paadre."

The words are a little less slurred—practice makes perfect, I guess. "Well…"

"Say, padre" —he's making a real effort to speak distinctly— "Ya wouldn't happen to have some spare change, wouldja?"

I fight down a sigh. "Benny, I do have some change, but…"

"Honest, padre. I'm headed down to MikkiD's for some coffee and a burger."

Isabelle's on her third round. Though I know she'll keep going for as long it takes for me to get to her, I hate to make her wait.

Experience has taught me that if I give Benny money, it will go for either more smokes or more whiskey. Luckily, I have an out, and I should be able play it quickly. "Benny, I remember giving you two dollars last Thursday night when you told me the same thing. And you told me you'd bring me the receipt to prove you bought food and not cigarettes or whiskey. But you didn't. So, tonight, you're on your own."

"Tat's fair, paaadre."

The slur is back in full force even as he pulls a piece of cardboard off the side of his walker. He hangs the sign from wire clothes hangers on the walker's front cross-bar. It reads, *Viet Nam War Vet—Every quarter helps—GOD BLESS.*

That done, he starts wheeling down toward the McDonalds. "Ya hafa gude evenin', paaadre."

"You as well, Benny."

Who knows? Perhaps he *was* telling the truth. And perhaps I have committed the sin of unjustified condemnation.

But now I'm free to go to Isabelle.

As I step into the inner eastbound lane, she stops her pacing and swatting at the air. She doesn't look at me, keeping her attention on the ground a foot or two in front of her. By coincidence or not, she has stopped just where the traffic leads me to walk up onto the south sidewalk.

It would be arrogant to think the Lord had arranged the traffic so I could cross all four lanes of Colfax at little more than a brisk walk. Nonetheless, I give Him my thanks.

I know using her full name will cause the swatting to start anew, and several minutes will pass before it stops again. So, "Good evening, Izzy."

Only then does Izzy look up to meet my gaze. "Father Grigori." It is not Isabelle who says this, it is Izzy's scattered, diffident gaze.

Everyone else to whom I minister addresses me, as is Catholic tradition, by my ordained name, "William." But not Isabelle. In fact, I don't know how she could know my given name. Just another one of the mysteries that is Isabelle.

From the basilica's portico, I had not noticed the light, open-hand shaped bruise on her left cheek nor the bruise around her right wrist. "Izzy, what happened to your face and wrist?"

"Michael is coming."

Still Izzy—is this her prophecy? But I don't care—what I *do* care about are the bruises.

"*Izzy*, what *happened* to your face and wrist?"

"Isabelle needed money, so she tried to turn a trick. But the Jane was a lesbian who didn't appreciate Isabelle's little Isaac."

This isn't the first time Isabelle has tried to prostitute herself to a woman who subsequently abused her when the Jane discovered that biologically, Isabelle is a man.

"I see." I want to take her right hand in mine to examine the bruise, to wipe the dirt from her face so I can better see the bruise there. But in the six months I've known her, we've touched only once. In the church's hospice. And she fled immediately afterward. But come to think of it, it was after this she started calling me by my given name.

Though it costs me terribly, I respect her self-denial of human compassion. "Who is Michael?"

"Michael is coming for Benny."

For no longer than it takes her to answer, *Isabelle*, not Izzy, looks up at me. Direct and self-assured, not afraid and confused.

By both her tone and the way her eyes hold—almost grip—mine, *Isabelle* implies I know this Michael.

It is always Isabelle who tells me what will come to pass.

And as always, the intensity of her gaze starts to fade.

She is Izzy once again.

And even though I know to expect it, I flinch at her first swat at the things she sees before her eyes but aren't really there. And as she turns and stumbles away, so she won't hear, I quietly pray, "May the Lord watch over you, Isabelle."

~ * ~

For the next hour, I stand in front of the Cathedral, inviting all who pass to the midnight Mass.

But my heart's not in it—another sin for which I will have to atone.

Michael. Archangel *Michael?* The Lord's warrior, His bringer of death? If it is the Archangel coming for Benny…

There are so many ways to die on Colfax, and so many do.

Worried for his physical safety, I keep an eye out for Benny. But I do not see him before it is time to go in to celebrate the Mass.

~ * ~

Attendance is sparse, as I give the evening mass. My heart is not in it—another sin to account for: my prayers are only half-heartedly for those to whom I offer the sacrament—mostly I pray the Lord will show Benny mercy this night.

But I soldier on for the sake of the parishioners who braved Colfax after dark to attend.

"Take this, all of you, and eat of it: for this is my body which will be given up for you. Take this, all of you, and drink from it: for this is the chalice of my blood, the blood of the new and eternal covenant. Which will be poured out for you and for many for the forgiveness of sins. Do this in memory of me."

The handful of elderly people in attendance line up in front of the Communion table. Many move slowly, very slowly, due to age and various infirmities.

To each I give a Communion wafer and say, "The body of Christ." To which each reply, "Amen."

To each I give a bit of Communion wine in a thimble-sized plastic cup and say, "The blood of Christ", to which each reply, "Amen."

Some return to their pew to kneel and pray, while some

simply leave.

When I served the right to all, I return to the lectern to give the sermon I failed to prepare out of worry for Isabelle and Benny. I look out over the handful of remaining souls, and then close my eyes asking the Lord for inspiration I am certain I do not deserve in light of my many sins.

I almost confess that I have no prepared sermon. That I don't know where to find the Lord's mercy and comfort this night. "I…"

My only thought is of Isabelle. "There is a young lady who used to attend this church. She…"

Nothing Isabelle has ever told me has been under the Seal of the Confessional and I have often told Monsignor James of her prophecies and other things she has told me, but those conversations have been priest to priest—I have never related her prophecies or anything else she has told me to anyone else. To speak of them now, before congregants who are looking for words of hope and comfort…

But I cannot help myself—there is something in her story the few congregants before me need to hear. "She feels she is no longer welcome in a house of our Lord." Perhaps this all I need say of Isabelle.

"But we are all welcome. God calls to us. Each of us. Even when we can't hear him doing so. I, myself…

"Shortly after I arrived in this country, I saw a poster in a church. It had a poem, 'Footprints in the Sand,' that touched me in a way very little else ever has. Perhaps you have seen it as well. I memorized it, but I will not recite it in its entirety for you now. It was about a man who looking back on his life at the time of his death, and saw a sandy beach. In places there were two sets of footprints and at others there was only one set. He saw the lowest points of his life were when there was only one set of footprints, and said to God, 'I don't understand why, when I needed You the most, You would leave me.' And God replied: 'My precious child, I love you and will never leave you. Never, ever, during your trials and testings. When you saw only one set of footprints, it was then that I carried you.'

"I…I pray you remember this: the Lord is *always* with you. He is with all of us. Even when… Even when it seems he is not."

Here I realized I've said all I can. So, I end with the blessing,

"We ask this in the name of Jesus the Lord. Amen. The Lord be with you."

Some of the parishioners respond, "And also with you." while others do not. If because they are not sure what to make of what I've said, I don't know. All I know is I've said everything I can. "May almighty God bless you, the Father, the Son, and the Holy Spirit. Amen." Feeling I have failed in my duty to them, I conclude simply, "Go in the peace of Christ. Thanks be to God." I bow and kiss the altar, and make my escape to the sacristy.

I close the door behind myself and lean back against it. Closing my eyes, I address the Lord in supplication, "Lord, I see only one set of footprints for myself. And Isabelle. I pray you walk with Benny tonight."

~ * ~

As I remove my vestments, I can't help but think about when I first met Isabelle.

It was just days after I had arrived at the basilica; I had not even led my first Mass, when the Monsignor approached me about a girl in the hospice. She had been badly beaten.

As he led me to her bedside, he told me Izzy and Isabelle's story.

Told me how Julia, one of the cleaning staff, had found Isabelle lying, nearly unconscious and bleeding, by the rectory door. He hoped I would be able convince her to go to the police to report the beating—she had told him only that Jane had done it.

When I first saw her, I could not believe anyone would do anything so brutal to such an obviously already tortured soul. But my own experience with the *Bratva* back home in Moscow forced me to acknowledge such things happen. Far more often than a loving God would allow. So often to the least able to…

The Monsignor introduced us: "Father William, this is Izzy. Izzy, this is Father William. I've asked him to look after you."

Isabelle did not reply.

At first I tried to console her, but she did not need consolation.

In a very matter of fact manner, Izzy—it would take me some time to recognize the difference between Izzy and Isabelle—told me that what had happened *happens*.

This was the beginning of my trek into the moral and

spiritual desert that is East Colfax.

I spent hours by her bedside.

It took me that long to convince her to tell me the story.

It was the same story Izzy had told me earlier today, only with more dire outcomes.

Then I tried to show her sympathy, but she did not want it.

Sympathy implies a connection, but the desert is a desolate place.

Eventually, she announced her need to relieve herself.

I offered to bring her a bed-pan and give her privacy, but in an act of will the likes I had not seen before and have not seen since, she forced herself up out the cot in which Julia had laid her.

With her first step, she stumbled and when I took her by the arm to steady her, she froze like a statue.

I said her name, apologized, worried I had wrenched her arm.

But she did not respond. Did not move.

Eventually, not knowing what else to do, I let go.

Only then did Izzy look at me and say, "Isabelle needs to do this for herself, Father Grigori."

I was startled by her use of my given name, convinced the Monsignor had given my name as "Father William."

Odd how only tonight it should come back to me this was the first time Izzy had called me Grigori.

But her poise forbade questions.

I escorted her to the restroom and then found the Sister Nurse to ask if Izzy had suffered physical harm not visible to the eye.

When I returned scant minutes later to the restroom, Izzy was gone.

The desert is also a lonely place, as I truly began to learn that night.

~ * ~

I am on my knees, praying for guidance regarding both Isabelle and Benny when there is a shockingly loud knock at my door.

"Father William! Are you awake? There's been a..."

Julia's voice trails off as I open the door. Her eyes are wide with fear, her mouth gaping with dismay, her aged, dark Colombian skin pale. Her right hand is still raised in a fist, as though she doesn't know what to do with it now. The other trembles at her breast.

"Julia, what is it? What's wrong?"

She starts to answer in Spanish, too rapid for me to follow, but stops herself after just a few words. She swallows hard, and her eyes plead for comfort.

When I reach out to touch her still raised fist, she starts and snatches it to her breast as well. I gently take both her hands and hold them between mine. "*Julia, está bien.*" My Spanish is not yet as good as I want it to be, so I continue in English. "Whatever it is, it is the Lord's will." Doggerel theology, but Julia's faith is a simple one.

This seems to steady her, but I can see the effort it costs her to suppress her normally charming accent. "Father, there is man in the courtyard." She swallows again, before adding, "I think he is dead."

It takes me a moment to process this, but then, letting go of Julia's hands, I spin and stride to the small window that looks out over Logan and the rectory courtyard. I thrust aside the heavy drapes and…

Red-and-blue lights flash balefully.

Uniformed officers stand around a body.

Paramedics rock back on their heels, remove an oxygen mask from…

The body lies in a smudge of something black against the courtyard's limestone and marble tiles.

Blood.

In this light I can't make out his face, but there, a few feet from the body, is Benny's unmistakable walker with its bright orange tennis balls.

I bow my head, close my eyes, and quietly utter "I commend you, my dear brother, to almighty God and entrust you to your Creator." I suspect Benny is already dead, so the Prayer of Commendation may not be appropriate, but when I look back at the sad scene, the Monsignor stands in the background, and I trust he has given Benny his Last Rites.

Then my eye is drawn across Logan to a person standing in a shadow. She seems to be standing witness, with her head bowed.

And as I realize who it is, Isabelle looks up at me.

~ * ~

I run down two flights of stairs like Satan himself is at my heels. Bursting through the rectory's front doors, I startle the two police officers still standing near Benny's body.

But even before I get to the sidewalk, Isabelle is gone.

~ * ~

As the Monsignor and I walk together back into the rectory, he volunteers that Benny died of a single small-caliber gunshot.

Suspects? None.

Motive? No money on the body. But for a homeless person like Benny, that means nothing.

His walker was his most valuable possession.

On the other hand, maybe he had just bought a pack of cigarettes or a bottle of whiskey.

~ * ~

Though I lay on my bed until the sun rises, I never really make it to sleep. For no reason I can express, even to myself, I know Isabelle was there when Benny was killed.

On Colfax, people have been killed for less.

Lord, it is I who need comfort.

~ * ~

I don't know what to do. If Isabelle witnessed Benny's murder, then she could be a target now.

But it's entirely possible the person who killed Benny was so drunk or high or both they don't even really know what they did or that they were seen doing it.

~ * ~

During the day, when my duties allow, I go out onto Colfax and ask after Izzy. Many of the people I speak to know of her, but no one seems to know where she spends her days.

~ * ~

The Monsignor, a very intuitive man, doesn't ask why I'd like him to take the evening Mass. Today is August 15th, the Night of The Assumption, so the evening Mass is starting later than normal

—at sundown, at 7:56 p.m.

By the time the Monsignor has begun his entrance procession, I am on Colfax asking its nighttime denizens if they've seen Izzy or know where she might be found. I walk a few blocks to the east and then back a few blocks to west of the Cathedral several times.

Having learned nothing of use, on my next eastbound trek, I walk an additional block before turning back to the west, and then walk an extra block in that direction.

It's a Friday night, and the traffic is insane. More than once I nearly become a statistic myself when crossing Colfax to speak with someone I've seen in Izzy's company.

Perhaps the Lord is looking out for me, but I take no comfort in this thought.

I am convinced it is Isabelle who needs His protection.

~ * ~

By nine o'clock, my search pattern has expanded to the east end of the 16th Street Mall. I've never seen Isabelle on the mall, and it's earlier than I've seen her anywhere, but many of the Colfax homeless panhandle on the mall until around eleven. I hope someone there might know how I can find her.

~ * ~

An hour and a half later, I'm back in my rectory cell. My feet and legs ache. I haven't walked so much in such a short period of time… Most likely, ever. And the hot, humid August weather has left me a sweaty and smelly mess.

Not wanting to waste time, I spend more time on a hand-towel bath than a shower would have taken.

As I put on my shirt, I immodestly look out my window.

As I do Isabelle looks up at me from the very spot where she'd stood last night.

Buttoning my shirt fully isn't possible as I run down the stairs, but modesty be damned.

This time, she's still there as I blow through the front doors. In seconds, I'm standing before her—it's Isabelle, not Izzy. Without thinking, I blurt out, "Isabelle, I've been looking for you all night."

Her eyes widen at the sound of her full name, and her hands start to twitch.

I fear even Izzy will retreat into swatting the air, and squash an urge to take her hands in mine in an attempt to keep her mind from fluttering away. Instead, I quickly correct myself, hoping to minimize the damage. "Izzy, I was worried about you."

Her jaw clenches ever so slightly, and her hands become still. It may not be Isabelle looking at me now, but at least Izzy is.

I want desperately to ask if she witnessed Benny's murder, but I fear this may not be a good tack to take either. Perhaps the tried and true. "How are you tonight?"

I'm probably kidding myself, but it looked like, for just a moment, Izzy, or possibly Isabelle, was thanking me with her eyes.

"Michael is coming."

My stomach plummets to my feet. I know she's just answered the question I wanted to ask. "Izzy…"

"Michael is coming for Isabelle."

The Earth seems to spin a day's turning around me in but a moment.

The next few seconds pass in a fraction of one but take an eternity to play out.

A glint of light behind Isabelle catches my eye.

A shape emerges from behind a trash dumpster in the Archdiocese parking lot.

A flash of light.

The sound of a snub-nose .38.

Isabelle gasping.

Stumbling a step toward me.

Her hands coming to rest, unbelievably lightly, on my chest.

The sound of the gun hitting the ground.

A guttural, angry voice saying, "You won't rat me out to the pigs, you bitch."

The sound of feet running away into the night.

Without being aware I'd taken a hold of her; I gently lower Isabelle to the ground.

"He's here," she says in an absurdly matter of fact way.

And suddenly, night becomes day.

Or rather morning, as the light illuminating Isabelle's face feels like the sun rising in the east behind me.

She is only nineteen years old, but her face has always looked many years older. Those extra, unwarranted years fade away in the golden light illuminating her face.

Isabelle is the beautiful young woman she was meant to be. Her dingy, stringy hair takes on a brilliant flaxen sheen. The dirt on her face evaporates. The only thing about her that doesn't change is the cornflower blue of her eyes.

And then she smiles—Isabelle smiles. "Grigori, I brought Michael for you."

I am stunned—Isabelle has never in my experience referred to herself in the first person.

Perhaps what she's said should scare me, but the look in her eyes tells me there was nothing to fear.

Following her gaze, I look over my shoulder.

"Child, forgive yourself and know the forgiveness the Lord God granted you the day you were born. Come with Me, and never know pain again."

In my ears, the Archangel's words are English. In my mind, I hear him in my native Russian. In my heart, the Latin of the Holy Church. And in my soul, every language ever spoken by any of God's creations.

He is beautiful. Divinely beautiful.

But not so beautiful as Isabelle, when I turn back to her.

Her eyes close, and as they do, she says, "I brought him to lead you out of the desert."

And as they do, the light of the Archangel fades away.

~ * ~

I am still standing there looking down at Isabelle when the police arrive. They try to question me, but the look of peace on her face arrests their natural suspicion. Their natural cynicism.

It is a look I am I certain Isabelle never knew.

But that is of no concern now.

All that matters is that Isabelle tells no lies.

And in this, and the light of the Archangel, I find a comfort that will last me all of my days.

~ * ~ * ~

P James Norris has master's degrees in Physics and Philosophy. In the 1980's, he wrote four spec scripts for ST:TNG. In 2018 he started getting short stories published by the likes of Moon Magazine,

Fantasia Divinity, Rhetoric Askew; his shorts have been included in three anthologies. He's written three one-hour fantasy TV pilots. He has five novels in various states of incompletion—maybe, some day, he will finish writing them. He lives in Idaho with his wife and a dog, two cats and four chickens.

His published works can be found at: amazon.com/author/pjamesnorris and at ocetacea.net/pjamesnorris.

Love Takes Wing

Corinna Underwood

That summer Ella's heart transformed from a hot, pulsating vessel of life and love to a hardened, brittle block of ice. She walked on water for the first time. It was no miracle. As soon as her toes touched the ocean, a vast expanse solidified, and a polar bear romped outside the beach house with her cub.

She tried drinking scalding teas to thaw herself out but only managed to take the smallest sip before they too became solid. She hid herself away at the beach house where there were no friends to help her hold up under her sorrow because she was afraid she would give them frostbite or she would make their huge hearts crack and explode.

It was all because of Walter. One moment he was there with his booming laugh and his restless energy and the next there was silence and stillness. She would never have been ready to lose her husband, but to have him snatched away was a cruel twist she could hardly believe. When she had begun to believe it, a tiny crystal of ice had formed in an instant between heartbeats, and it had steadily grown through her vital muscle.

Time heals they say. Over the fireplace, Walter had hung a clock that always made Ella laugh because of its oversized face. But now it offered her no solace. Its hands were clenched into fists that sucker-punched her with every tick.

She stopped hearing the birds singing and her heart froze a little harder. Walter had loved the birds; there was every kind of feeder and nesting box in their small garden. He loved their sense of freedom he'd said. But the hummingbirds were his favorite, with their wings in a blur. Flying jewels he called them.

"I'll come back as a hummingbird" he once said. And she had believed him. He knew everything about them and would feed her facts about them until she came to love them too. Now, she sat by the window watching the feeders, not daring to touch them lest she turned them into nectar popsicles. No hummingbirds came.

One morning she decided to go outside after all. She stepped out into the sunlight and noticed her herb garden was in disarray. Walter had planted it for her on their first anniversary. He had laid the stone himself in the shape of a wheel with different herbs between the spokes.

"It's the wheel of life," he'd said. "Our life together."

She began to pull out the weeds. Each one turned into a brittle starfish before releasing its hold on the earth. And tiny slivers of ice fell from Ella's eyes onto the ground where they twinkled for a moment then disappeared.

Ella stood stretching her taut back and rubbing her stiff fingers. Suddenly her ears began to hum and she wondered if this was the end. Perhaps she would be locked in perpetual stasis; a broken-hearted tribute to cryogenics. But she realized the buzzing was not in her head. It was coming from inside the beach house where she had left the door standing open. It was so loud it had to be at least a small swarm of bees. But as she peered around the door there was no swarm, but the hum was louder. Then she saw it.

A tiny silhouette, stark against the windowpane where its wings blurred into seventy-eight beats each second. She watched its sapphire throat and emerald wings glisten in the sunlight like priceless silk. It suddenly stopped hovering and came to rest on the kitchen counter. Head cocked, it turned to her and their eyes met for a long moment.

Ella's lips moved silently in a sound shape something like 'water.' She sat at the table on a throne of ice, wondering what to do, how to set the tiny bird free. But he seemed in no hurry to leave and she could not take her eyes off him. Then suddenly he took to the air again and began to fly at the window, beating its tiny body against the glass.

"Oh please, please stop!"

Ella jumped to her feet. She reached up to release the window's catch but the pane only frosted over. The hummingbird turned, hovered at eye level for a moment then dived into Ella's imploring hands. Before she could snatch them away, the bird had nestled in her cupped palm. Fear tremored through her whole body. The tiny bird held on tight, but it did not take on arctic whiteness like everything else she touched. Instead, it seemed to pulsate, and she could feel its tiny heart beating at thirteen hundred and sixty beats per minute.

Ella felt a strange sensation in her palm. It seeped slowly up her arm to her shoulder. She realized it was warmth. A warmth she hadn't felt in three months. The hummingbird rose. It hovered so close to her cheek she could feel the subtle draft from its wings. She felt a momentary flicker in her ear and watched as the bird floated to her still outstretched palm where something glistened. It dipped its head and sipped elegantly. Then at the crook of her elbow and the nape of her neck. Her skin was glistening everywhere and when she looked down at the floor there was a pool at her feet. Beneath the thrum of the hummingbird's wings, she could hear her heart pound. The flying jewel darted out into the sunlight. Ella ran to the doorway and squinted in the bright sunlight. They were back. All of them. The finches, the sparrows, the buntings, and the hummingbirds.

In the evening, Ella walked down to the beach for the second time that summer and took a chance. She dove straight into the waves, wondering if they would close over her head in a sheet of ice. They did not. They felt soft and warm around her like Walter's arms.

~ * ~ * ~

Corinna a British author, uprooted and transplanted to the U.S. She has published stories and poems in print and online. She is also the author of multiple books including, *Haunted History of Atlanta and North Georgia, Murder and Mystery in Atlanta,* and *The Darkside Chronicles*: a collection of mysteries with a paranormal twist. When She's not writing, you'll find her sowing seeds of imagination in dark and mysterious places.

School

Justin Zipprich

Sunday 2/8

Dear diary, I'm a ten-year-old boy who probably won't make it till eleven. I've got a sickness but I'm not sure what kind. All I know is that I'm not as smart as the other kids and I look different too. It's sad so I won't think about it now.

Today is a sunny day and I'm sitting on the porch with my new birthday gifts. I got a fluffy teddy bear, a new diary and of course, I have the daisies.

I love to sit and watch the daisies. I could watch them all day long. They're very beautiful as they move with the wind without a care in the world. They are so lucky. They get to stay out in the sun all day, and they never have to worry about going to school.

Just the thought of going back to that place tomorrow makes me sad. Nobody likes me there. They only like making fun of me because of my sickness. Their favorite thing to do is make pig noises as I pass in the hallway. I never need to look in a mirror because the kids at school describe me well enough as it is.

They tell me that I have a fat round face, huge eyes, a big tongue, and short stubby arms. They like to call me Piggy. They also love the fact I have to take my special classes due to the fact that I'm not too smart. One time my dad took me to take a smart test, I scored a fifty. That seems like a good score to me, but what do I know? When I'm in class the other kids like to sit out in the courtyard and make faces at me through the window.

It's not like I don't try to defend myself, but when I do it just makes things worse. My words don't come out real well. They are so clear in my mind but when they come out of my mouth it sounds jumbled and thick, at least that's what they tell me. I don't want to think about that now. I just want to think of the daisies. They are always here to make me happy. I see brightness and happiness in the daisies. I feel better now. Maybe tomorrow will be a good day after all.

Monday 2/9

Today was another bad day. I tried to stay positive and hope for the best but it didn't work. There's this one boy, Timmy, he's the meanest of them all. I know it's not nice to say but if I had to hate someone, it would be Timmy. He likes to gather around a bunch of kids, and have them laugh as he makes fun of me. His favorite thing to do is to pull my pants down in front of everybody. They all laugh and I start to cry, but that just makes them laugh even harder.

It seems that no matter what I do, the kids are always mean. My dad loves it when I hug him so I thought that could work. It didn't. When some kids are mean I try to give them a hug. They don't like that. They call me gay and then shove me away. My dad says gay means happy but the bullies don't think so. School is very confusing.

It'll be okay though; when dad gets home he'll make me my favorite food, spaghetti. Then everything will be happy again. Until then it's just me on the front porch with the beautiful daisies. They are the very best things next to spaghetti.

Tuesday 2/10

I usually take a shortcut through the forest, but today I decided to take the long way home from school. When I passed the park I saw a lot of boys playing with their mothers. They all looked so happy. I wish I could be as happy as them. I used to have a mom but she left dad and me when I was small. I'm not sure why she left but dad says it was because she was confused.

I think it was my fault, but dad says she just didn't understand how special I was, so she got scared and ran away. It doesn't matter though because I have my dad and he is all I need in the world. He is my best friend. Dad was in the army, and he's the toughest guy I know, he could beat up all the bad kids at school with one swing! Dad loves to show me all the awards and medals he won while he was on duty. Sometimes he even shows me some of the tools he used against the bad guys.

I know they're dangerous and I'm not allowed to touch them, but I promised I wouldn't and he trusts me. Besides, he keeps all the bad things locked up. He locks them in the adult drawer and he hides the key under his pillow. Sometimes dad lets me sleep in his bed, and those are my favorite nights. Well diary, that's it for today. We'll talk again tomorrow.

Wednesday 2/11

This won't be a long journal; today was a very bad day. When I was coming out of class, Timmy, and a bunch of older kids were waiting for me. Timmy told them all my mom left me because I was a weirdo and that nobody likes or loves me. I told them my dad loves me and that he could beat all of them up!

They didn't care and told me it was a lie. They said my dad didn't love me, and that he just puts up with me. I know that's not really true but it just hurt my feelings so bad. I don't ever want to go back to school again. I'll just tell my dad that my heart is acting up again, and I'm not feeling very well. I think it's a broken heart. I don't want to see the world anymore. I just want to sit alone in my room for a while.

Sunday 4/18

I've been allowed to stay home from school for the last couple months. I've spent most of that time in my room, alone in my bed. I thought it was time for an update, diary, so you don't get worried about me. I told dad how sad I was, and that I didn't want to go back to school, and he said that was okay for now. He invited a doctor to our house. She's a very nice lady. Her name is Ms. Sarah. She comes over twice a week and just talks with me.

I told her how I missed my mom and that I get sad sometimes. She gave me some breathing exercises to do when I get worried about things. She told me that it wasn't my fault that mom left, and that my dad loves me and is very proud of me.

Speaking of dad, he showed me all kinds of cool things while I was home. He showed me the medals he got for fighting the bad guys in the far away place. He got a medal of honor for when he saved a bunch of his friends and a bronze medal for being very brave.

He also showed me all the cool tools that he used to use. He showed me these goggles that help him see in the dark. I put them on and I felt like a secret agent! I'm real good at remembering how his special tools work, like how a salt rifle works. It uses little beads that come out of the end and hit targets. You always have to be careful with that one.

The best thing he showed me was his favorite tool of all, something called a hanger nade. It's a cool little thing that reminds me of a pinecone but there's much more to it. There is a special pin that you pull. As soon as you pull it you have to run far away. Dad says he used it to keep bad people from hurting him. He showed me how it works but told me I'm never allowed to touch it.

He says if they are used right they make the bad people go to the bad place. I always wonder where this bad place is. Sometimes my dad brings me to this giant toy store. I don't like it cause it is very noisy. I always say that I want a new toy, but I forget how scary that store is. Inside there are all these bad kids that run around. They throw the toys and yell as loud as they can. I pick the first toy I find just so we can leave as fast as possible and go somewhere quieter. To me that is a very bad place, maybe that is where the bad people go.

I had a really fun time with my dad. He reminded me that I'm very special, and that I will do great things in my life. I needed that quiet time with my dad, and now I don't feel half as sad anymore.

Monday 4/19

Dear diary, it's the morning of my first day back at school. I'm feeling very positive that today is going to be a good day. I'm sure everyone missed me while I was gone. Who knows, they might even greet me with hugs! You know how I like those. I can only hope for the best and I'll let you know how it goes.

~ * ~

I am very tired of hoping and praying for good things to happen, it never works out the way I want it to. Today was officially the worst and saddest day of my entire life. It's hard to even talk about, it was just that bad, but I'll try my best. After I got out of class, this boy Michael came up to me and said that my dad was waiting outside to pick me up.

I had been in work groups with Michael before, and I thought he was my friend. I guess I was wrong. Since he seemed like a neat kid, I followed him outside. I wasn't sure why my dad was here at my school but as usual, I was excited to see him. When I got outside my dad wasn't there. Instead it was Timmy and a group of his mean friends. I should have known it would be Timmy.

I knew it was a bad news situation so I tried to run but two boys grabbed and pushed me into a big circle of bullies. When I tried to beg them to leave me alone, my words didn't come out right and they just laughed at me.

They threw me on the ground and started hurting me. They were all kicking my arms and legs with their hard shoes. All I could do was roll around on the dirty ground, praying it would stop. I was crying hard, I couldn't help it. After what seemed like hours they finally gave up and went away, leaving me hurt and crying in the dirt.

When it was finally safe, I got to my feet. I was hurting all over, and bleeding from my nose. I didn't want to go back into school so I just walked home. I also didn't want dad to see my bruises and be sad for me so I was lucky that he was still at work when I got there. I went to my bed and crawled under the covers. It's hard to write under here.

I really didn't want dad to see how hurt, and beat up I was so I stayed under the covers when he came into my room to say goodnight. I just pretended that I was asleep. While laying here I decided that it is up to me to do something big to keep the bullies from hurting me. I need a very smart plan.

Tuesday 4/20

My dear diary, it's just past midnight and I just came up with a genius plan! If I can't keep the bad kids away on my own then maybe I can use a bad people tool instead. I remember when dad told me about the little hanger nade, and how it is good at keeping bad people away. It's so easy! If I do it right then those bullies will go to that bad place where they won't be able to hurt me anymore. I still can't figure out where that place is. It could be an island or a scary forest or maybe even that loud toy store I don't like. Wherever it is, I know they won't be able to make fun of me anymore and that is good enough for me.

All I have to do is pull the pin, put it in Timmy's backpack and run far away. Then he'll never bother me again; at least that's how I think it works. Dad will probably be pretty mad at me, but he'll also be proud that I defended myself like he used to do in the army. Tomorrow is going to be a very exciting day indeed. For now I'd better get some rest.

Wednesday 4/21

Good morning diary. Today is the big day and I couldn't be more excited! Things are finally going to be okay for me and that thought makes me very happy. Last night while dad was sleeping I snuck into his bedroom. As quietly as I could I took the key to the adult drawer from under his pillow. I was sure he would wake up when I tried to take the key, but he must have been having a very good dream because I got the key without waking him.

My teacher says that if you know something but you don't tell anyone, it's the same as lying. I guess that means that this is the first time in my life that I have ever told a lie. My dad never realized that I had the hanger nade in my pocket. He didn't even feel it when he hugged me goodbye. I know it's wrong to steal but it might be my last hope of stopping the bullies and finally being happy. It's something that I have to do on my own.

All this time I had no idea it would be so easy to turn my life from bad to good. Since mom left, the only person who loves me is my dad. Everyone else hurts me in all kinds of ways and I can't take it anymore. Now I know that all I needed to make the bad people go away was this little hanger nade. Soon it will be just dad and me, the person I love the most in the whole wide world. He is everything to me, and I can't wait to see how proud he is when I get home and tell him the great thing that I've done. After years of being hurt, the hanger nade will finally make me happy again.

When I get home from school I can sit outside with dad, and watch the daisies, and I'll never be sad again. Goodbye diary, I'll talk to you soon.

~ * ~ * ~

Justin Zipprich is a freelance writer and blogger based out of Las Vegas. He is an admirer of the written word and the amazing worlds that these words create. Although he loves his blogging work, his true passion will always be the world of fiction. He has written a multitude of short stories, numerous full-length screenplays, and is currently working on his debut novel.

He is proud to have had his previous work published by Necrology Shorts, Foliate Oak Literary Magazine, Fiction and Verse, and Whisperings Magazine. He has also received several nominations for his screenwriting efforts."

Strawberries

LCW Allingham

A lock buried in the north, beneath the path. A lock buried in the south in the strawberry patch. A lock in the east and the west. These provided a barrier through which evil could not pass. That is how I knew the boy was trouble.

I watched him start up the brick walkway and when he hit the barrier, he stumbled, fury twisting briefly over his face before he put his mask of sweetness on and pulled out his phone.

Freya's phone chimed.

Freya danced from her room, her favorite floral skirt flowing around her long legs. "Lance is here, I'm out, Mom."

"Wait a minute." I kept my tone even although my heart pounded like a Beltane drum. "I want to meet this boy."

"Mom!" Freya sighed. "Please."

"Why can't he come to the door?" I asked. "Why do you have to run to him?"

"I'm not running to him." She kissed my cheek. "Just cut him a break, okay?"

Then she was out the door. What could I do to stop her? I was unprepared for my nineteen-year-old daughter to date a monster. She'd always used good judgement. She'd always been able to spot a snake in the strawberry patch or her dating pool.

How had this boy gotten in? Perhaps I'd become careless.

From the window, I watched Freya take his outstretched hand, watched as he squeezed her fingers just a little too tight and tugged her off balance toward him. She smiled brightly and he looked up at me and nodded.

The gesture spoke of victory.

Then he pulled her to his car, parked in front of the neighbor's house. He hadn't even been able to bring his Nissan into our driveway.

What was I going to do?

I checked my binding spells. They were all in place. I knelt before my altar and I called upon the goddess.

Keep my daughter safe, please! Shrivel her affection for this boy and let it die.

The goddess was silent. I was missing something.

An offering? I burnt incense and put out a chalice of vodka. Others used wine, but my goddess always preferred vodka from me. I kept a big bottle just for her.

Yet when I prayed again, she still did not answer.

I collected the crystals from the corners of the house and replaced them with stones that had been cleared and charged under the last full moon. I set an amethyst grid under Freya's bed for clarity and protection. I smudged the house with cobalt and sage,

I checked the locks. One beneath a brick on the walkway to the front door. One buried in the strawberry garden. One at the base of the cypress tree outside my bedroom window and one near the lilacs outside Freya's window. My property was protected. But when she was out of the house, my daughter was not.

When she came home, she was different. Her smile was dreamy and her gray eyes glazed. I followed her to her room, pretending to listen to her description of the date as I scanned her body for injury. There was nothing to see, but somehow, he had marked her. I could feel it on her, like a dark, throbbing bruise right across her heart.

"He's really funny, Mom," Freya said as she brushed out her auburn hair with the mother-of-pearl handled boar bristle brush my mother had given her. I hated that brush, but I never told Freya. She thought her grandmother was kind. "He's got a dark sense of humor, like you."

"Well I hope I get to meet him sometime. Do you think he'll come to the door next time you go out?"

"I'm meeting him at the pool hall tomorrow night. But maybe next time. Oh, and he's going to come with me to the strawberry festival. So, you'll definitely meet him then."

The strawberry festival was a month away. She was already making plans to include him in our special tradition.

Goddess, what am I missing?

~ * ~

Freya didn't say her own things anymore. It was always "Lance said..." or "Lance thinks..." or "Lance did..." and when I said I wanted to know what she thought she laughed like it was a funny joke.

He had his own apartment. They had met at Osiris College, the very small, private college Freya attended because her father used to work there. She could live at home and save money and keep her waitressing job where she made great tips. He had no family nearby, no reason to be invading our peace.

"Why did Lance choose Osiris?" I served her chamomile tea after another date to the pool hall. Lance liked the pool hall. Freya never cared for pool before. She looked tired, her eyes smudged with mascara and her lips raw from his stubble. She'd been having trouble sleeping.

"He likes the campus." Freya sipped her tea.

"Is he going to go home to visit his family this summer?" I asked.

"He doesn't have anyone to sublet his apartment," she said. She brushed an errant strand of hair from her face and the wide sleeve of her shirt slid up to show the edge of a finger-shaped bruise, wrapped around her arm like a snake.

"So, he's not even going to visit for a week?" I asked.

"Geez, mom! It's a twelve-hour drive and he can't take the time off work!".

She never used to snap at me. The mothers of her high school friends use to call me. "Lucinda, what are you doing with Freya that I'm not? You two are so close, and she always has nice things to say about you. My daughter can't stand to be around me!"

"I treat her like an adult," I would say, careful to keep the smugness from my voice. "I trust her to make her own decisions."

None of them ever wanted to do that. Trust a teenager? Keep their hands out of their daughter's life? No. Mothers needed to force their daughters down a straight and narrow path. No sex. No drugs. No parties. No fun. Be a nun until you are in college, and then we will throw you to the wolves, in a white dress.

Yet here was my Freya, who had embraced her freedom with restraint, without restriction, and was now willingly wrapped in the webs of a spider.

"I'm staying over Lance's apartment this weekend," she said, with that punishing tone I used to hear her friends use against their mothers.

Goddess, help me.

~ * ~

I set a new grid beneath her bed; fire opal for protection against danger and mistreatment, pietersite to recognize falseness and open up intuition, moonstone for feminine strength. I put carnelian over the door so bad intentions could not enter the house. I smudged all her clothes and cleansed all her jewelry and wove chains with her hair so the goddess could always find her and guard her.

Freya spent less and less time at home. She stayed at Lance's apartment five nights a week, sometimes going over straight from work. The nights she was home, Freya was agitated, and quick to snap at me.

She didn't help me make dinner or clean or even tend the gardens where our strawberries began to blush. When I asked her to, she sighed heavily.

He was claiming her. Hickies on her neck. Little bruises on her wrists and arms, her back and thighs, fingers pressed hard into her precious skin. She kept them covered, but her flesh had grown inside my womb and I could see where it cried out with pain, even beneath long sleeves in June.

"I'm worried about you," I said one morning before she ran off to work. "You don't look well."

"Thanks a lot, Mom," she snarled.

"You can tell me if something is wrong. I will always listen to you and I will never judge you. You know that, right?"

"You're so full of shit. I know you hate Lance! You can just say it!"

"Freya…" I had been careful to never speak ill of him. I knew it was the surest way to run her off. Freya's own father had taken on a god-like quality to me when my mother had announced he was no good. I had been so quick to trade my mother's control over me for his.

"You think I haven't seen the crystal grids beneath my bed?" Freya cried. "Fire opal? Really? I can make my own decisions."

"I just want you to be happy," I said softly. I never hid my craft, nor did I force it on her. I had not been ready to be inducted into the secrets of my family until I was twenty-two, pregnant and abandoned. It was a choice I thought Freya would make when she was ready.

She had always quietly appreciated my protection spells, sometimes watching me work, selecting crystals for the grids, bringing home rocks and feathers for my charms, helping me hang and dry the herbs for potions.

"I am happy!" she shouted. "I'm happier than I've ever been in my life! So just stay out of it!"

She slammed the door on her way out and the carnelian fell from the top of the frame and cracked on the terracotta floor.

Goddess, what do I do?

~ * ~

We worked tentatively for the strawberry festival; few words spoken between us. I collected the perfectly ripened strawberries into crates. Freya made pies when Lance was working.

We had won the strawberry award ever since Freya had started helping me. She had been crowned the Strawberry Princess two years ago. Our berries were known to be the best.

The gardeners of our little town would beg me for my secrets but, they could never reproduce what Freya and I had. The strawberries were the children of my mother's garden, perhaps the only pure thing to come from her home. They knew our voices, our reverent hands. They felt the bond between Freya and I, the magic only produced by our love for each other and the earth we tended.

There were rotten strawberries in the patch this year. I pulled the plants that produced them and burned them the night before the festival. I prayed I removed them in time.

Freya put on her favorite red dress, with amaryllis print, and a flowing, knee-length skirt. She wove her hair into braids. She came out of her room an hour before we had to leave with her face twisted in despair.

"Something's wrong," she said. I looked up from my packing to see she was right.

Her dress, hung oddly on her narrow frame, its scarfy skirts tangling around her legs, the cap sleeves digging into her arms, like manacles, above a faded yellow bruise twisted around her elbow. The scoop neck fluttered around her chest, avoiding the curve of her breasts.

Her hair was dull, not its usual sunset richness. Her ends were dried and frizzing, and fly-aways formed a fuzzy halo around her head.

Freya's face was pale and gaunt in spite of her careful make-up, and her eyes, welled with tears.

That boy. It was that boy. His claim clung to every part of her now, feeding off her vitality. Freya began to cry. I ushered her into the bathroom and pulled the braids from her hair.

"I'll get you the lavender and peppermint soap and you just scrub up. Then we'll put aloe and hibiscus oil in your hair and try again. Try on my constellation dress. It always looks good on you."

Freya let me take care of her. She took my potions. She cleansed her face with witch hazel and let me apply my blessed mascara to her lashes to clear away the blindness that had overtaken her.

She let me clean him off her and wrap her in the dress I had bewitched with glamours and spiritual armor.

We were late to our stand, and could have been disqualified but my daughter was herself again. Freya glowed as we unloaded our crates and pies onto our folding table, with our hand carved wooden sign that said, "Haven's Strawberries". Freya's friends from high school ran over to help.

"You haven't been returning my calls!" one of them said.

"Let's get together next weekend," Freya said. "I have a couple days off. Maybe we can go to the beach."

We had our stand set up just minutes before the judges started around, sampling strawberries.

"You look lovely, Freya," Mayor Gross said. "Done your first year of college?"

"Yes Ma'am," Freya said.

"Dean's List?" Mayor Gross's fingers hovered over the strawberries, trying to select the best one.

"Yes, Ma'am. I've kept up my GPA"

Mayor Gross nodded and finally selected her strawberry. "Freya, if you are looking for work over the winter holidays, I have a paid internship available."

"I would love that, Ms. Mayor." Freya smiled.

Mayor Gross looked at her strawberry. "I don't know how you grow them so big, Lucinda." She finally took a bite. "And they're always so sweet! They're like the most strawberry-tasting strawberries I've ever had!"

Freya started to flicker just before they gave out the prizes. She stood on her toes to try to see through the crowd gathered around our stand. Her smile became strained. Lance was supposed to be here.

She plastered on a smile when Mayor Gross presented us with the blue ribbon for best fresh strawberries.

"Every year!" our stall neighbor, Bernadette Samson cried. "You're going to have to teach me whatever witchcraft you're using, Lucinda."

Bernadette won first prize for best strawberry jam. When she was younger, Freya wanted to compete for all the prizes. She knew we could win but I told her we had an unfair advantage that could quickly have us ostracized in our little town we loved so much.

Freya went around to buy some of everyone's goods. Jam, strawberry shortcake, strawberry cream, strawberry soap, and four jars of strawberry lavender butter, supporting our neighbors whether we liked them or not. I learned the importance of community when John turned his back on me and our daughter. When our friends ignored my calls. Thou shall not suffer a witch. At least not if she won't convert to Christianity for a shotgun wedding.

Freya disappeared into the crowd looking for Lance. He said he would be here. No doubt she told him where to meet her, how to get there, and yet now she was looking for him, in case he got lost and forgot how to text.

She wandered back with her bag of treats, dejected.

"How are you doing, sweetheart?" I chanced the question

"I just…I'm anxious for you to meet Lance." Freya surveyed the crowd again.

I kept my teeth from obviously clenching. How quickly would she forgive him if he never showed up at all?

They called Freya for the crowning of the strawberry princess on the stage in the front of the park. All of the former princesses stood behind the mayor while she announced a young woman who excelled in character, community service, and academics. It was a nominated position, and candidates were never announced but circulated amongst a group of teachers, employers and mentors for secret voting. I had voted every year except when Freya's name was on the ballot.

Freya shined on stage but, her eyes were scanning the crowd

looking for Lance. Still looking for Lance. I could see his coils wrapping around her, pulling the smile from her face, the pride from her stance, dragging her down before my very eyes as the new princess was announced.

I would have to make Freya an onyx charm to keep her on course.

She was so distracted that when all the women moved forward to welcome the new strawberry princess, Freya thought the ceremony was done and started to leave the stage. Someone caught her arm and Freya blushed.

It was when she was hugging the new princess that I spotted Lance, strolling up through the crowd with a cigarette hanging from his mouth and his eyes locked on Freya, like a cat stalking a baby bird. *My* baby bird.

Freya was laughing as she strolled off the stage, arm in arm with friends, when he struck.

"Babe!" he barked.

She spun toward him, her face alight, and I watched as he set his expression, a casual, questioning twitch of his hands, a cock of his brow, all so subtle everyone else would miss it, unless they understood.

I understood. The expression blamed her for something.

Freya understood. Her face fell and she ran to him, reaching for him. He jerked back from her and she recoiled, reaching her hand into her hair instead, twisting an auburn strand around her finger and tugging as she tried to cajole him.

"I've seen those two, over at the pool hall." Bernadette appeared beside me as I watched the exchange. "I can't tell your girl who she can date, but you should know, Lucinda…"

"I know," I said.

"I figured you did." Bernadette's voice was solemn. "If you need to talk to anyone, my two girls are married now. One I talk to. One I don't."

"Thanks Bernie." I patted her shoulder, but kept my eyes on Freya.

She was gesturing toward me. He was glowering at her. She was pleading. Apologizing. For what? for smiling. For laughing, for enjoying herself without him.

I felt a strange power collecting around me. At first it startled me, and then I recognized it and shook it off. This was destructive magic that would hurt my daughter if I let it out. I knew that for sure because I had often been on the receiving end of it when I was her age. I had never told Freya this kind of power existed, just like I never let her know about people like Lance and all the ways I encountered them when I was a young woman. I let her think her father was the white knight. Her grandmother was the kind matriarch and I was selfish. I pushed the power down, into the earth.

But before it was completely gone, the boy glanced over at me, and he saw it on my face. He put on his mask of charm and took Freya's hand. Now she tugged away from him, but he tightened his grip and forced her hand up to his mouth for a kiss. She melted with his poisonous touch and he pulled her into his arms, kissing her forehead.

I made my face smile. So did he, but he kept his eyes averted until Freya introduced us.

"Mom, this is my boyfriend, Lance. Lance, this is my mom," Freya was trying to smile too, but he had shaken her. Shaken my careful protections right off her. Her hair was already frizzing, her skin losing its glow.

I stuck out my hand. He had one arm around Freya's shoulders and the other hand gripping her upper arm. This is *my* girl, his stance said as his green eyes pretended to sparkle warmly at me. My outstretched hand forced him to let go of her arm, and his shake was a little too firm. I pushed the anger down, down where it wasn't going to hurt anyone. "Lucinda Haven. It's a pleasure to finally meet you, Lance."

Freya twitched at the word "finally". Shit. I had messed up. Lance's smile stretched wider.

"It's great to meet you, Lucinda," he said giving my hand a very brief but extra hard squeeze and jerking it toward him, pulling me off balance. "I've been after Freya to introduce us. I hope we can all get together for dinner sometime. Freya tells me you're an amazing cook. Do you have any of your wonderful strawberry pies left? I'd like to try one."

"I'm sorry, we sold out very quickly," I said.

"Actually, I saved one for you." Freya tugged loose from Lance to retrieve a pie she had hidden under the stand. She handed it to him, proudly, and he took an appreciative whiff of it and tossed it onto the table.

"Well, Freya wants to show me the rest of the festival. I guess this is a big deal for you two. Freya being a princess and all. It was really nice to meet you, Lucinda." His false eyes danced. He already knew he'd won.

"Bye Mom," Freya said weakly as Lance tugged her off.

He plucked at her skirt as they walked away. "I thought you were going to wear the red dress. This one is kinda slutty."

Then they were gone in the crowd and that power, that force gathered around my feet again, waiting for me to call upon it.

No, no. I could not.

"That looked surprisingly friendly," Bernadette said.

"He called me Lucinda," I said, my voice flat and monotone.

"You gonna kill him?"

I could. I really could.

Goddess, contain me.

~ * ~

I was ready to leave the festival after the encounter, but I had obligations, and I hoped Freya would come back. I prayed she would come back, if just to help me pack. It would have meant his control over her wasn't complete. She never came back. He probably dragged her home with him as soon as they left me. I gave his pie to Bernadette.

When I got home, I dug through Freya's laundry until I found a tank top with one of Lance's blond hairs on it. All the possibilities spread out in front of me, but for now, I just wanted to keep Freya safe. Let her see what he was doing to her.

I bound the hair with a white ribbon. Let him reveal his true self to her. Remove all his glamours. It wouldn't last forever, with only this one discarded hair, but maybe it would be enough.

I called to the goddess under the moonlight as I wrapped the hair. I prayed for her assistance. I put it in a circle of malachite to break the ties he had with Freya, and burnt incense. I left three gold chalices of vodka on the altar with a plate of fine, rich, dark chocolate.

Freya's sobs woke me just after three am. She was not in the house, but collapsed at the end of the walkway, just before the northern lock that protected our home from negative influences.

An Uber idled at the curb, the driver leaning out the door, unsure what the hell to do with her.

I wrapped myself in my flannel robe and ran out to her.

The driver jumped out, "Look, she's in a bad way. I asked if I could take her to the hospital but she insisted I take her here. I don't even know—"

"Thank you for bringing her home," I said, conjuring a twenty in my pocket and handing it to him. "I will take care of her."

"She was hiding behind a gas station," he said.

I collected my sobbing daughter into my arms. The back of her dress was ripped. Her skirts were muddy and her legs were scraped and bleeding.

"Thank you," I said again, my voice indicating it was time for him to go. He got the idea. I picked up Freya. She was light and insubstantial. When I started toward the house, she began to shiver in my arms.

The lock in the north.

Freya was so enmeshed with that boy she could not cross my barrier. Without setting her down I kicked up the brick it was buried under.

The barrier was broken. For the first time since we had moved into this house, when my little girl was six years old. I could feel things rushing past me. All the nasty things I had kept at bay for so long. I had kept my daughter so safe, she'd been unprepared for the violence that waited in the world.

I placed Freya on her bed. I ran a hot bath with sea salt and prepared a diffuser with pine needles, bay leaves and basil for protection, lavender and rose for sleep. The open barrier nagged at me. What if he came for her?

While the bath ran and the herbs steeped, I set the brick back over the lock. The foul wind blowing through my front door stopped. The negativity was in my space now but I would clear it. It would take time. It was a nasty ritual but, for now, I needed to care for my daughter.

Freya had stopped sobbing but tears still ran down her swollen cheeks. I helped her into the bathroom, without a word. A word could shatter her now. I let my hands, my aura, my prayers, my gentle care convey my love, her safety, as I carefully peeled her dress from her body.

Her back and breasts were bruised. There were red splotches on her arms, skin twisted beneath angry fingers. My binding spell had been useless. Why had the goddess forsaken us?

I helped her into the bath. Freya hissed at the heat but her tears dried at last as she curled her knees up to her chest and clutched them. I poured the water over her shoulders, her head, gently washing her body and hair with our new strawberry soap. The dried blood from a small, gash at her hairline ran down her face. I washed it all, washed her clean, and, at last, as I wrapped her in a plush towel, she spoke.

"I hit him first," she said, her voice cracked and ragged.

I nodded but still said nothing. Her return was tentative, a thin auburn hair, wrapping around my finger, begging me to hold her as she climbed. I could not tug or it would break.

"He was being so... He can be so...angry." She choked. "I thought if he just saw what I loved, he could understand it was good. That he could be here too. That I would share all this with him. But it made him angry instead. He yelled at me for it. He made fun of me for the strawberry festival. And I just... I told him to shut up and take me home. And he laughed at me, and said I was being a brat, and then he started to...he wanted to...and I didn't want to because I was mad. There are so many things I like that I let him tell me were stupid. But you, and our town, and the strawberry festival, and...those are not stupid. You are not. You're my mom and I love you and if he can't...so I told him to stop."

She didn't need to justify any of it to me. But she needed to do it for herself. Goddess help her, she needed to convince herself she was not wrong to love the things she loved, the things that loved her back.

"He wouldn't and I tried to push him and he just held me tighter and so I...I told him I would hit him, and he just laughed at me, so I just got so mad and I hit him. I did hit him first, Mom."

"Okay," I said, wrapping her in a clean, flannel robe and leading her back into her room.

"So, it was my fault," she said. "I started it."

Freya searched my face now as I sat her down on her bed. She was so young, so vulnerable. I had never before seen my daughter look like this. She's always been powerful, strong, confident. I hated him. That black anger, now that it had gotten into my house, gathered around my feet, but now was absolutely not the time to let it in. I took a deep breath and opened myself up to the goddess.

Help me help my daughter.

I felt her cooling hands on my shoulder. I felt her voice run through me as I looked into my daughter's haunted gray eyes.

"No," I said.

It felt like there should be more to say, but that was all the goddess gave and my daughter collapsed against me, more substantial, crying cleansing tears as I brushed the knots out of her hair and kissed her cheeks and forehead.

We stayed like that for a long time and then Freya whispered into my shoulder. "I'm done with him."

Again, the goddess spoke through me. "Okay," I said.

Goddess, thank you.

~ * ~

While Freya was home, Lance showed up at her work. When he got aggressive, insisting Freya was there and he was going to see her, her manager called the police and Lance ran off. I should have known that would not be enough.

Two weeks after Freya returned to work, he called and one of the new waitresses gave Freya the phone.

When she came home, she had already made her decision.

"I'm not going back to him, Mom," Freya said. "But I need to meet him in person, one last time, for closure."

So many crimes have been committed in the name of closure. My heart sank. I could not help myself when I asked, "What if he hurts you?"

Freya's face clouded. "He feels terrible about how things ended. And I hit him too. We just want to talk a little bit, in a public place, Mom, so we can end on decent terms and move on."

I didn't believe that. I'm not even sure she believed that. All we had done to build her back up now teetered on a knife's edge, ready to fall back into ruin.

There was nothing else I could do. I had done all I knew how. Did I just accept this? Let her go and make her mistakes, be broken down, and, maybe someday, be killed by this beast that claimed her?

It is the only choice a mother has. A typical mother. They might fight, and call the police, and scream and rage, but in the end, they cannot keep a daughter safe.

I am not a typical mother.

I am of the Goddess.

The daughter of a very powerful witch with a talent for dark magic.

So, after four years of estrangement, I called my mother.

"It's Freya, isn't it?" is how she answered the phone. I wondered if she had gotten caller ID but I suspected she'd just known, the way she'd always known. Just that annoying, smug, knowingness crawled right under my skin, awakening all the old resentments.

"Yes." I bit back on all the angry words that wanted to spew. Mother always knew best. What to wear, what to eat, who to date, with words and magic that cut right to the bone.

"There were three rings around the moon last night, and I saw an owl outside my window this morning. The crows have been gathering around my house for two months and telling me all sorts of wicked things and two of my windows have cracked. That's just the omens, Lucy. If I told you what the spirits have been telling me..."

"I'm sure you will, Mom," I said. "But I just don't..."

"You need to get rid of the boy, Lucy," my mom said. "All things point to the boy. He's a liar who wears masks of charm."

"How do I get rid of him and not hurt Freya?" I asked. "If I move against him, she'll never forgive me."

My mother was silent for a moment. It was so unlike her I checked my phone to see if the connection had been dropped, but no, she was still there.

"Mom?"

"What price would you pay to keep your daughter safe?" she asked.

Would I do for Freya what my mother, mistress of manipulation, had done for me?

~ * ~

Freya had a good relationship with John, her father. He moved to Boston when she was a teenager. She spent Christmas and Thanksgiving with him, holidays that meant nothing to me. He never forgot her birthday. He called her once a week. He had been a decent father, and he cared for our daughter. He was a good man to her.

It was not the same with him and I. We met when he was in grad school and I was getting my bachelors in horticulture. He was my TA and he was handsome and charming and came from a normal family, like I so longed to be part of. He had a cool apartment and fun roommates who did normal things.

I would go home to my mother's dark house, full of judgement and strange smells and talismans made of bones. My mother who thought my normal, handsome, smart boyfriend was not good enough for me. My mother who shoved me out into the world that ostracized me for the strangeness she instilled in me and then criticized everything I did there.

John was not a bad man. But the closer we became, the more he came to know me, the real me that I kept carefully hidden in public, the more he tried to fix me, shape me to be normal like him, and I was a willing student.

Until I got pregnant with Freya.

There was a sudden rush to get married that I didn't understand. He told me it was the thing to do.

I was swept along to engagement parties, wedding dress shopping, suddenly flanked by his friends and sisters who were now called my bridesmaids. They told me to hide my pregnancy so his mother wouldn't find out. Oh, and by the way, I would have to be confirmed into the church before we got married.

The church told me all the ways I was sinful, all the ways I was wrong, that I was dirty in the eyes of God. I realized all I wanted were the warm, embracing arms of the goddesses who had filled the house of my childhood.

I moved out of John's apartment and returned to my mother's house. Her embrace was not warm, but her door was open.

John and I fought. He didn't really believe in his religion but he certainly did not believe in mine. He cut me off, turned his back on me and the baby and told stories to his friends and family about all the wicked ways I'd wronged him.

I was devastated and broke. All my money had gone toward a wedding I wasn't going to have.

And the whole time my mother whispered: I told you so.

I raised Freya under my mother's thumb, rebelling by telling her stories of her father's love, protecting her from the darkness in our house with a strict reverence to a goddess of light.

My mother derided me. I had nothing in the world but Freya.

When Freya was five, John suddenly appeared at the door, his eyes wide and his hands shaking as he passed me a check for back child support.

"I'm sorry," he said. "I'd like to meet her."

I thought at the time he had just come around. Did I not see my mother's influence woven all around him? Perhaps I couldn't believe she would ever let me go.

I was finally able to move out of my mother's house, start my own life, and pursue my bliss. Strawberry festivals, community charms, supporting other women who had no one on their side.

"Do you love your daughter enough to give her up, Lucy?" My mother met me at the little tea shop just outside my town.

"I have tried everything I know. And she was so close, but now she claims he's changed."

"Of course she thinks that. She's an idiot." My mother laughed when I bristled. "You thought you raised her to be so wise, Lucy, but she's still nineteen, and you did her no favors wrapping her up in your little white magic bubble. You should have told her the truth about her father. Told her there are people out there who use control in lieu of love."

"Like you?" I snapped.

My mother grinned. She was still a beautiful woman in her mid-sixties, with porcelain skin and raven black hair. She looked like a French supermodel. Or a witch. "I prefer a healthy dose of each. Now, will you invite me to your home so I can see what needs to be done, or are you afraid I will pollute your little sanctuary?"

She followed me to my house and pulled into my driveway behind my car. I watched warily as she crossed the threshold of the lock barrier without so much as a flinch. Such a spell would not keep such a powerful witch as my mother at bay, but it would give her pause. If she could cross without issue, that meant she was not a negative influence in my home. Still, it was hard to believe my mother had no ulterior motive.

"Let's get started, Lucinda," she said.

Goddess, protect me.

~ * ~

We burnt incense with cypress, mint and a pinch of belladonna, bound with sandalwood oil. I prepared a red sauce full of onions and garlic, to serve over pasta with dandelion wine and mint cakes. An hour before Freya and Lance arrived for dinner, I removed the lock from the walkway, opening up the path into my home my mother and I had carefully laid out.

We prepared a new altar and opened the portal. When all the pieces were in place, darkness would enter my home. I was inviting it.

My dining room table was adorned with a linen tablecloth, woven with runes by my mother's coven. It was my mother's favorite for the last night of the lunar month. The night of reverence for the underworld gods.

"Bring Lance to dinner to meet your grandmother," I had said. Freya had been grateful for the invitation.

Just the fact she was not suspicious showed how well I had guarded her from the truth about my mother.

She sent me a text to let me know they were on their way. Lance was still in the honeymoon period of his abusive cycle so he agreed to prove to Freya how changed he was. But he was beginning to slip. It wouldn't be long now until Freya took a fall or caught her hand in the car door.

"Don't wimp out on me, Lucy," my mother said as I placed two black glazed ceramic vases on the table full of vibrant blue wolfbane flowers. Would Freya recognize it all when she arrived? Would she see what we intended?

But Freya's face was bright when she pranced into the house, Lance lagging behind her, his charming mask carefully arranged on his hateful face. I saw my mother's face falter a bit at the sight of my daughter. They embraced tightly and I smiled at Lance. I shook his wretched hand.

"Lucinda," he said. "Thank you for inviting us."

Us. He said "us". Out of habit I pushed back against the cloud of power that collected around my feet. Then I shook off the inclination and let the darkness in, taking his hand with a grip tighter than his own.

"It's past due." I watched him squirm. "Please, would you like a glass of wine?"

He blanched. "You know Freya and I are underage."

He said it like I was clueless. Like I didn't know he would get her drunk and push her to do things she didn't want.

"Oh, honey," Freya said, "Mom doesn't care about that. Try some."

My own daughter served Lance the wine of wrath, marking him for judgement.

Goddess, forgive me.

~ * ~

Lance tried to sit at the head of the table. Freya quietly tried to correct him, but he brushed her off. My mother took his arm and led him to the seat beside her without a word. No one told him why we served food and wine to the empty place as we started dinner, and he didn't dare to ask. Sitting beside my mother subdued him, as we knew it would.

When the clock chimed seven o'clock, there was a rumble in the house we all felt. Freya laughed nervously and my mother smiled, wide and wicked.

The dark goddess Harek climbed out of the mirror portal and looked around my house. The kids couldn't see her, the darkness rolling off her gray skin, the sharp white teeth that shone through her parted charcoal-colored lips.

Harek sat at the empty seat at the head of the table and raised her chalice to drink. Freya's brow furrowed and Lance's face went white. Her presence was so strong they felt her there. I felt her there, the tendrils of her darkness pulling gently at my skin. We were not strangers, Harek and I.

The goddess observed the boy, her black crowned head swaying side to side as my mother and I continued to converse as if all were normal.

I hated tricking my daughter. I had sworn I would never do it.

But I would break all my vows to keep her safe.

When dinner was over, Harek stood. She moved like a streak of running ink to where the mint cakes waited for desert and touched the last one on the right. Her endless eyes met mine, and my head throbbed. Mother cleared the table, and I served the mint cakes. When I placed the one she touched in front of Lance, Harek nodded at me. Then she streaked back to the portal and tumbled away.

If the mint cakes were examined, no one would ever find a

thing wrong with any of them. There was no poison, no venom, nothing toxic to a human being. Just flour, sugar, eggs, oil and fresh mint.

When Lance started to convulse after we cleared the dessert plates, mother called an ambulance. Freya wept and held him as he foamed at the mouth. She rode with him in the ambulance and stayed with him through the night.

Freya texted me the next morning to let me know the doctors thought Lance had a stroke, that he was out of critical condition but very weak and would have to be in the hospital for a while.

She came home, after three days by his side, to get her things. "I'm moving into Lance's apartment, and I'm going to take care of him. You can't stop me."

I didn't try but I called my mother.

"You must have patience, Lucy. The boy is debilitated. The goddess made her judgement. Have patience and Freya will find her way out."

So, I had patience. For months I had patience. I learned from her father Freya had dropped two classes to have more time to work and take care of Lance. John flew out to try to talk some sense into her. I learned from my mother Lance was impotent, had limited use of his right side, and was too weak to pin Freya down when she made him angry. Freya was confiding in my mother, who somehow had managed to pretend she was more supportive than me.

And finally, after three months, Freya called me.

"Lance is going to live with his father in Portland and I'm not going with him," she said. "You got your way. Are you happy?"

"Are you?" I asked.

She sniffed. I could sense the relief pouring off her, even over the phone. She was ready to be done with him. Lance had done all he could to continue to abuse my beautiful girl as she cared for his weakened shell. He cut with words. He hit with guilt.

But he'd lost his grip, and Freya had been able to pull away at last.

"I could have been," she said, "But you decided for me, didn't you? I'm going to live with Grandma. Don't call me."

She hung up without my response. My mother had gotten her way, after all these years, taking Freya as her own. My bitter laugh filled my empty house before dissolving into tears.

That night, under the waning harvest moon, I tore the strawberry patch up from the frosty ground. I burnt all the plants except for two, which I potted for Bernadette.

I sowed the garden with pumpkin seeds. I sang them a song I'd never sung before. I placed a chalice of vodka on the altar for Goddess Bridget, and a chalice of dandelion wine on the altar for Goddess Harek.

Goddesses, show me the way forward.

~ * ~ * ~

LCW Allingham is an author, editor and artist in the Philadelphia area. She is a founding member of the Utter Speculation series, and her short work has appeared in several other anthologies.

There was
Never Enough Time

H. N. Hunt

Bella feels the world crumbling around her. She hadn't under-stood exactly what was happening until this precise moment. It always seemed like the sort of thing that happened to others, not to her. She heard the stories but who wanted to believe them?

There are people around her and she can't make out what they're saying but it doesn't matter because Matt is bleeding and the world is falling apart for her. She is lying on her belly in the detritus of the alley, pressing her face against his chest and people are talking but none of this is bringing Matt back now, is it?

And Matt himself is running a hand over her head, the gesture so familiar and somehow so final Bella can't help a whimper. She can't fix this. Nothing she knows can fix this.

"Easy, Bella," Matt says and though his voice is low, she can hear it just fine over the chatter and sirens behind and around her. "Don't worry, girl. Be good for Karen, okay?"

But Bella doesn't want to be good. Bella wants to howl at the injustice of it all because what did Matt do to deserve this? They walked this way all the time and nothing had ever happened so why now? Why this time?

Then there are men in uniforms and they are coming to Matt. But, although Bella recognizes them as paramedics, she knows they cannot help Matt. She can smell death already clinging to him.

Then hands are pulling her back and she fights, lashes out with her voice because she would never hurt anyone, not even now but she can't be away from Matt because if she's away from him then it will be over, and he will be gone. He is her world and what does Karen know? She doesn't want to be a good girl and she doesn't want to go with Karen.

"Bella, please." The voice is Karen's and despite her thoughts, Bella calms down, recognizing at last the smell of the hands that have her. They are touching, stroking, trying to convey and pull comfort at the same time. Bella doesn't want to, but Karen is an ice floe of familiarity in this artic sea of uncertainty and Bella leans into her, resting her face against Karen's abdomen.

"It's okay, Bella," Karen says though it is not. Her voice is as choked as Bella feels and Bella knows if Karen could, she'd be howling in tandem with her. "We only have each other now, Bella," Karen says as the paramedics exchange grim looks. Karen is more realistic than most people and she knows as Bella does Matt is not coming back.

"You've got to help me, Bella," Karen says, her voice thick, her arms heavy around Bella's neck. "Please, help me."

And Bella knows she will. Her world is over but here is Karen and Karen needs her and Matt asked her to be a good girl. So that is just what Bella will do. She presses her nose into Karen's neck and gives her tail a thump and promises herself she will be a good dog for Karen.

~ * ~ * ~

H. N. Hunt lives and works in Pennsylvania. She spends most of her time reading and writing and playing with her dogs, who have not figured out the concept of personal space. She has had work published in a variety of venues and hopes to see it published in more still.

Tatters

Leanbh Pearson

She wanted an iron heart. A heart that didn't feel. If she had such a heart, she wouldn't feel the anguish enveloping her. She fluttered her hands uselessly at her collarbones and imagined opening the cavity below and peeling her ribcage apart. She'd thought she'd recovered from the pain but clearly her mind was telling her otherwise. It was treacherous sometimes. Her mind. Everyone said so. Everyone said how the pain she felt now would pass just like it had before. But she only felt it growing like a poisonous plant taking root inside her heart. If her heart were made of iron, then the plant would surely die. The awful thing would wither and die within the iron confines of her heart. She assumed her iron heart would then rust from the rot contained within.

She looked at the pale sunshine filtering through the net curtains of the lounge room. The sofa felt hard as stone beneath her. She was fragile, she knew this without any doctors or her friends telling her. The body she once had was withering around her mind and if only she could hold on a little longer to the tiny spark of sanity that remained, she might outlast the pain. She shifted her position to relieve some of the pain and tapped her fingers against her chest, half-expecting to hear the hollow thud of iron beneath. There was only the sound of flesh hitting flesh and the rhythmic pulse of her heartbeat beneath her fingers. She sighed. The pain was a constant insurmountable wave that crashed upon her body. She knew with every wave her mind collapsed a little more, a piece of it washed away as if it were a sandcastle on the shore. She felt each fragment of herself fading—search for it as much as she wanted—she could never get those pieces of herself back. *My mind is pulling apart. I'm tearing into tatters and soon there'll be nothing of me left but shreds of who I was.*

She settled back against the sofa, hands clutched to her chest and silently cursing her weakness. The betrayal of everything she was and all she might become hinged on outlasting the disease that robbed her daily—hourly—of who she was. She shook her head. She couldn't fight this. There wasn't enough of her mind left to fight this illness. She leaned back against the sofa and let go. In a desperate sigh, she stopped fighting and let the pain take her and hoped in giving up the fight, her heart would become an iron mechanism that couldn't feel. She might survive the hopelessness of delivering herself up to the illness, pain and tortured thoughts of her mind. Instead of wishing for a future that looked less likely and bleaker each day, she wished for the iron heart and to let her mind dissolve into tatters. She wouldn't feel and wouldn't remember any of the dreams she'd once had for herself. She relinquished the fight and ignored the tears that slipped down her cheeks in silent protest.

~ * ~

There's silence. It's golden and luscious and she stretches cat-like on the bed. She's always been gifted with long limbs that were the source of envy from other women and desire from men. She hates it, this beauty that's only skin deep. The silver lines of self-inflicted scars covering her body shimmer like scales as though she's a creature from forgotten myth. But she's as trapped as any exotic creature—a thing to be admired and caged until she's cast away. She knows that's happened already and feels the bars of her prison between her too-thin fingers.

The darkness swarms around her. It beats at her like a live and winged thing, fierce and terrifying. In response, she rakes her fingernails down her face, trying to tear the tatters of her mind free, as though gouging rotten flesh from her cheeks. The beast inside her roars. It wants freedom just as she does. The monster throws itself against the iron bars of her will. The chambers of her mind bend but do not break. She can't let it free, can't let it taste daylight and let it consume all that she is.

~ * ~

Moonlight now. There's no daylight anymore. She's not felt true daylight for days, years. Or has it been decades?

She holds firm against the madness inside her. It stalks in the dark corners of her mind, trying to keep to the shadows where she might forget it. There's no hope of that. She can feel its restless prowling and its keen gaze as it watches her. She stands tall and readies herself. It lunges forward with an abyss for an open maw and wild, hungry eyes.

~ * ~

She screams, grabbing fistfuls of her hair. The locks tear free in a long and filthy hank. She drops it to the wooden floor and stares at the limp and discarded remains in the muted light. Memories stir. She'd been bright and clean—a beauty in golden light no one could resist. How things had changed—how the darkness had changed her.

The monster wakes. It stalks the confines of the chambers in her mind and its cunning eyes miss nothing. She is naked before it—exposed and unprotected from a piercing gaze that sees all of her. It knows every inch of her body and mind. Too late she realizes she's defenseless before it.

~ * ~

She snarls and scratches at her hands, trying to keep the claws of the beast within her flesh. Are the tips of talons piercing through her skin? Blood drips to the floor. She rushes at the light slanting through the window and roars at it with soundless fury. Her hands slam palm up against a dirty windowpane. Blood smears the toughened-glass surface in a scarlet haze. She stands motionless, mouth open in a rictus of defiance. Breath coming in ragged pants.

There's only broken pieces of herself to hold the monster at bay now. It has to be enough. She can't let the madness take her. It's both her weakness and her strength. There's a terrible price for those who embrace it. *Am I willing to pay?* She shudders at the thought. *I might lose myself to the monster.* Would it be the first time? Or would it be again? She screams, voicing her fear—a fear that she's unable to defend herself.

Deep within the shadows of her mind, the monster stirs. It watches her with bright and pitiless eyes. It waits. She's prey now. All that's left are tattered pieces of herself. The monster gnashes its teeth, the fragments of memory and hope swallowed in its maw. The darkness gathers around it like a rippling forest of inky shadows.

~ * ~

She remembers—only the smallest pieces of the past—when the monster in her mind wasn't the thing she needed to fight. There had been another illness. There had been another fight which was brighter, harsher than the darkness. She looked at the bent and knobby joints of her fingers. There had been hope once that she'd overcome this broken body. *How can this feeble body be strong enough to fight the monster?*

She struggled to recall. She'd fought the pain of illness for years—for the length of several lifetimes. That was true, wasn't it? She shook her head, unsure whether the memory was a true one or something the madness had conjured. No. She was certain there had been a time before when the darkness hadn't invaded her life. A time before the madness consumed everything she'd been.

She looked down at her hands and bent the joints. Pain flared—white-hot—eclipsing the madness and the grief of hopes lost. *Yes, I'd hoped to beat this illness and instead I'd let a disease fester and grow within me. The darkness had blossomed and the monster thrived in a world of hopelessness. In that place, I'd become only tatters of my former self. I'd forgotten who I was and what the world truly was.*

Her hands were pale as bone in the muted daylight. She uncurled her fingers and let the pain remind her she was alive. She wasn't the monster in the darkness—a being driven by rage and despair—she was here in this broken body. Compared to the darkness and the madness, her broken body seemed a thing of beauty. In the chambers of her mind, the monster gnashed broken teeth and screamed with hoarse brutality. She closed the doors in the dungeon of her mind and gathered the tatters of herself about her like a cloak. She would do more than survive the pain. She would thrive.

~ * ~ * ~

Leanbh Pearson lives on Ngunnawal Country in Canberra, Australia. An LGBTQIA & disability author of horror & dark fantasy, her fiction features in numerous anthologies. Always aided by her canine assistants, her writing is inspired by folklore, fairytales, archaeology & the environment. She has judged the Australian Shadows Awards, Aurealis Awards, received an AHWA mentorship, participates on convention panels & is a member of the HWA & SFWA. Leanbh's alter-ego is an academic in archaeology, evolution and prehistory.

Follow her at leanbhpearson.com. Twitter, Facebook and Instagram @leanbhpearson

Fifty Matches

Gregory J Wolos

I

"The Darkness Dash is just a mile," my daughter Mary tells me over the first breakfast we've shared in years. "That's the length of Loathsome Cave. A lot of the young men race—fathers too, except the old and the sick ones. The cave's a shortcut people here use all the time—otherwise it would take hours to hike around Hallowed Mountain. Inside, the path stays right next to the creek. But for the Dash you're not allowed to carry light—no lanterns or torches. You've got to feel your way through. Don't worry about falling into the creek, though. It's only a foot deep. Smashing your head on a hanging rock would be much worse, so keep your hand in front of your face. But they've been doing the Darkness Dash forever, and, so far, everyone's survived."

Mary doesn't allow her gaze to slip down to the orthopedic boot that stabilizes what's left of my right foot. She was just about to begin grade school when I left for the war, where the mortar shell that killed two of my trench buddies shattered everything below my ankle. Less than a year after my return, her mother, my dear Kathy, succumbed to the Spanish flu, and I sent our little girl from the infected city to live with her aunt down in this less populated part of the country. Now Mary's twelve, and her resemblance to her mother fills me with both joy and pain. We exchange monthly letters, and I've traveled here in part to honor her request that I be present at her baptism. The photographs I've sent since we separated don't show my injury. In one I'm posing in uniform with her and her mother shortly after my return from Europe. Kathy and I are seated, and little Mary stands between us, her plump hand resting on my knee.

"Every year there's a big picnic," Mary says. "Everybody comes. The Dash is first, and we—the Saint John the Baptist Evangelical Church Baptism Class of nineteen twenty-four—march through the cave in a procession behind the racers. We get to have a lantern, of course. We'll sing hymns as we go. It's supposed to be lovely, with all our voices echoing. When we come out, all the picnickers—the racers, their families, and the families of the kids getting baptized—will cheer for us. We'll keep marching right along Winston Creek to where Pastor Lee will be waiting to baptize us, one by one."

~ * ~

And so two groups gather this morning at the entrance to Loathsome Cave: about fifty Dashers, and the dozen or so Sunday Schoolers ready for baptism. The children, including my Mary, gather around William, their teenage youth leader, who will lead their procession. The Dashers are in festive spirits. Not much of a mixer, I stand aloof from them, though I feel their glances: I'm both a stranger and a cripple who leans on a walking stick. One of the younger men offers me a sip from a bottle he's been passing among his friends.

"It's damp in there," he says. "This will help keep off the chill."

"Maybe after," I say. I tap my cane on the ground. "I need all the stability I can muster."

"Well, no need to worry. You'll make it through. If you panic in the dark, just sit and wait—the Sunday school kids will collect you. Every couple of years a straggler or two need help." He takes a swallow from his bottle and laughs, looking back at his companions, who are watching us converse. "Usually it's somebody who can't handle his liquor. Some of the church folks—the old biddies, mostly —don't countenance the drinking on account of the solemnity of the occasion—the baptisms, you know." He bends toward me, and I smell the whiskey on his breath. "But for most of us the party starts right here."

Youth leader William is also the Dash's official starter. He waves a gold watch over his head. "Gentleman," he calls, "it's two minutes before your noon start. Please make your way to the cave entrance."

Before shuffling to the mouth of the cave, I catch Mary's eye. She stands on tiptoes and gives me a bon voyage wave. She wears a white dress and a crown of flowers atop her honey-colored hair. All I want to do is stare at her—I could keep it up for hours.

"Gentleman, get set!" Upon young William's announcement, I yank my attention from my daughter and limp forward to join my fellow racers at the mouth of Loathsome Cave. Jingling the warning bells we wear on our wrists, we sound like a herd of impatient sleigh horses.

"Go!"

I shove my way past my shouting competitors and lurch inside, where the light gradually diminishes. When the cave bears to the right, I stop dead in sudden and absolute darkness. It's as if I stand on the edge of a cliff. Gulping a breath, I stagger forward.

~ * ~

And now I'm deep within Loathsome Cave, as alone as I've ever felt in my life. My bad foot aches, and both knees bleed through the torn fabric of my trousers after a dozen stumbles. In the pitch black my wristlet bell jingles like a lost lamb's. Just below me, paralleling the path I ease down blindly, Winston Creek gurgles. It's been a while since I've heard the shouts, curses, and tinkling bells that initially pursued me like Harpies. As far as I can tell, I'm leading the Darkness Dash.

I thrust my cane into the darkness before I dare each step. My eyes are useless, but when I shut them, I seem to stumble more often. It's impossible to order one's thoughts without light. As I claw my way forward, I fantasize about my exit at the end of the race: I will feel my way around a corner, and a brilliant circle of blue sky will bloom like a morning glory. Kathy's sister Millie will be waiting among the picnickers. She's a sturdy woman, unmarried and childless until she agreed to take in her niece. I send her a monthly sum for the child's necessities. Millie greeted me with a cool but cordial nod at the train station. Nearly a dozen years older than her sister, she's at the far edge of middle age, and doubtlessly has guessed I mean to steal back the child who's provided her with a companion, a purpose, and a source of income for the last half dozen years.

But deep in Loathsome Cave, a failure to concentrate exacts a cost: the wall of stone dips away, and, as if a rug has been pulled out from under me, I'm weightless—until my knees, then my hands, hit the path. Again. My wristlet bell jingles as I rise. I find the wall and lean on it, catching my breath. *Don't smash your head*, Mary warned, and I picture her in her white dress, waving to me as I turned toward the cave entrance. But the image lingers—do I see her mock my limp for her giggling friends when she thinks my back is turned? I feel my scowl—but how much can I trust what I envision in the darkness?

"Christ-Christ-Christ-Christ-Christ—"

I hear the muttering a moment before I'm nearly run over.

"Hey," I blurt, "I'm here!" Hands paw me, like I'm being sculpted from clay. I grasp a wrist and squeeze.

"Christ—" A gust of breath. "You the guy with the cane? I was pretty sure you were ahead of me. Damn, it's dark."

"Pretty dark," I echo. "Pretty damned dark." I hold tight to my new companion. Then he laughs, and I laugh too, mirthlessly, like the laughter I remember in the trenches of France. Our wristlet bells tinkle in unison.

"'The tintinnabulation of the bells,'" my companion says. "That's Poe."

"He's always burying somebody alive, isn't he?"

"Sure. Drunks and madmen and such. We left the drunks behind for the Sunday school kids. There'll be drink aplenty after we get out of here."

"A fine motivation," I say to distinguish myself from the teetotalers.

"Let's get moving," he says. "You keep the lead—that stick of yours comes in handy."

We forge on together through the darkness. I become aware of each yip or moan I release. My companion growls "Christ!" every few feet.

"Is this your first dash?" he asks.

"Very first. My daughter talked me into it. She's getting baptized. You?"

"My fifth. I knew I hadn't seen you before. Your daughter's Mary? I saw you talking with her. She's my sister's age."

"Your sister's getting baptized, too?"

"Naw—ouch! —we favor a different church."

"Hold up," I say. My cane has found a gap. I tap ahead and find firm footing. "Okay—" My companion's hand is on my shoulder. "You've done this 'dash' four times? Does experience help?"

"Done it in the dark four times, and with a torch or lamp, maybe twenty, thirty more. But, no, experience doesn't help much. Dark is dark—it sucks the time out of things. Time and distance. Who was it in the Bible that got stuck inside a whale? Job?"

"Jonah."

My companion snorts. "I know my Poe better than my Bible. Got to be some kind of sin in that."

We creep along for what feels like hours. My cane taps. Our wristlets jingle. The creek laps faintly at our side.

"Wouldn't it be funny if all the Dashers wore those hats that jesters wear—the ones with the bells—instead of these ones on our wrists?" my companion asks.

"You know," I say, "I didn't hear your bells before you caught me."

"Oh—an old Dasher's trick. You can cup your bell in your hand. It muffles the sound and you can sneak up on folks. Problem is, if you do that, you can't really use two hands to feel your way forward. There's worse that goes on," he continues. "Some folks carry matches. They spark 'em up if they start to panic."

"You bring any?" If I had a match, I'd be sorely tempted to light it.

"Naw—You've got to draw the line somewhere. Quieting the bells is one thing, but beating the darkness is the whole point, isn't it? Had a Dasher go nuts once, did you know that? The year before my first Dash. He came out of the cave swearing he'd seen all kinds of things—demons and devils, virgins being sacrificed on an altar, god knows what else. Rumor is he's locked in a hospital somewhere. His people moved out of town." We pause. My companion sighs. "I guess I wanted to see for myself what it's like to come face to face with the Devil. You think that's what this darkness is? The face of Satan?

"I'll tell you after we're out," I say. "In the daylight. Let's move."

"I don't think it's much further," my companion says. "Got a kind of clock inside that's telling me we're close. Feels like we're rounding a turn. 'Let there be light.' That's God talking right there, not Satan."

I inhale sharply—there's something different, as if my blindness has lifted. A new dimension redefines our position: space. We can see ahead of ourselves.

"Here we go, here we go!" my companion nearly shouts, and as I turn back to him, the whites of his eyes stand out. His teeth, too—he's smiling. It seems I've spent the bulk of my time crawling through Loathsome Cave with a Negro. I'd seen him in the crowd before the race.

"Hello," he says. "Name's Mercury. They call me Merc."

"Chester," I say. "Chet." Never in my life have I kept company for such a long time with a black man.

"Just a little further round here and we'll see the way out," he says, then pauses. "You hear that?" His head snaps around, the mass of his hair a different kind of black. "Bells jingling? We're getting caught—let's go!"

We stumble on, leaving behind the perfect blackness. The creek and cave walls twinkle. Another slight turn, and there's the opening a hundred yards ahead, so bright I wince. We look behind us—nobody. We're panting and laughing at the same time.

"You step out first," Merc says.

"How about together?" I ask. "They'll have to declare it a tie."

"There's no tie they're gonna let you have with me," he says. "Today I'm beating only one kind of blackness."

I look him in the eye, ready to protest, but I can see there'll be no arguing with him.

"You know," he says, "this cave used to be part of the Underground Railroad. That train's traveled pretty far, but it's nowhere near pulling into any station. Not by a long shot."

I see the figure of a man at the opening. He stoops—he's staring at us—and then his arm shoots up in the air. He pivots and runs out of the cave.

"Go on," Merc says, pushing me forward. "I'll be right behind you."

I wobble out of Loathsome Cave, and I'm immediately bathed in sunlight and cheers. "The winner!" I hear declared amid the whooping and clapping, and "Who is he? He from around here?" I'm blinking so fast as my eyes adjust that I can't absorb the full scene—a sea of smiling faces, a blue sky and the greenest forest I've ever seen. I smell roasting pig, and my stomach flip-flops. A pewter mug appears in my hand. Anticipating water, I lift it to my lips and suck in the foamy head of a beer.

"Look," somebody shouts, "here comes Merc!" and there's a smattering of applause. I turn to see my companion paused in the opening of the cave. He's holding something in his hand, and at first I can't make out what it is.

"Hey," another voice cries, "Merc's got a match. That's a

disqualification."

A few lackluster boos arise, before my Dash-mate brings the lit match to his lips, shrugs, and blows it out. The crowd quiets. "Couldn't beat the cripple anyway," he says, shaking his head, and the boos turn to cheers. Hands slap my back, and the beer spills down my chest.

"Here come some more," somebody yells, and out of the cave totter three Dashers who immediately shield their eyes, then wave to their supporters. Left alone, I glance around to see where Merc has gone and find myself staring into the stern face of my wife's sister. Unlike the casually attired picnickers celebrating the Dash, Millie is here only for Mary's baptism, and she's wearing her best Sunday suit and a veiled hat. I toss my wrist bell to a nearby child and wedge my mug between the roots of the closest tree.

"Looks like I won," I say.

My sister-in-law nods. "And you're a mess. Your trousers are torn. You're covered with dirt. The children will be coming soon. Your Mary. At least rinse your face and hands off in the creek. And run your fingers through your hair. You saw her before you started your silly race?"

I nod. "She looked beautiful. And devout." In the light of day, the idea she'd mocked me seems silly. Sporadic shouts and cheers rise and fall as more Dashers spill out of Loathsome Cave. "I'll see you after I wash up," I tell Millie and hobble along the creek, acknowledging the congratulations of grinning strangers. I aim for a spot downstream far from the revelers and pass a small table dominated by a massive Bible. Here the creek feeds a shallow pool that's easily accessed from the shore—a perfect spot for baptisms. I yank off my boots and feel the creek mud ooze around the toes of my good foot. My bad foot is numb, and I dig it deep down into the silt.

The sips of beer have gone straight to my head, and I almost lose my balance as I squat to splash my face with water. I note the peak of Hallowed Mountain rising starkly against an azure sky, and I realize I'm no longer squinting. How many millennia had it taken wind and water and sun to carve out this valley? Again I smell pork —it mingles with the scent of the pine trees covering the upslopes on either side of the creek. Has anyone set a plate for the winner?

A hundred or so yards downstream Merc stands among a

handful of Negroes. I raise and lower my hand. *Cripple*, he'd said about me. And he'd intentionally gotten himself disqualified. What, I wonder, are the compromises he makes to survive in this community? He faces me squarely and points. The rest of his company look my way. I assume he's just told them I won the Dash. And then I notice my rear end is wet. When I rise from my squat, I discover the water that had only been up to my ankles has risen to the middle of my calves. The tug of the current nearly topples me. The creek has overlapped its borders and is spreading onto the shore. My cane is floating away, and I barely manage to grab it by its tip. I look back at Merc, and he's still pointing in my direction. I pick up my boots and scramble up toward the pine trees, but the rising water outpaces me. I look back toward Hallowed Mountain and my heart nearly stops.

The crowd at the mouth of Loathsome Cave is rapidly dispersing, half on either side of the swelling creek. Folks are splashing up among the trees. Those closest to the cave are already waist deep in surging water and cling to each other for support as they struggle toward higher ground. Downstream, Merc and his company are following suit. Picnic baskets bob away—and there goes the table set up for the baptisms. The Bible is gone. The toes of my good foot smash against submerged roots.

I see Millie up among the trees ahead of the rising water, her arms encircling the waists of two women also wearing their Sunday best. The heads of all retreaters pivot back and forth from the direction their headed back to the mouth of Loathsome Cave. As we stare, the water suddenly surges with even greater force, cascading like Niagara Falls. *Where are the Sunday School children? Where is Mary?*

II

The cause? The collapse of a rain-damaged dam twenty miles distant, constructed with state and federal money at the turn of the century in the failed hope of encouraging industrial development in the region. Because of the area's unique topographical features, when the dam burst, the water inundated the unpopulated valley through which Winston Creek runs. The results? A swollen water course, a submerged cave, and a new lake.

All the of the Dashers have been accounted for. But after five days, there's still no sign of the unbaptized youth of St. John the Baptist's Evangelical Church. Not so much as a waterlogged garland of flowers, let alone a body, living or otherwise. Newspapers sent reporters, who, after complaining how difficult it was to navigate the transformed terrain around Hallowed Mountain, left after a few days. "No bodies, no business," one was overheard muttering.

Attempts at rescue by the local police and fire departments have come up empty: volunteer divers have found the current at either end of submerged Loathsome Cave unnavigable. Family and friends of the missing have set up camp on the "baptism" side of Hallowed Mountain and wait, grimly and planlessly. My sister-in-law prepares meals and coffee at the fire beside our tent, one of the dozens erected among the pines above the new lake. Her Sunday best outfit is rumpled and soiled. She asks me to join the prayer circles she leads, but I decline. I'm too busy practicing holding my breath.

I'm up to five minutes. The cave is a mile long. If the current travels at ten miles an hour, it should carry me from start to end in about six minutes. What have I got to lose? I've got to try to find some sign of my daughter. Merc, always near, is the only one who knows of my plan to float through Loathsome Cave. "You're going to get banged up," he says. "You okay with cuts and bruises?"

I shrug. "No choice."

"What about we put you in a barrel? You'd have air in there at least."

"Won't work. Can't see anything in a barrel."

"Can't see anything in a god-damned underwater cave, either."

"But I'll be able to feel if I bump into anything that's not rock —I'll—maybe I'll be able to tell what it is."

Merc nods, blinking slowly. He picks up a pot next to his campfire. "You can strap this to your head—it'll keep you from knocking yourself silly."

By evening I can make it to Merc's four hundred count without taking a breath. "That's over six and a half minutes," I gasp. "First thing in the morning I'm going in."

~ * ~

I rise at dawn. The promontory of Hallowed Mountain will block the sun until noon. I peek into our tent—my sleeping sister-in-law is wrapped up tight in her blanket, her Bible clutched in her hand. Last night she got into a heated argument after her prayer meeting with another St. John the Baptist's Church congregant who insisted the unbaptized Sunday schoolers were doomed to perdition. "Might as well just accept it, Millie," the woman said.

"Blessed are the children," my sister-in-law retorted with iron jaw certainty.

Merc appears at my side. "It'll take you a couple of hours to hike around the mountain to the cave entrance," he says. "I'll show you the trail. No reason you won't shoot right through the cave. I'll be looking out for you on this side. If anybody asks where you are, I won't admit to knowing until, well, things shake themselves out." He claps me on the back. "I hope you find what you're looking for."

I salute him with my cane and settle the pot on my head.

"You look like Johnny Appleseed," Merc says. He holds out a small metal cannister. "Got fifty matches in there. Maybe they'll come in handy."

"I thought lighting a match was cheating," I say, smirking as I pocket the cannister.

"Different rules for this race," he says. "See you in a couple of hours."

~ * ~

The only time I've been on this side of Hallowed Mountain was for the start of the Darkness Dash. The rushing river-that-used -to-be-a-creek sparkles in the late morning sun. The flat land where the racers and the Sunday school children had gathered has disappeared. The water pushes right up to the mountain's blank base. I pause at the water's edge, probing with my cane for the best entry point. Closing my eyes, I imagine floating in total darkness. Will it feel like flying? Birds call to each other from the trees as I strap the cooking pot atop my head with a thin belt I fasten under my chin. I remind myself that, should I slam into rocks, I mustn't gasp. I pat the sheathed knife at my side. Something soft—how swiftly can I cut off a swath of cloth, a clump of hair—anything that offers proof of the children's fate? No matter what I do or don't find, if I make it through, maybe others, better prepared, will follow. The children mustn't be left in perpetual darkness.

I have sliced off my trousers at the knee. My boots I leave on shore. Taking my cane is a last-minute decision. I'm shivering as I plant my good foot in the water, and I immediately feel the current grab my leg. My scarred foot follows. The sun is already behind the mountain—it's shining on the heartbroken campers on the other side. I count breaths—on the fifth inhalation I stagger forward until I'm waist deep. The cold water shoves me toward the base of Hallowed Mountain. I lift my feet and submit to the current, trying my best to ignore the whispers of doubt: *no air, no light, a mile.*

Inhalation six: I fill my lungs and dive. The cave's mouth yawns before me, and then I'm swallowed by darkness.

~ * ~

We sat in a packed theater, Kathy and I, five years before the war. Our attention was riveted to the movie screen, on which a locomotive, still some distance off, sped toward our seats. Uneasy titters filled the theater. The engine hurtled toward us like a black avalanche, smoke billowing from its stack. Mesmerized by its ever-expanding headlamp, we were caught in the train's path. Some in the audience screamed and buried their faces in their hands; some stood and stumbled over their neighbors' legs towards the aisle. I drew Kathy close. Her hair smelled of lavender. She dug her nails into my palm. Then a flash of light, and the screen went blank, leaving the crowd buzzing with thrilled relief. Kathy's lips touched my ear. *I'm pregnant*, she whispered in the dark theatre.

~ * ~

A memory, so like a dream, born from a thirst for light. *Air and light, light and air.* Do we breathe in dreams? My eyelids flutter—open, closed, there's no difference. How far have I traveled? I imagine my war buddies swimming beside me in this darkness, as silvery bright as mercury in their uniforms, their faces as expressionless as the faces on coins.

The chin strap of my pot-helmet is too tight. Can you choke when you're *not breathing*? I lose my cane as I claw the cave roof. *Air pockets*? The flesh is torn from my knuckles. *Air, water, light, dark.* If the blood from my hands left neon-red trails, I'd be easy to follow.

I'm carried forward relentlessly. The dream soldiers disappear.

Did Mary really limp? *Dearest Father* she begins each of her letters. Her correspondence is like a locked diary: she names people I don't know, places I haven't been, activities I can't picture. She'd summoned me for a baptism, not an exhumation.

Time—my pulse hammers in my ears, counting off the passing seconds. Am I moving fast enough? The stiff bodies of what must be actual fish glance off me. A hiccup now would kill me. I slap my thigh and find my knife. If I strike something soft, I must grab for it and slice. Hair, fabric—what about flesh?

Dots of light flare like fireflies around my face—a sign I've reached my limit. I gulp water—I hear myself coughing—retching. Somehow, I'm upright—my feet touch bottom. Wheezing, I suck in air.

"Hello?" The word reverberates in my clogged ears. Then a chorus of bleating voices cascades down on me: "Who's that?" "What's there?" "Have they come for us?" "Praise Jesus!"

"I'm here," I sputter. "Where are you?"

"Up here—" "Here—" "Here—" "Here—" Then the first, deeper voice again. It must belong to William, the youth leader:

"Whoever's there, it's us—the Sunday school class. The water came fast, and we climbed up here. There's kind of a shelf—like a platform. We—I—dropped our lantern. But we're all here. All thirteen of us. We're very hungry. We've been sharing a sack of cookies. There's just crumbs left."

"Is Mary there?" My teeth are chattering. "It's me, your father."

"Yes, Father—how did you find us? It's so dark. How many days have we been here?"

"I have my watch—" William says. "I wind it, but I can't read it."

I'm faint with exhaustion and relief. "Five days," I say. "Winston Dam burst." I squeeze the small cannister in my pocket. "I've got matches," I say. "Is there any way you can pull me up? I'm reaching toward your voices now—can you hoist me?"

A hand closes around mine and squeezes, and I grunt with pain. My knuckles must be deeply gashed.

"We've got you," William says. Hands flutter over me like a flock of birds coming to roost, and I'm dragged upward out of the water. Bodies swarm against me—is there so little space?

"Father—" Mary's voice cuts through the mewling of her

Sunday school classmates. "I knew you'd be here—he survived the war," she announces. I'd hug her, if I knew which body was hers.

"Matches," I repeat. "I've got fifty matches. We can strike them against the cave wall. But they're like gold—there has to be a purpose for lighting one. They'll last just a few seconds."

"Can't we use one just to see ourselves?" Mary sounds like her mother. "It's been dark for so long."

"Light one, light one!" the others chirp.

"One, then." I shake the cannister close to my ear as if it contains a pair of dice, then unscrew the cap and finger out a single match. "Take me to the wall," I instruct, and I'm pushed and tugged until I bump into the side of the cave. "Keep your distance when I light it. You don't want to blow it out."

With an invisible flourish, I strike the match. It's small flame glows in my cupped hands like a golden apple. Oohs and aahs rise around me. Somebody claps. When I lift the burning match, I see glittering eyes and smudged faces. Shadows waver on the cave's roof and walls. Below us the water surges darkly. There's the youth leader, a head taller than his charges. His watch glints in his hand. And Mary? A wreath of shriveled flowers crowns her tangled hair. The match flickers and goes out, plunging us back into darkness. The children groan.

"Forty-nine left," I say.

~ * ~

In the darkness of Loathsome Cave, the Sunday school class and I listen to William:

"We were marching along the path, singing hymns, reciting psalms. We thought there might be some stragglers from the Dash, but we didn't come across any."

I won, I nearly declare, but keep silent—you can't bask in glory without light.

"Believe it or not," William continues, "we were reciting the Twenty-Third Psalm. We'd just gotten to 'he leadeth me beside the still waters,' when there was a huge roar. The creek overflowed, and we were splashing in water up to our ankles, and, in seconds, our knees. We were nearly swept away. I told everybody to grab hands. Thank God we were right here, the only spot in the cave where we could climb out of the flood."

"And then we lost the lamp," somebody says.

"I set it too close to the edge and it fell in," William says. "We've been waiting in the dark for the water to recede."

"And then you came to save us, like Jesus," another voice says.

"Your parents are worried." My voice echoes through the pitch-black chamber. I don't tell the children they're presumed drowned and I'd come in search of bodies. "How far are we from the cave's exit?"

"Maybe halfway," William says. "If the water's this high here, it'll fill the cave to the top the rest of the way. It's a miracle you made it from the entrance to us. How'd you do it?"

"I held my breath and let the current take me," I say. "It was a pretty rough ride. Without my helmet I wouldn't have made it. It's a cooking pot." I reach up for it, and my wedding band pings against the metal. I loosen the chin strap and ease the pot off my head. "That's how I'll get out, too, I guess—hold my breath. It'd be too hard for the kids. Honestly, I don't know how long it'll be before the water goes down. When I bring word you're all okay, we'll figure out the next steps. What do you need most? Food?"

"Food, yes. There's plenty of water."

"Maybe we can float food to you from the entrance," I say. "We can put it in waterproof baskets, and when they reach here, you can pull them out."

"How will we see them?" William asks.

"We need a net," Mary says. "We can make one out of my dress. We can tear little holes in it and stretch it across the creek. Then we'll catch whatever floats by."

Other girls volunteer their dresses, too.

"We'll use yours, Mary," I say. "I'll trade you my shirt. It's too short to stretch across the water, but it will cover you fine."

"I'm ready," my daughter says boldly. "We don't need to waste a match—we can exchange in the dark."

I peel off my wet shirt. Somewhere near my daughter is stripping off her dress. "No peeking," she says. I feel a breeze when she waves the dress at me, and I grab the fabric with one hand and hold out my shirt with the other. It's snatched away.

"Thank you," Mary says. After a moment she murmurs, "Hey, the buttons are all wrong. They're on the opposite sides—okay, there we go."

~ * ~

Match 49 flares as I flatten Mary's dress out on our rock perch, which is larger than I first thought, maybe ten by twenty feet. I poke the first net-hole with my knife. I glimpse the children, who stand in a semi-circle around me. My shirt hangs down past my daughter's knees. A second before the match goes out, she sweeps her hair out of her eyes. I cut the rest of the holes in the dark.

The children drag a huge rock across the platform for anchoring the net. Mary lights matches 48, 47, 46, and 45 while William and I, up to our armpits in the creek, find an outcropping to knot the fabric around. When we finish the job, William is spent.

"I don't know how you did it," he pants. "That current is impossible."

"The better for my ride out of here." I've avoided thinking about my exit strategy. I barely made it in—I'll have to duplicate a miracle to make it out.

"I've got to leave now," I tell William. "What do you need besides food?"

"Definitely more matches. A lantern would be great. Another bucket, for keeping things sanitary."

"Check. When I bring word you're all okay, things should really get moving. Maybe they'll call in the Army Corps of Engineers if the water doesn't recede—maybe they can divert the flow somehow. But I can't imagine it'll take more than a month to get you out."

Some of the children groan.

"You'll catch some fish in your net," I say as a diversion. "You can have a fish fry."

"Then send us some firewood and kindling, too," William says.

"We could use your pot," Mary says.

"I need it to get out, but we'll float you a fry pan and some other utensils. And I'll leave my knife. About your watch—"

"We shouldn't waste matches just to see the time."

"No. But how long does it keep going after you wind it?"

"It's guaranteed for forty hours."

I calculate. "If you wind it now, you can keep track of its ticking. When it stops, wind it again, and then a third time. That adds up to one hundred twenty hours: five days. You can scratch lines into the wall. You'll have a kind of calendar, at least."

No one speaks. The water rushes by in the dark.

"Right," William finally says. He'd left his watch with my daughter while we'd been in the water working on the net. "Wind it now Mary. That'll be number one."

"If you have 'time,' you can be organized," I say. "Forty hours is around a day and a half. Make a schedule—when to sleep, when to check the net. You should practice doing things in the dark. But it will all be easier if we can get you a lantern." I slide my knife from its sheath. "William—I've got my knife—I'm holding the handle out. Where are you?"

"Wait—" Mary says. "I know we need to save matches, but can we light one more? So we can see you to say goodbye? Match number forty-four, right?"

"It's up to you," I say. I'd love to see her.

"Light it," the children clamor. "For 'goodbye and good luck!'" "Light a match!"

"Okay," my daughter says. "I'm lighting one now, here at the wall."

A scratch and flicker, and weak yellow light paints the cave's interior. I place my knife in William's hand. The children, backlit, are strung out like paper dolls cut from black paper. It's as if they're saturated with darkness. Except for Mary, who holds the burning match in front of her face. She fixes me with a gaze—her eyes gleam like jewels. She's misbuttoned my shirt, which hangs unevenly above her knees. The wet bandage binding her ankle is coming loose.

"Hug," she says, a moment before the match sputters out.

"Hug!" the children echo, and suddenly a dozen pairs of arms encircle me like eels. Mary whispers in my ear.

"Thank you—thank you for coming."

"I'll tell Aunt Millie I found you," I say. "I'll tell all your folks you're doing okay. Alright—see you soon!" I secure my pot-helmet, find the edge of the stone floor and sit with dangling legs. I shove off and am swept away with shocking speed. Goodbyes echo behind.

I inhale until it feels like my chest is going to split. There's still air above me, but I don't dare risk another breath. About halfway, William said. Maybe I'm near the point where Merc caught up to me during the Dash. Has he seen my cane emerge on his side of Hallowed Mountain? If I never appear, then the waiting mothers, fathers, brothers, sisters, pastor and congregants won't know to cease mourning and to send supplies instead.

My helmet grinds along the cave roof and my face is pushed underwater. *Blind—blinking—blind—blinking.* Not the belly of a whale —it's an enormous serpent I travel through sightlessly, battered by every set of its endless ribs.

Lights out, lights out, we would shout in our trench during midnight shellings. Then one night there was a burst of light, and I woke up in a hospital with half a foot and two fewer friends. There was a threat of gangrene, the doctors said. I might have lost my leg. I might have lost my life. If I had, maybe Kathy and Mary both would have moved to Millie's ahead of the Spanish flu. But there would still have been a procession through the cave, a burst dam, a flood.

I slam against rock after rock. *Don't breathe, don't breathe,* I repeat until the words start to lose meaning. In the trench I'd tucked photographs of my wife and my baby girl into my soldier's helmet. Today my daughter hugged me before I left her behind in the dark —I never told her I won the Dash. How did she hurt her foot?

Just one breath—when I lift my head, it's hammered so hard my teeth ache.

The fireflies are back, sparking like they did before I found the children. All like a dream. The flashing bugs become a blizzard of feathers: daisy-sized, they gently pummel my face, my shoulders, my legs.

The feathers knit together, unspooling in a long white skein —I'm chasing the train of a wedding gown. A lost bride turns her head, but her face is veiled. Who is it—my dead wife, beckoning me to join her? My daughter, expecting the future I promised? I reach for the fabric, but it disappears, and my hands swat at utter blackness.

Everything I think I see is a trap, a dream composed of imagination's perverting light. *Don't breathe.* All that matters is forward momentum—*don't stop.* And if it *has* all been a dream? What if I was finished before I found the Baptism Class of 1924, and the rest has been make-believe—no platform, no children, no net, no plan for supplies. *No matches.*

I frisk myself—I must have left my knife and shirt—and the matches—*somewhere.*

Before I found the children alive, how did I intend to use my knife? Slice off *what?* Even my imagination is out of light—I can no longer—or refuse to—visualize.

The current splays me across a pillar. Pass it on the right or left? Left. I'm tossed upward. My helmet comes loose and sinks. I wrap an arm around my head for protection. I should have gone right.

I'm stuck—I'm jammed into a crevice, laid out on my back, my head pillowed on stone, my legs pinned so firmly I can't feel them. I haven't the strength to flail. It's as if I'm becoming part of the cave. Water washes over me in the permanent darkness. How many minutes have I held my breath so far? Is there really a gold watch back in the cave keeping time? Seconds become forever.

Don't.

Breathe.

Why not? Without time, there's no past and future. No one will ever be missing or be missed. But it would have been nice to have seen one more bit of light. One more match.

~ * ~ * ~

Over one hundred of **Gregory's** short stories and reviews have been published in journals like *Glimmer Train, Georgia Review, Michigan Quarterly Review, descant, Florida Review, The Pinch, Baltimore Review, Tahoma Literary Review,* and *Southern Humanities Review.* His work has won awards sponsored by *Solstice, descant, Gulf Stream, New South,* the Rubery Book Awards, *Emrys Journal, Gambling the Aisle,* and the White Eagle Coffee Store Press.

Gregory's story collections include *Women of Consequence* (Regal House Publishing, 2019), *Dear Everyone* (Duck Lake Books, 2020), *The Thing About Men,* (Cervena Barva Press, 2022), and *The Green Ray and Other Stories* (Scantic Books, 2022). His novel *Kika Kong vs. the Dead White Males* was released by Adelaide Books in the summer of 2022. For full lists of his publications and commendations, visit gregorywolos.com

Gregory's stories often reflect Kafka's assertion that a literary work "should be an ice axe to break up the frozen sea inside us."

The Dark

Brian Rothstein

I jolted awake in a pitch-black room, my pajamas drenched with sweat. The bed in which I lay was hard and unfamiliar with only a thin sheet and blanket to cover my body. I knew I wasn't in my home, but had no recollection of where I was or how I'd gotten there.

"Vanessa?" I called out to my wife. No response. I felt for her in the darkness, but her usual place on my left was vacant. "Vee?" I called out again. "Are you here?"

Silence. A knot formed in my stomach.

My last memory was of us driving in the car. I had reserved a table for our sixth wedding anniversary at Le Provencal, the French restaurant where we first met. Everything seemed fine, so why couldn't I remember anything else? Did I drink too much at dinner?

I needed light. If I could see where I was, it might jog my memory. I reached out my arm and brushed across a flat wooden surface. A nightstand. I fumbled for a lamp, finally grazing an upright metal rod. My fingers groped for the switch and I flicked it on.

Nothing.

I took a deep breath and exhaled slowly to calm myself. There had to be a rational explanation. The power was likely out and Vanessa had gone to check. That would account for her absence.

But why weren't we at home? Could we be at a friend's place? That seemed unlikely since it was our anniversary and we'd have wanted to be alone.

What else? If I'd gotten drunk, maybe Vanessa did the same and neither of us could drive? That made sense. If we both drank too much, we might have gotten a hotel room to sleep it off.

A hotel! Yes, that must be it! The power had gone out in the middle of the night in our hotel room. Surely Vanessa had gone to the lobby to see what was going on. That explained everything.

I sighed with relief. Still, I wanted to find Vanessa, so I embarked to find the lobby as well.

I swung my legs out of bed and placed my feet on a cold

linoleum floor. Odd, since most hotels I'd known were carpeted, but I shrugged it off and placed my hands in front of me, feeling around the room. I made contact with a wall and shuffled to the right, slowly edging along until I felt the ridged molding of a doorframe.

Another room. I swept my hand across the inside wall in search of a light switch until my fingers touched a small plastic bump. I flipped it upwards but remained in darkness.

Wait…

No power. I smirked at my foolishness as I slid through the threshold and continued following the wall.

Suddenly a spasm of pain shot through my shin and I cried out an expletive.

I reached down to discern my attacker and felt something cool and smooth. I rapped it with my knuckles and heard the hollow clink of porcelain. "Fucking toilet," I muttered.

I grimaced and forged ahead, forming an image of my surroundings as I explored the layout of the bathroom. I passed a countertop and sink, then a metal rack filled with plush towels before finding a small window.

A refreshing breeze washed over my still sweaty forehead as I slid the glass upward. I rolled up my sleeves and stretched out to feel the crisp night air on my skin, but my hand clanged against a piece of metal. I tried further to the left, yet once again found the path blocked. Inch by inch, I extended my arm, this time to the right, praying for it to poke through the barrier—but I met only more iron.

My heart sank.

Desperate with frenzy I grabbed the metal rods and shook with all my might, but the bars held firm.

My first panicked thought was of Vanessa. Where was she? Was she safe? I went to call out her name, but muzzled myself before the words left my lips. The last thing I wanted was to draw attention if we were in danger.

I slumped to the floor, my breath rapid and short. Had I been kidnapped? But who might want to harm us? I'd made no enemies, and to my knowledge, Vanessa hadn't either. Did they want money? Was this a case of mistaken identity? Were we simply victims of circumstance at the wrong place at the wrong time?

I inhaled deeply to prevent myself from hyperventilating. I needed to remain calm so I could find Vanessa and escape. But how? If one window was barred, the others would be as well. Without power, the phone wouldn't work either.

There was no way I was getting out; someone would have to come in. I'd wait behind the door until it opened and ambush my jailer from behind.

A burst of energy enveloped my body and I shot to my feet. I needed a weapon—something to smash over my guard's head and knock them unconscious. I hastily groped my way out of the bathroom and retraced my steps to the lamp. The base would make a perfect bludgeon.

I ripped the cord from the wall and clutched the heavy metal neck tightly in my hand. The bathroom had been to my right, so this time I went left, swiftly creeping forward in search of the entrance to my prison. I brushed across a protrusion, then another, equidistant but lower.

Hinges. I'd reached the inside of the shut door. I pressed my back against the wall and readjusted my grip on the lamp. At some point, the door would swing open and I'd take my captor by surprise, knocking them senseless with a blow to the head. All I needed to do was wait.

Patiently I stood, still and silent like a cheetah ready to pounce. The faint tick of a wall clock grew louder, and I focused on its rhythm, each beat another second.

Tick…Tick…Tick… Fifteen minutes passed. Then thirty.

Tick…Tick…Tick. An hour. My thoughts raced. Would someone ever come? Was I trapped, doomed to die with this room serving as my coffin?

Fear overtook me. My heart galloped in my chest, and I felt as if I might faint from angst. But then, as states of delirium often produce, a crazy idea entered my mind.

I reached down and gripped the door handle. It couldn't possibly be…could it?

Gently, I twisted the knob, waiting for it to click to a halt, yet it turned further and further until the latch bolt disengaged. I inched the door open expecting a ray of light to illuminate my surroundings, but I remained shrouded in blackness. My other senses would have to guide me to Vanessa.

I eased the door wide enough to slip through and crouched down, readying myself for a new labyrinth. However, the potent smell of disinfectant hit my nostrils and I stifled a sneeze. Fucking allergies. This was no time for them to act up.

The faint sound of voices came into earshot and I perked up my ears. They were getting closer. I scurried back into the room and shut the door, reassuming my attack position. One person I could handle, but two? I gulped and wiped my sweaty palm against my pant leg as the muffled voices became audible. To my surprise, the speaker was female.

"I'll tend to Mr. Hayes," the voice said. "Would you mind checking on room two-oh-four?"

"No problem," another female replied.

My brow furrowed in confusion. My guards were women? And who was Mr. Hayes? How many other people were being held prisoner?

Before I could process the information, the knob jiggled and a waft of air hit me as the door lurched open. Now was my chance! I burst from hiding and swung the lamp with full force in the direction of the doorway.

The blow connected with a thud and a body crumpled to the floor. I darted outside, feeling my way along the wall with frantic urgency before stumbling across another door. I slipped inside hoping for respite, but a man called out, his voice old and frail.

"Hello? Who are you?"

I dropped the lamp, and despite the dark, instinctively held up both hands in a show of peace. "Please, sir, I mean you no harm. My wife—she's missing and I have to find her."

"I don't know who you are," he mumbled.

"I'm a prisoner too, but we can find a way out. Please," I begged. "My wife is missing. Help me!"

He paused and took a few labored breaths. "You don't belong in here."

"I don't know where 'here' is!" I shouted.

Shit. That was loud. Very loud. The old man attempted to answer, but I shushed him and listened. To my dismay, footsteps approached the door and it creaked ajar.

"Is every—"

I charged at the voice. Our frames collided, sending a woman sprawling with a shriek of surprise.

The commotion did not go unnoticed. Another voice

screamed for security as I scampered away, careening through the darkness in a panicked flurry.

Suddenly, my foot tangled around a cord and I tumbled to the ground. A hand clenched my pajama leg, but a ferocious kick freed me from its grasp and I bounced to my feet.

"Stop, Mr. Barnes!" A parade of now male voices called my name in vain, but I continued to flee, crashing blindly through the unknown before my face smashed into a solid wall. Blood gushed from my nose and I teetered from the blow, staggering backwards against another wall to my left.

"Mr. Barnes!" The voices grew louder. I repressed the pain and whirled to the right, desperate for an escape route, but a third wall sealed my fate. I was trapped.

The patter of footsteps behind me slowed to a halt and the sounds of panted breathing closed in. My heartbeat thumped in my ears like a snare drum. Flight was no longer an option. That left me but one choice—fight.

I spun around and exploded toward my captors as if someone had shot me from a cannon, violently swinging my fists like a madman. I took one by surprise, landing multiple blows to his soft flesh before a collection of muscular hands grabbed my arms and pinned them behind my back. A sweeping kick took out my legs and I dropped to the floor. Right away, a knee dug into my back and a forearm pressed my face into the cold linoleum.

I yelled and thrashed with every ounce of strength attempting to break free, but a sharp object jabbed my neck. The vigor instantly drained from my body, and with one final, weak flail, I faded from consciousness.

~ * ~

I awoke again in a pitch-black room lying comfortably on my back. My head felt foggy, like a bad hangover, making the memory of the previous horrors seem distant. Had it all been just a bad dream?

"Vanessa?" I called out into the darkness. No answer. I reached for her, but my arm jolted to a halt, fastened to the bed with a thick strap.

My blood ran cold. It was no dream.

A surge of adrenaline flushed the haze from my brain and I

yanked each of my limbs to no effect. All four were bound to the bed. I writhed against the restraints with all my might, but they wouldn't budge. Angry and afraid, I screamed in primal rage.

My shouts drew attention, for not a moment later I heard the door open and the click of high heels approached my bed.

"Mr. Barnes," a soft woman's voice said. "You can't keep doing this."

A hand touched my shoulder and I gnashed my teeth.

"Please, Mr. Barnes," she continued. "If you're going to misbehave, I'll have to sedate you again. You don't want that now, do you?"

"Fuck you," I snarled.

She sighed and turned my right palm upwards to access my vein.

"Wait, don't," I blurted. "I'll stop, I promise."

She released my wrist. "Do you know who I am?"

"No," I shook my head. "I can't see you. Why can't I see anything?"

A chair scraped across the linoleum.

"Mr. Barnes," she said. "I'm going to sit down and have you listen to something. What you're about to hear is going to be difficult, but it's the truth."

I snorted in derision. "How can I believe a word you say?"

"You can't. That's why *I'm* not going to tell you anything… *you* are."

A tape clicked on and my own voice began to play.

"Michael, it's me—I mean you…us." My voice was pained with compassion. "The woman you're talking to is Dr. Wagner. Please be kind to her. She's only trying to help."

I lay speechless at the shock of hearing my recorded self.

"This is difficult for me to explain since I know how you'll react, but everything I'm about to say is true. You have to believe me—well, believe yourself. You don't remember what happened, but we were in a terrible car accident with Vanessa. A semi-truck ran a red-light and plowed straight into our sedan, knocking us down a ravine. You suffered a severe brain injury, which is why you don't remember. You're an amnesiac."

The Michael in the recording cleared his throat. "The amnesia is anterograde, meaning you can't remember anything that happened after the injury. You'll remember for a few days, maybe a few weeks, but new long-term memories no longer develop and you eventually…forget."

A lump formed in my throat.

"But these are the facts. The windshield shattered during the accident, sending glass shards into both your eyes. The doctors at Mercy General did all they could, but they couldn't save your sight."

I attempted to cry, but no tears fell from my damaged eyes.

"That's where you are now—the psych ward at Mercy General Hospital. Since you're hearing my voice, you're certainly strapped down to the bed, but don't panic, okay? Nobody is going to harm you. You're restrained for your own protection and for the hospital staff. You become dangerous when you think they're trying to hurt you."

Recorded Michael took a deep breath. "And the last part is Vanessa…" My voice on tape quivered, barely able to choke out the next words. "She…she didn't make it."

A deafening ring flooded my ears and the rest of the message faded into the background. "No," I muttered, shaking my head. "She can't be…"

As much as I wanted my denial to be untrue, a strange feeling of déjà vu signaled otherwise. My beautiful wife was dead. Never again would I feel her touch. See her face. Hear her voice.

I wailed in anguish and Dr. Wagner placed a gentle hand on mine. "I'm so sorry, Mr. Barnes. I'll give you some time alone." She placed a small remote in my grasp. "Just press the button if you need one of us. We'll undo the restraints as soon as it's safe."

Her heels tapped into the distance and the door snapped shut leaving me sobbing with grief in the empty room, not only in mourning for Vanessa, but in dread of the fresh hell that would repeat itself the next time my memory failed.

~ * ~ * ~

A distant relative of famed Prohibition-Era gambler Arnold Rothstein, **Brian Rothstein** is a freelance writer with an M.A. in Communication from Arizona State University. Growing up in sunny (and oftentimes too hot) Scottsdale, Arizona, Brian spent his childhood summers engrossed in books where his love for writing began. Today he still resides in Scottsdale with his wife, Alayna, and dog, Chungus.

Angel of Death

P James Norris

1 - The Hiker - *Ante Mortem*

Tears fell from her cheeks like the raindrops falling from the dark, swollen clouds that obscured the sky from horizon to horizon. Her grey, tattered, ankle-length dress whipped about her in the wind, and was soaked through. But her long, dark hair lay dry as though there was no wind or rain. Indeed, no rain touched her skin, not where her simple dress's straps left her shoulders and arms bare, not where her wind-blown skirt exposed her calves. Only her dress and sandals were touched by the elements, and the swiftly running creek water in which she stood.

She had no need for clothing to protect her from the elements. Nothing of this world had touched her for longer than she could remember.

Even so, her skin was cold, but not due to the wind or rain.

Moments ago, lightning had struck a tree not far from her—she knew the distance to the tree to the foot, to the inch, to the smallest fraction of an inch. Not because she wanted to, but because it was a site of immediate death.

She wept for the all the living things killed outright in that tree. The father robin burnt to char in midair as he returned with a gullet full of food for his five chicks. The mother robin impaled by a piece of bark, a piece of natural shrapnel, as she brooded their chicks, trying in vain to shield them from the rain and wind.

And for those who would die in the seconds, minutes, hours, and days to come as a direct result of the lightning. She knew to the tiniest fraction of a second how long it would take for each of the chicks to die. For each of the thousands of living things that made the tree their home. The tree would die as well, though its final, true death would take three months, five days, twenty-one hours...

She gritted her teeth, squeezed her eyes shut. Forced the countdown to the tree's end from her consciousness. Likewise, the family of squirrels who made their home in a hollow left by a fallen branch not far from the robin nest, the numerous centipedes, beetles, myriad of flying insects, and the colonies of moss that hung from the tree's branches.

Surely many of the animals that had made the tree their home would survive, but they were unknown to her—she could take no solace from their good fortune for the lightning had not marked them for death. To her, they were as invisible as to any other…

She was no *person*.

Not anymore.

Suddenly she felt an unearthly, glacial grasp on her right shoulder.

A voice produced by no larynx rasped, "It is time."

Without looking over her shoulder at the black-robed figure standing there, or at the hourglass she held in both hands, she replied, "No, there are thirty-eight grains left."

She looked down at the broken body of the young hiker at her feet. The torrential downpour had weakened the earth's hold on the rocks along the gulley's rim where the man had been walking. His weight had caused them to slide apart from one another, and him to tumble twenty or so feet down into the creek. He had come to rest face up, but had broken his right ankle, bruised several ribs, and hit his head on a rock, knocking him senseless.

If the water in the creek weren't rising because of the rain, he would, no doubt, have eventually regained consciousness. Stumbled back to his car. Or called for help using his cellphone.

But the ever-deepening water would soon cover his face.

When it did, he would drown.

If she did not touch him, did not release his soul from its Earthly bond before the final grain of sand fell in her hourglass, did not release his soul before he died, his soul would remain bound forever to his body. He would become a ghost. Knowing he was dead and unable to move onto his final, natural destination, unable to interact with the world around him, he would slowly go insane.

His insanity might give him the strength to affect the physical world. He might become a poltergeist, and in his insanity terrify and possibly harm anyone unlucky enough to pass nearby.

When only thirteen grains of sand left remained in her glass, she knelt in the creek beside him. Her black tresses fell into the water, framing his face, unmoved by the running water that was killing him as it filled his lungs.

His eyes opened and found hers just inches above his face. There was fear there, having nothing to do with the physical facts of his situation, if he even understood them.

But he knew he was looking into the eyes of his Death.

A change came over him as her right hand moved toward his chest, as the last few grains of sand fell in her hourglass. His mouth moved, and though only bubbles escaped, she heard his last words. "You're so beautiful."

Her hand came to rest open-palmed on his chest, and as the last grain of sand in her hourglass fell, Robert Anthony O'Callaghan died.

2 - Robert Anthony O'Callaghan - *Post Mortem*

In a moment lasting twenty-eight years, five months, three days, and a number of minutes and seconds that held significance only to Bobby and those who loved him, everything he was, had ever been, had ever hoped to be, flooded through her.

~ * ~

His new—born son wailed as only a baby could. The doctor held Jonathon Quigley—Cassie's grandfather's middle name—O'Callaghan up to Bobby as though for his inspection.

Every one of their friends who'd already had children had told him all newborns were ugly except to their parents. Bobby pursed his lips, and couldn't help but think, "Nope, not even when they've wiped all the blood and goo off you..."

He looked down at Cassie, whose beautiful hair was plastered to the side of her head with sweat, and who was panting like she'd just run one of her 10K marathons. "Look, love, you've given birth to a wrinkled, hairless little monkey."

She swatted at his thigh with her hand, but clearly didn't have the strength for a serious effort. "But he's *our perfect hairless little monkey,*" *she replied with a smile as the doctor handed little Johnny to her to hold in her arms for the first time.*

~ * ~

"*With this ring I thee wed,*" *Bobby said as he slipped Cassandra's wedding band onto her long, delicate ring-finger. He looked up and saw tears of joy threatening in her beautiful green eyes. Her red hair, a much more lovely red than his frankly orange hair, framed her face.*

"With this ring I thee wed," Cassie said as she slipped an identical band on his finger.

~ * ~

His right arm hurt, but for some reason, he didn't care. His mouth felt like it was full of cotton, and there was an almost overpowering taste of blood-iron.

A voice he couldn't identify said, "Your son's very lucky, Mr. and Mrs. O'Callaghan. People who are sober during accidents like your son's... Well, their bodies often fight the accident instead of just going with it and come out much worse for it. And people with a blood alcohol content as high as your son's usually aren't wearing their seatbelts."

"Well, we really tried—"

Bobby thought, Mom, why are you crying?

"—to drill into him the importance of always wearing his seatbelt."

Some corner of his mind was still clear of the pain and drugs and understood. He had driven home. Or tried to, even after Greg and Bill had tried to convince him he was too drunk to drive.

But that one coherent corner of his mind couldn't tell him if he actually managed to say, "Oh, Mom, I'm so sorry," *out loud, loud enough for her and his Dad to hear it.*

~ * ~

Every moment of Robert Anthony O'Callaghan's life, every self-perceived success and failure, all his joys and pains, all the pride and all the guilt, even memories he didn't know were still part of his mind and soul surged through her.

His entire life flashed before her eyes, past her ears and across her skin, just as it had for him, but only in a matter of heartbeats.

Her right hand, as it always did when the deceased's soul blasted through her, came to rest between her breasts, where there was no heartbeat to be felt.

~ * ~

When her vision cleared of the memories of Bobby's life, she saw him standing in front of her, in the rapidly rising creek, on the far side of his body. His corpse.

As she stood, she saw the rushing creek water flow through his insubstantial form.

The falling rain pass through him.

The wind carried a leaf torn off a tree above the gulley through him.

Her motion caught his attention, and his eyes, which had been staring at his body, met hers.

She saw concern in his eyes.

Knowing him now as intimately as she did, she knew his concern was for her.

"Miss, are you all right?"

The dead often didn't understand where they were, their situation. Their minds blocked out their death, the minutes and even hours leading up to it.

Unlike them, Bobby O'Callaghan knew he was dead. She could see the memory of the painful fall down the side of the gulley in his eyes. The desperation as the water rose around him, unable to lift his head as it began to flow into his mouth, into his nose.

But his first thought upon rising from his body was of her, of the tears still running down her face.

Even if she had not *known* Bobby O'Callaghan's soul, she would know from this what his final destination would be. Where he would spend eternity.

And then he saw her companion behind her. For an instant he recoiled in fear, taking a step, and then another, back away from her.

Again, she felt the ice-cold, skeletal hand on her shoulder.

At this, Bobby took a step forward, his hands flexing, the incorporeal muscles of his torso tensing. He meant to protect her, to fight on her behalf.

If she asked him to.

No, this one would not be cut down by her companion's scythe. Would not spend eternity in Hell.

This one was destined for Heaven.

Again, her companion rasped, "It is time."

Bobby's eyes narrowed.

"He means it's time for you to move on."

"Move on to where?"

She lifted her hourglass in both hands, and as she did, the

sand began to glow. Within moments, its buttery light illuminated the entire gulley. It was warm, brighter than the sun, and infinitely more comforting.

Human eyes, living eyes, would have been blinded by the glass's light. If it were meant for them, if the light could be seen by the eyes of the living. In any case, there were no living eyes here.

But Bobby was exalted by the light, and he stepped toward it.

Bobby O'Callaghan had caused his mother such pain the night he had driven drunk. And he had felt such guilt for that one stupid act. But he had been a good man.

Perhaps precisely because he had felt such guilt.

The upper base of the glass blocked the glowing sand, its brilliant light, from her direct view.

It was not meant for her.

It was meant for Bobby.

Bobby took a second step toward her, and as he did, his form began to fray. With his third step, he trod into his forgotten body.

He was little more than a wisp of smoke.

Even to her eyes.

3 - Mary Elizabeth Morely - *Ante Mortem*

Mary stood before her make-up stand and ran a brush through her long, straight, dark hair. In the stand's mirror, she saw William walk up behind her.

As she set the brush down, he wrapped his arms around her waist. "You are so beautiful, Mare."

She smiled. "You know 'mare' means a female horse, right?"

"Well, y'know, you have long legs like a horse. But you also know I mean it like an ocean of the moon." He nodded toward her image in the mirror. "It's fitting, with your dark hair and dark eyes."

She looked at her reflection—her eyes were a dark, midnight blue.

"But didn't you tell me once it was also the root of 'night-mare'? Something like a supernatural being that caused nightmares? Old German for 'succubus'?"

Mary's degree was in Middle English literature—she and William had met in a graduate seminar on the use of Greek and Roman mythology in 14th and 15th century European art.

"No, not 'succubus' —that's a female spirit who seduces men in their sleep. 'Mare' referred to an incubus—a *male* spirit who seduced *women* while they slept."

"Well, in either case, there's sex involved." He jerked his head toward their bed. "Whatcha say we involve ourselves in some sex rather than going to this dinner party of your advisor's?"

He leaned in to nuzzle her neck as she said, "No, I can't be a no-show."

He blew gently on her neck, making her shiver, and looked at her again in the mirror. "You sure?"

When his right hand started to move up her stomach, she took both his hands in hers, and pulled them away from her. She tilted her head to force his mouth away from her neck and said, "Now who's the incubus?" Letting go of his hands, she turned and put her hands on his chest, pushing gently.

His eyes widened. "My seductions give you nightmares?"

She laughed and stepped around him. "No, of course not. And Dr. Jones's parties aren't the nightmares you make them out to be." Stopping at the bedroom doorway, she looked at his crestfallen face. "Now be a good boy and come along."

He sighed. "If you insist."

~ * ~

At the front door, Mary grabbed her purse and pulled out her car keys.

William walked past her, through their apartment's front door, and onto the patio. He turned back to her with his arms spread and a smile on his face. "It's a beautiful night—let's walk!"

From the door's threshold, Mary felt the night's cool air, but it was warm enough. "Sure, why not?"

As they walked the quiet city streets, Mary asked William for the umpteenth time what it was he disliked about her advisor and received the only reply she did: "He just rubs me the wrong way."

At the party, William mingled for the first hour or so, but then parked himself on a couch in the corner of the living room, leaving Mary to make the rounds and rub elbows with Jones and his guests, the other professors and students from the Literature Department.

When she had done her duty by her advisor, she walked over to William to tell him they could leave. "Great, let's get out of here."

He stumbled ever so slightly as he came to his feet. "Damn, right leg's fallen asleep."

There was no slurring of his speech, but she asked teasingly, "You sure that's all it is?"

"Well, maybe not *all* it is." He gestured at the three bottles on the coffee table in front of the couch. "Herr Professor has good taste in beer, at least."

William suggested they walk back through the park between 8th and Main. "It's romantic with the moon and all the stars out," he said, and she agreed.

Halfway through the park a wind came up, and with it came clouds. The temperature dropped, and they both pulled their coats more tightly around themselves.

The central part of the park had no lights, but the path was wide and easy to follow even in the cloud-obscured moonlight.

Mary had no warning when a shadowy man-shape stepped out from behind a tree just a few feet in front of them. The moon was behind the hooded figure, but Mary could see an arm held out to its side. Moonlight glinted off something metallic in that hand.

"Gimme yaa money," a man's voice slurred.

Just as Mary realized the man was holding a knife, William stepped in front of her and pushed her back a step with one hand.

William said, "We don't want any trouble." He held his hands out by his side.

"Don' care wa you want."

Over William's shoulder, Mary could see the man take a step toward William.

"Gimme yaa money," he repeated.

William took a step forward, and Mary whispered, "William." She'd never been so terrified in her life.

William said, "Look, I'm going to reach for my wallet," as he swung his right hand back as if to warn Mary to stay back.

Suddenly, the man charged them.

Mary saw the knife-hand swing forward and then William's body blocked her view. She screamed William's name as he surged forward.

The moon disappeared behind the clouds.

Mary could only see two shadowy shapes struggling a few feet in front of her.

William gasped. And staggered back. And fell to the ground.

Screaming William's name, Mary ran forward two steps and dropped to the ground next to him.

He was holding his stomach, and something dark was seeping out from between his fingers.

She put her hand on his chest.

His heart was pounding.

He reached up with a hand covered in blood, reached for her face but fell short—his hand came to rest on her jacket, between her breasts.

The boy said, "I just wanted the money." For some reason, his words were no longer slurred.

Mary looked up.

For an instant, the moon came out from behind the clouds, and Mary could see the mugger's face clearly.

Their eyes locked.

He looked confused.

The boy couldn't have been more than 18 years old. Blood-shot eyes. Bags under his eyes. Sunken cheeks. Scabs on his chin, his forehead.

Meth, Mary thought.

The boy turned and ran.

"Mary, I feel so cold."

William's heart stopped beating.

~ * ~

The police arrived.

Told her she had called 911 on her cell phone—it was on the ground next to William. There was blood on it.

Paramedics arrived.

The police took Mary's statement.

The paramedics took William's body.

~ * ~

"Ashes to ashes. Dust to dust."

~ * ~

For days she did not leave her and William's apartment.

She would stare for hours on end at her jacket—with the

jacket unzipped, the bloodstain did not look much like a handprint, but she knew it was.

Friends stopped by.

Dr. Jones stopped by.

They all uttered meaningless platitudes.

~ * ~

The police never found William's murderer.

But Mary did.

There was a pawnshop not far from the apartment. One day, she went there. Bought a gun.

Every night thereafter, Mary walked the park along the path William and she had on their way home from the party.

She wore the jacket she had worn that night, the one with William's handprint rendered in his blood between her breasts.

One night, a shape stepped out from behind a tree and into her path.

A glint of moonlight reflected off the knife in its right hand.

Mary drew the gun she had bought for this purpose even as the boy said, "Gimme ya money."

She recognized the voice.

It wouldn't have mattered if she hadn't.

Mary pulled the trigger once. Twice. And again.

The boy fell backward.

Mary walked up to him and looked down at his face.

His eyes were even more bloodshot. The bags under his eyes more pronounced. The cheeks more sunken.

She said, "William didn't deserve to die. But you do."

The boy tried to say something, but blood bubbled from his mouth.

Mary knelt beside him, unconcerned with the knife still clutched in his hand. She placed her free hand on his chest.

Waited for his heart to stop beating.

~ * ~

"Police! Drop the gun!"

Mary did not know how long she had knelt next to the body of William's killer.

Did it matter?

She looked over her shoulder and was blinded by the bright light of the policeman's flashlight.

"Drop the gun!"

Mary looked at the gun still in her hand.

Did it matter?

William was dead.

She stood.

As she turned to face the police officer, she heard the report of his gun.

She could not see him.

Standing before her was a figure that stood at least two feet taller than her. It wore a black, tattered robe that whipped about it even though there was no wind. At her eye-level, one skeletal hand held an hourglass. Somehow, she knew there were only a few grains of sand left in the upper bulb. In the other fleshless hand, It held a scythe even taller than It was.

Her gaze moved up to its hood, and saw a skull. The eye sockets were empty. Fleshless cheekbones created the illusion that It was grinning.

The lower jaw moved as the robe flapped in the non-existent wind to show the spine, the fleshless rib-cage below the skull. "You have murdered."

Its visage was terrible, and Its voice should have turned the blood in her veins to ice.

This was her Death standing before her.

But she was already as cold as she could be. Had been since William uttered his last words.

Her attention was drawn down as the bullet from the policeman's gun emerged from Death's robe. It left no hole and moved so slowly Mary was able to follow it with her eyes.

In the periphery of her vision, she saw Death begin to swing Its scythe.

Just before the last grain of sand fell in Its hourglass, the scythe passed through her.

A fraction of an instant later, the bullet ended her life.

4 - Mary Elizabeth Morely - *Post Mortem*

She looked over her shoulder and saw her body sprawled

across that of William's killer.

The policeman cursed and moving to kick her gun away from her hand, passed through Mary's Death as though It was not there. The officer asked no one in particular, "Why? Why couldn't you just drop the damn gun?"

Death stepped aside so Mary could once again see It.

She could see tears running down the policeman's face. He looked like he could hardly be much older than the boy who had murdered William.

Death rasped, "Compassion has been lost to you."

She turned to Death and screamed, "He murdered William for the money we had in our pockets. He deserved to die!"

"Death is the end of all things. It is not a dessert." Death stepped toward her.

She brought the hand holding the gun up, but it was empty. She no longer wore her jacket, jeans or shoes. Instead, she wore a simple, white strap dress and sandals.

"You will find compassion again at my side." Her Death held out the hourglass. "Take the glass."

"No. I just want to die."

"You are dead." Death released the hourglass.

She thought she had been cold before, but now…

The hourglass began to float toward her.

"Take the glass."

Her hands took the glass from the air.

5 - Mary Elizabeth Morely - *Per Mortem*

Over the days, years or decades that followed, she became an Angel of Death.

At first, she had refused to touch the dead and learned what could happen when she failed to do so.

Time ceased to have meaning for her—perhaps it had no meaning for the dead.

Or Death.

For much longer, she had scoured the memories of the dead to find a justification for their deaths.

~ * ~

With Bobby O'Callaghan's fourth step, he said, "It's so beautiful."

And as he took his fifth and final step in this world, a single new tear spilled from her eye as she said, "So are you."

Her companion rasped, "Release the glass."

She was so stunned she almost didn't understand her companion. It had never asked anything of her except to take the glass and to release the dead. "What?"

"Release the glass."

She turned away from Bobby O'Callaghan's body to find her Death had reached out Its free hand toward her.

Trembling, she did as It asked.

"You have found compassion again."

The sand in the hourglass began to glow.

"Its Light is now for you."

She looked to her Death's eyeless, fleshless visage.

But the Light was even now washing out Its form.

And in Its place, she saw William beckoning her to join him.

~ * ~ * ~

P James Norris has master's degrees in Physics and Philosophy. In the 1980's, he wrote four spec scripts for ST:TNG. In 2018 he started getting short stories published by the likes of Moon Magazine, Fantasia Divinity, Rhetoric Askew; his shorts have been included in three anthologies. He's written three one-hour fantasy TV pilots. He has five novels in various states of incompletion—maybe, some day, he will finish writing them. He lives in Idaho with his wife and a dog, two cats and four chickens.

His published work can be found at:
amazon.com/author/pjamesnorris
ocetacea.net/pjamesnorris

In a Sea of Night

JT Seate

Bodies whirled and twisted on the dance floor to the booming beat of *Play That Funky Music, White Boy*. The blind girl sat at a table with a girlfriend and her guide dog, tapping her foot to the rhythm.

"Would you like to dance?" I asked.

She looked in the direction of my voice. A smile crept across her face, an honest good-natured smile that more than offset her unfocused gaze. She didn't know whether I was short, fat, or ugly. All she knew was someone had asked her to dance.

"Go ahead. I'll watch Bandit," her friend told her.

Some inflection in her friend's voice must have told the girl I was presentable, but I don't think it mattered. Her Golden Retriever lay patiently under her table. His soulful, brown eyes looked unsurely at the stranger who'd asked to borrow his mistress. The blind girl patted the dog's head and I led her toward the square of hardwood on the lounge's dance floor.

"I'm not very good," she said.

"Neither am I. What's your name?"

"Beth. What's yours?"

"Spence."

The pounding beat ricocheted off the walls. Most everyone in the lounge was up, their feet gyrating in personal, frenzied interpretations of a fertility dance.

"I think we have a little room to maneuver here," I shouted.

She smiled trustingly and began her own variation of booty shaking. With her arms raised above her head, she resembled a Spanish *Contessa* clicking castanets, enjoying the freedom of her own space.

"You move beautifully," I told her.

She didn't answer, caught up in the rhythm of the song. Her enthusiasm was contagious. I moved as sexily as I knew how, forgetting my efforts were lost on my partner.

Finally, the white boy was no longer playing the funky music.

"Thank you, Spence." She reached out and touched my arm

to show her appreciation and to give me the opportunity to lead her back to Bandit.

A slow song wafted from the speakers—*Unforgettable*.

"Are you all right with one more?" I asked.

"A tummy tickler? Sure."

She melted against me the way every man hungers for, clinging like a vine long familiar with the stone it intertwines, our bodies coming together as if each was a perfect partner of the other. Her head against my shoulder, she hummed along with the music.

Other couples swayed languidly. In that moment of closeness, I considered how attuned her remaining senses must be. When the song ended, I guided her back to her brown-eyed boy who waited expectantly, his muzzle resting on his paws.

"Thanks again," Beth said.

Her friend gave me a curt smile as I ambled back to a corner of the bar feeling I'd done my good deed for the evening.

Beth and her girlfriend finished their drinks and left. I would never see her again but I often thought of how adept she'd been at making the most of her situation, how her blindness didn't interfere with many of life's pleasures. It was an important and ironic lesson because within a few days, I would be as blind as she.

~ * ~

The turning point in life on Earth started for all of us on September 6, 2023. My alarm sounded at 6:45. I slapped it off seeking a few more precious moments of quiet, holding my job at bay. I rolled over expecting to witness the sunlight streaming through my bedroom window.

Nothing but darkness, not even a shadow, as if our sun had abandoned the galaxy, the thick blackness of the darkest night imaginable. I closed my eyes tightly and rubbed them with the heels of my hands before opening them again. No reassuring golden glow, only the gloomy nothingness of a coalmine deep in the bowels of the earth. My hands reached out with fingers curled into claws, as if I could pull away a black shroud of extreme night and reveal the familiar world of light and images. I grasped only air.

I was a newspaper reporter. I rely heavily on my senses and it was clear that I was as blind as the Cyclops in *The Odyssey*. I furiously rubbed my eyes until they burned, to no effect, then fumbled for my bedside phone while fighting a wave of panic, knocking a picture of my latest girlfriend from my nightstand in the process. I heard the glass crack as it hit the floor.

Feeling the raised numbers I tried Mary Ann's number. Her recording answered.

My emotions warped beyond panic to a deeper plane of terror. Was I in some kind of limbo, perhaps dead, where darkness was a perpetual companion? "It must be a nightmare, has to be," I said, willing my words to be true.

My next impulse was to dial the newsroom. Jimmy from the night shift answered. "What?"

I could hear shouts and the scurrying of people in the background. "It's Spence. I…I can't see!"

"You and everybody else! Nobody can see, man! It happened about three hours ago. It's like the end of the world. We're getting reports in from everywhere."

"Nobody?" I said dumbly, momentarily setting aside my own sightlessness. "I'm going to come in and see what I can do."

"That's just it. No one can see to do shit! We're all caught in the same trap, apparently all ten billion of us. We're down here running into each other. There's nothing to do but try and contact our families."

I had no family to contact. "What do they think caused it?"

"Hard to say, and the couple of scientists and doctors we've got on speed dial aren't willing to speculate yet. All we've got is radio and TV. The UP wire is useless. There's a lot of talk about how long our audio systems will stay up. Trust me, stay home."

I reluctantly hung up. Surely I could get to my computer and start on the story. Then the overwhelming force of the situation slammed into my frontal lobe and unleashed a tremble that proliferated from my spine into my extremities. *No written stories, no pictures, no newspapers, unless they are in braille.* Here was the story of a lifetime and I couldn't write it.

Transportation? A city full of hysterical people running and falling, smashing into each other in panic—a Three Stooges world. "It'll be okay," I whispered without conviction. "Machines and electronics will still work. Most everything is computerized. Blind people get around all right."

I found the TV remote and punched in the numbers for

CNN from memory. The fact Big Brother was on the air gave some comfort.

"We must all pray this condition is only temporary," a female talking head cajoled. "We should stay in our homes and remain calm."

I tried to convince myself this was good advice.

"Specialists from around the world are communicating to try and determine what has happened," she continued.

It was obvious the "specialists" were clueless at the moment. I felt a new sensation—shortness of breath, racing heart, tingling in my fingers, not to mention unadulterated terror. I fought to keep my attention on the newswoman wondering how she was dressed, or whether she was dressed at all. A twisted part of me wondered whether things like clothes mattered anymore.

In other disasters someone eventually came to the rescue. Now everyone needed rescue. As a newspaper guy, I'd seen hurricanes, floods, tornadoes, earthquakes, and war rip peoples' lives apart, but that was the point. That is what made this phenomenon so different. I had *seen* all those things. Now, I couldn't see to find my shoes.

No sirens blared outside. In every other crisis or catastrophe, sirens always screamed from patrol cars and fire trucks. *There won't be any more of that unless it sounds to direct people toward the food.*

Food!

God, how long would that last?

"Let's hope we'll be able to laugh about all of this soon," a man said with false capriciousness to the woman on the news. "Just now coming in… The White House has issued a statement that the nation is now under Martial Law. Everyone stay in your homes and for those not fortunate enough to be home, stay where you are."

Something other than sugar plums danced in my head. This century had already brought major changes. In spite of most news outlets' best efforts, society had fallen victim to cancerous idiosyncrasies. Politics was based on nothing but misdirection and lies with false deities driving the world into false realities. Truth had been lost.

At this point, I would have screamed if someone on the street hadn't beaten me to it. Banging my shin on a piece of furniture, I felt my way from bedroom to hallway, my arms extended like Frankenstein's monster. I realized I was crying. What kind of cruel joke was Mother Nature playing? I thought of the blind girl I'd danced with…Beth. I pictured her poise and grace. For her, just another day was beginning. For me, my life could be altered forever. Today could be a precursor to the end of the world.

My blind journey continued as I stumbled through a house no longer familiar toward my front door. I negotiated the passageway with a spastic dance step of my own, trying to think positive. Then I heard another scream.

"I'm blind. Oh God, someone help me," a woman cried from somewhere.

Had a mad scientist gone Stephen King's "super flu" or Covid one better? Had some demigod released a poison agent that first stole your sight and then took your life? Blindness might just be the start. My thoughts were racing helter-skelter, out of control. Something had gone hideously wrong and thrown my universe into the blackness of sight and mind.

I felt for the bolt on my front door and forced it open. The earth had turned toward the morning sun after all. Although I couldn't see, its resplendent rays warmed my face and the deep blackness lightened a shade to dark gray. Thank God for the sun. I began to have hope, thinking this state of affairs might be improving.

The woman's voice again, screaming. It sounded like she had stopped in my front yard. I thought it might be my neighbor, Emily, the one who liked to play the Blues on hot summer nights.

"Who's there?" I called out.

"Spence? I'm blind."

The most ludicrous thing I could've said would be, "so am I." It was too insane, too impossible. "Talk to me," I said. "Let me come to the sound of your voice."

This horrendous phenomena wasn't mine alone to bear and I took a measure of comfort in that. I wasn't isolated. Feeling for the woman, my arms moved to the right and left as I slowly approached. I ran into something and almost stumbled. It was the woman, kneeling in my driveway.

I dropped to a knee and put my arm around her. "It's all right," I said ludicrously. "I have you."

"I can't see!" she wailed.

Her warm tears fell on my knee. I was as naked as a frequent dream. I'd have a jolly time explaining this to the cops if they showed up, my thoughts in terms of a normal world.

"Is it you, Emily?"

"Yes. Can't you see me?"

"No, I'm afraid I can't."

"What's happening? Is everyone in this town blind?" she screamed.

"Let's go inside. I'm squatting here in my birthday suit. I'll try to call someone."

She reached out and touched my bare chest to confirm my statement. We stood and I found my way back to my front door with Emily in tow.

Another person yelled from down the street. At first I thought he'd seen me in the buff and was threatening to call the police. Then I realized his wails entreated anyone to call the police, as his eyesight had abandoned him.

I ignored his shouts and led Emily to my sofa. Feeling around and finding the telephone I knew to be in the kitchen, I tried 911 again.

I'm sorry. We are unable to connect your call at this time. Please try again.

Trying to put the phone in the pocket of my nonexistent robe, it only slid against my tingling thigh.

"What has happened?" Emily asked for the second time between gasps for air.

"I don't have a clue." The kind of headache caused only by the truth was setting in, but I needed to circumvent my fear as I dialed Mary Ann's number once more. This time she picked up. "Mary Ann. Are you all right?"

"You mean, can I see?" She hesitated then added, "Have you turned on a TV or radio?" Her voice was strangely calm, frighteningly so. "It's worldwide. The whole world has gone blind, Spencer. The entire world."

My nakedness meant nothing. All of us were naked, emotionally.

~ * ~

Then the madness began, taking the shelter-in-place edict to even further heights—the madness of a society thrown into darkness, blind people groping about in a lightless void. Life as I knew it had ended in the blink of an eye, so to speak. Fashion, sport, traditional warfare and commerce, all vanishing in an instant. Humankind trembled on the brink while scientists squabbled and tried to find the mysterious genetic code that had swept across the face of the earth, to no avail. The teaming masses, now in a land where prestige, power and appearance no longer mattered, prayed for salvation.

For those too desperate to move on, there was always a bullet. Jumping out of a high window was also popular. The media named this means of self-destruction "finding Heaven's Gate." Those who were blind before the apocalypse became the gurus of the future. And life, somehow, went on.

In my youth, I'd heard a tale of a beautiful woman who took pride in her delicate feet above all else. She soaked them in warm oils. Then Lanolin was applied to the soles, arches, and ankles. The result was feet of perfection without calluses or blemishes. They were powdered and perfumed to smell as fetching as they appeared. It was no wonder the woman took such pride in her tantalizing feet, for she had no arms.

The moral? Make lemonade, I suppose. Eventually, the world accepted its blindness in much the same way, leaning on its remaining senses. It took a while, a great while, but seeds were harvested and distributed to all who could find their way to the distribution centers—all those who had weathered the necessary adjustments and had chosen to keep living.

I no longer worked for the paper or anywhere else for that matter. Existence had become basic and unfettered. My former manicured yard became home to a patch of earth that contained carrots, potatoes, tomatoes, and onions just for fun. Things I could feel. Things for Beth and me survive on.

As I said, I never *saw* Beth again but I did find her. She had been helping out at one of the distribution centers. Believe it or not, she recognized my voice. By some twisted quirk of marvelous fate I'll always be thankful for, we became a couple.

All of us still had music stations and talk radio but I didn't listen much, except when someone came on to tell us how to do something, the blind way, to make life a little easier. But I had what I needed…all there was *to* have.

~ * ~

Beth put a Blues ballad on the music machine and returned to the porch next to Bandit and me. I'd become fascinated by the heartfelt lyrics and liquid rhythms of the songs. I have poor Emily to thank for my learning the meanings behind the music. She'd just disappeared one day like so many others had. Lost, dead, or just moved on, who's to say?

My relationship with Mary Ann had shattered as thoroughly as her picture on my nightstand. Much about her had been based on appearances. I hoped she could find a way to live with the new reality of "being."

"Have you heard what they're saying about the latest vaccine?" Beth asked me. "Early tests have shown slight movement can be seen for up to twenty minutes with each dose."

"Where have I heard that before? Stay tuned," I replied as I found her hand and brought it to my lips, kissing it tenderly. "Did I ever tell you about the time I danced with a blind girl, before all of this? She was happier than I was when I could see. Gone is gone, and over is over, but now I understand what blindness strips your life down to: the awe and wonder of someone's kind word or touch. I guess the word is dignity. That's what she had—personal dignity."

I could sense Beth blushing as she nestled into the space between my arm and chest. "When I first lost my sight, I cursed when I dropped something," she said. "Then I learned to rejoice when I accomplished some little task." She turned her head and kissed my neck. "It doesn't really matter whether you see again does it? Not really?"

"We always want what we can't obtain. That's civilization's way. If suddenly there's a serum, I'll be the first to get in line. But I can tell you that for the first time in my life I'm content with who I am and what I have."

"Me too," Beth replied as twinkling stars gathered overhead, their pinpoints of light beaming from suns burned out millions of years before. We could have been the only two people in the world.

I looked into an indifferent cosmos. Even though I couldn't see the brilliant lights tacked against the backdrop of blackness, I knew they were there. I still felt their magic and wonder even though I could only imagine them. I thought about my fellow humans feeling their way along, looking for meaning in their forever altered lives. "Here we are on this bipolar blue bauble in a sea of night that alternatively displays nurture and destruction," I said to Beth. "Yet it still turns as it always has and the universe doesn't care if its creatures have eyes or wings or dreams. Everything just is."

"Let's dance again," Beth suggested. "I can put on *Unforgettable*. Let's dance in the dark, Spence, like before."

"Yes, let's dance."

~ * ~ * ~

J. T. stands on the side of the literary highway and thumbs down whatever genre that comes roaring by. His storytelling runs the gamut from Horror Novel Review's Best Short Fiction to the *Chicken Soup for the Soul* series. His memoirs and essays report fact while his fiction incorporates fantasy, horror, or humor featuring the quirkiest of characters.

The Slipping Away

Lee Conrad

Franklin Freemantle left his manager's office feeling better than when he initially went in, but not by much. The shakes had faded. The stares of his co-workers followed him as he walked back to his small cubicle. He fell into his chair, emotionally exhausted. He had dodged a firing this go around, but time was running out.

"Well?"

The voice was from Doug in the next cube.

"I guess I am going to be around for a while. Nia will be relieved, especially with us sending our daughter off to college in the fall. I don't know how I could face my daughter and tell her university is out."

Doug leaned his heavy body into Franklin's cube. His wrinkled shirt had a button missing, and he hadn't shaved that day. "I am so sick and tired of this. Every quarter, they force more of us out the door. Bastards make money hand over fist, but they would rather shove us out to the street and keep sending our work to another country. And I am just a perfect target for them… senior, on the old pension plan, and overpaid in their eyes. Surprised I have made it this far. Which reminds me, did you hear about the new dress code?"

"What new dress code?"

"No grey hair allowed."

"Good thing I'm younger than you, Doug."

~ * ~

At the end of the building, the manager stepped out and straightened his purple and black checkered tie. Casual wasn't his style. He wanted to stand out. Brian Holden was in his early thirties and determined to advance in the company. He took this low-level manager job a year ago but wanted more and would do anything to get it. He marched to another cubicle and spoke. A woman in her late fifties stepped out and with head hung down followed the manager to his office.

The meeting was short, not even enough time for the woman

to sit, and the manager didn't offer her a chair. He wanted this over with as little talk or pushback as possible. Brian handed her the envelope with the separation legal documents and her last check. Delia Hightower stepped out of the office and burst into tears. A few co-workers went to console her. Others stayed away like she had the plague, fearing her fate would be theirs if they got too close.

Franklin walked up to her and put his arm around her. He had known Delia for years. They joined the company when it was a small start-up call center. Divorced with a son in another state, this job was her life. Delia took the job seriously and put in more hours than others. When others quit during Covid, she worked from home and put in extra hours. But that didn't help her. As Doug said, her grey hair had done her in.

"Shit, Franklin, not only do I get canned, but I also have to train a replacement from the Philippines. If I don't, they won't give me my severance. Bastards."

Franklin walked her back to her cube to help her clear out and box her belongings. She sent her company email contact list to her personal email and added client names and information.

~ * ~

Towards the end of the day, more cubicles had emptied. The ever-noisy chattering into phones and the clacking sound of keyboards subsided. Boxes had been packed with personal items and family pictures. Some fired employees wrote obscenities on copy paper and taped them to the walls of their cubes. One simply said *you are next*.

"Franklin, let's go to the café and get some coffee. That last client gave me a headache," Doug said.

The complex they worked at had two parts. An indoor walkway connected the extensive area that housed the cubicles, nicknamed "the cattle pen" by the workers, to another building three stories high. In the middle was an atrium with a café on the ground floor. Ringing the atrium on the second and third floors were the executive offices, and above it all, a glass roof shaped like a pyramid. It was inviting and open.

"Some of us are meeting at the Hillcrest Tavern for a few with some of those that got fired today. Want to go?" Doug said.

"Sure, let me call Nia. I need to tell her I am okay anyway. I should have done it earlier. She's probably worried sick."

The Hillcrest Tavern was in the middle of a strip mall between a cell phone store and a liquor store. Nothing fancy, but close enough to work to fill a need. Today there was a need, and if you needed more, the liquor store was always open late.

The bar had filled up early and the tables filled with a mix of people now out of work and those still working but wondering who was next.

"Don't tell me. More jobs are gone, right?" Ryan, the bartender and owner said, as Doug and Franklin walked in. "I can always tell when business picks up in the early afternoon and in the middle of the week," he said, shaking his head.

Doug settled his bulky frame on a bar stool and ordered a double scotch on the rocks. Franklin ordered a beer.

"First one on the house, guys. Least I can do," Ryan said.

"I'm going to sit here while you act your usual crusader self," Doug said with a raspy chuckle.

"Don't know what I can say anymore, Doug. This slash and burn has been going on for so long, morale is at rock bottom. When that union organizer was talking to us, we should have listened to him. But he is long gone, and those of us left are on our own."

Doug took a slug of his scotch. "And no age discrimination here, oh no. They just throw a few of the youngsters into the mix to keep the government off their backs."

"You figured that out by now? I'm going to see who made it and who didn't. Don't get too drunk."

Doug smiled and gave Franklin the finger as he walked away.

Delia caught his eye and waved to him.

"Hey, over here, Franklin. You have got to hear this."

Delia was sitting at a table with Damien, a younger worker. He came into the company with a bunch of new hires, all under thirty a few years ago, when the company made a push to hire just millennials.

"You okay Delia?"

"I'm alright now that the shock is over. Got some prospects I'm going to work on tomorrow. If I get a bite, I am out of there. Screw their replacement training. I have vested rights in the old pension and some money in my four-oh-one-k. I'll survive. Being single helps. Wouldn't want to go through this with a family. I don't know what I'd do. But anyway, you have got to hear what Damien found out."

"Okay, Damien, fill me in," Franklin said as he sat down and sipped his drink.

"Well, remember our old manager, Elaine? We couldn't understand why she left so abruptly last year. I ran into her the other night at the Lost Dog Cafe. Hard to believe, but the company is even scummier than we thought."

"Yeah, hard to believe," Franklin said sarcastically.

Damien continued. "She was told by corporate to select people on the old pension plan, track them and note every time they had a sick day, were late for a meeting or moved out a deadline. Then build up a case for deficient performance and fire them. This is on top of the quarterly culling of the herd. In exchange for this, they promised her a bonus for each employee on the old plan she could terminate from the payroll and the pension plan. She quit instead of doing it. Said she couldn't live with herself if she got that low and dirty."

"That explains a lot," Delia said. "Franklin, remember when I told you Brian got angry when I got a thank you email from one client, and they copied him on it? Then the impossible assignments that three people usually handled? He said I missed deadlines but couldn't substantiate those claims. Or that "others on the team" complained about me. When I asked for details, he said it was confidential. Yeah, Damien, scummier than we realized."

"Wonder who else was targeted," Franklin said, looking over at Doug. Franklin had seen the dark changes that had overcome Doug in just a short time. He knew Doug and his wife had separated. That would put anyone in a tailspin, but Doug couldn't seem to pull himself together. He wondered if something else was going on.

Franklin turned his attention back to the conversation.

"A bunch, I would think," Damien said. "When Gloria was on chemo, she felt like crap, but Holden, instead of showing any sympathy, gave her more work. Of course, she fell behind. And guess what? Fired for poor performance. Most people don't talk about it. They blame themselves and keep it inside, eating at them until bam…something breaks. The pressure must have been immense. Lessons learned…don't get sick and don't get old in this company."

The night ended with the more sober ones giving former co-workers a ride home and a shoulder to cry on. A few cars would be left in the parking lot to be picked up in the glare of a new and unsettled day. Promises of keeping in contact left hanging in the air.

"I'm glad I carpooled with you, Franklin," Doug slurred. "I wouldn't want to hit anyone. Just taking myself out would be just fine." He made a screeching noise and mimicked turning a steering wheel.

Franklin knew Doug's moods, but lately, it had gotten worse. It was like he was giving up on life. Formerly a well-dressed man, neat in appearance, he had, as they used to say, gone to seed.

The ride to Doug's place was quiet. A passed-out passenger usually is. Franklin pulled into the apartment complex Doug had lived in since the breakup with his wife. The long hours of the job and trying to stay ahead of the game wreaked havoc on relation-ships. He helped a staggering Doug to his apartment, thankful it was on the first floor.

"Come on in for one more Frankie buddy," Doug slurred.

"Time to sleep for both of us. See you at the sweatshop."

"Screw'em, Frankie, screw'em." Doug had wrapped his arms around Franklin, threatening to send them both to the concrete walkway. "Okie dokie. I see myself in. Thanks for the ride."

They thought the firings were over. They were wrong. The bean counters in finance saw the company was light on its quota of people getting fired. An insatiable beast hungry for more. Stockholders clamored for higher dividends and Wall Street wanted results. Memos went to managers throughout the company to make it happen.

Again, Brian Holden hunted his prey among the cubicles. People held their breath. He walked past Franklin's cube and went into Doug's.

"You can tell me right here, Brian."

"No, Doug, come to my office."

Doug shuffled towards the manager's office. A sideways glance at Franklin showed a face of despair.

After five minutes, Doug walked back the way he came. Shoulders slumped, he passed Franklin's cubicle and headed towards the Atrium.

"You okay buddy?" Franklin called out.

Doug seemed oblivious to everything around him and kept

walking.

Damien went over to Franklin's cubicle.

"Is he alright?"

"He needs to just chill for a bit. Let's give him a little time, and then we'll go sit and talk with him."

Within minutes, an alarm went off and the PA system announced, "Security to the Atrium."

Franklin's thoughts went to Doug. "This can't be good," he said. He stopped by Damien's cubicle. "Damien, let's go."

They sprinted to the Atrium and on arriving saw people huddled about, some in shock, others crying.

Off to the side of the floor was the crumpled and battered body of Doug. He wasn't moving. Security guards surrounded the lifeless body.

"No, no…" Franklin turned away.

"What happened?" he asked a woman behind him.

Tears running down her face, she told Franklin and Damien how Doug calmly walked through the Atrium and climbed the stairs to the third floor and stood facing the front of the general manager's office.

"He turned, threw some papers in the air, walked to the railing and then…jumped over," she said between sobs. "Oh my God, why?"

An ambulance arrived and the EMT's quickly worked on Doug, but it was of no use. The damage was too great. He was gone.

The site shut down for the rest of the day and workers were told to go home.

One of the workers called the local media and when they contacted the company, a spokesperson said it was unfortunate and a tragedy but Doug had been depressed over the breakup of his marriage. Nothing to do with the company.

After the funeral, Franklin, Damien, and Delia met at the Hillcrest Tavern.

Losing Doug and the shock of his suicide overwhelmed them, and a hollowness seeped into their being.

Franklin cleared his throat. It was hard to talk about Doug in the past tense. He half expected him to walk into the bar and order his usual scotch on the rocks.

"I talked to Doug's ex-wife at the funeral. Yes, they had problems, but she said he was under a tremendous amount of pressure from work and was drinking more. He got angry at the simplest things. All they did was argue. She couldn't take it anymore, so they separated. She expected Doug would come to his senses and they would get back together. The thing is, she said he was fine up to the time Holden took over. That's when everything went downhill."

"But why didn't we see what was happening to him?" Delia asked.

"He slipped away from us, and we ignored the signs. We were caught up in our own survival and didn't see it until it was too late," said Franklin. "And it was the company's fault, no matter what their corporate mouthpiece said. If our manager is doing it, then you can bet others in this company are. They drive people to the brink, and some go over. They have blood on their hands."

Franklin looked at Delia and Damien. "We need to talk to some people about this. We can't let what happened with Doug happen to anyone else."

"Well, we can contact someone in the media," Delia said. "This is probably going on in other companies, and more than we know. You can bet they are covering it up. They will not admit they are driving their workers to suicide."

"The media will treat it as a story of the day and move on to happy news. We need some long-term help with this," Damien interjected, stabbing his finger on the table.

"I agree, Damien," Franklin said. "It really is up to us. We've seen it firsthand. I am sure we can find some local mental health experts we can talk to about this. You know, give us some guidance. And we need to talk to our co-workers. Let's break the silence and make a promise...no one else slips away. No one."

A soft rain was falling as they left the tavern, hearts heavy but with a new determination. They had made a promise and they would see it through.

~ * ~ * ~

Lee Conrad lives in upstate New York with his longtime love and their three rescue cats. His stories have appeared in Fiction on the Web, Literally Stories, Ariel Chart, Sundial Magazine, The London Reader, Books 'N Pieces and Written Tales.

Visit him at: facebook.com/leefrederickconrad/

Suppressed Shadows, Silver Scars

Malina Douglas

Aarno clenched his jaw, aware with acute discomfort of the dark shapes moving behind the locked door, and within him. Erja stared at him, eyes searching and hungry, but he would not answer her. He could not form into words the shadows that darkened his films, his life. He had known them so long they were part of him— a horrifying blackness that gnawed at his soul. The clock ticked.

Within him lay minefields of questions he did not want to answer. The attack, the psychiatric hospital. Lost years. Gaps in his life that he couldn't explain. Like chunks of a text blotted out. The secret in the next room, so perilously close.

And if he were to tell her, if he were to let that awful thing out that he was hiding in the darkness—as chaotic as his rough, repulsive self—she would recoil. She would run out of the room and slam the door behind her and probably never come back.

And he would fail.

He lit candles. Two long tapers, that he set into little brass holders. His hands were shaking so much, he dropped the lighter. *What if she were to find out?* The prospect was terrifying.

Beyond the long shadows produced by the tapers he saw her face. Calm as Töölönlahti Lake, revealing nothing. He would kill for that calm.

~ * ~

They were on the second glass of Merlot when the sounds began. Short, high-pitched eruptions that broke through the tenuous connection he'd been building all evening.

Erja paused, glass in hand.

"What's that?"

Aarno slicked back his dark hair the way he did when trying to impress someone. They were sitting in his Helsinki flat. It was just after midnight. The triple glazed windows revealed only faint lights; black smudges. A clouded sky. Starless.

"Oh, that's my, uh—dog." He rubbed his neck. "She hasn't been out for a while." He took a quick sip of wine. Put the glass down. A disonorous clatter. He winced.

Erja narrowed her eyes at him. She wore a grey dress tight as a sealskin that came to mid-thigh. Her legs were encased in black stockings, feet in wool socks she absently rubbed against each other. Her fur-lined boots, left at the door, had flopped down and folded over themselves like leeks. Her pale, silken hair was looped and fastened behind her head, and her face was as composed as a fresh-fallen snowfield. The lines on her forehead were so faint he could hardly see them. When he thought back, it struck him with force how ordered she looked then. All clean lines like a Carolus Enckell painting. Not like…after. She could never have been prepared for what happened after.

"Now, what was I saying about Wes Anderson's camera angles…"

Sounds again. Higher pitched and more insistent. Aarno tensed.

"That's definitely not a dog." Erja's brow creased.

The sounds pierced the thickening curtain of fog produced by the Merlot and the glasses of champagne before it.

Aarno clenched his fist until his nails dug into his hand. *Not now.* He willed himself to stay calm.

"Just a moment." He got up from the sofa, strode across the plush eggshell-white carpet and leapt over the part where the floor squeaked. He pulled open the freezer and grabbed a packet wrapped in Clingfilm.

Erja studied his movements. Something red flashed in the packet.

"What's that?"

The sounds were increasing in frequency.

Aarno ignored her. He ran to the opposite wall, unlocked a stout door, opened it a crack, threw the package in and slammed it shut. The whining cut off abruptly.

He locked the door.

Aarno heard the rip of the packaging, growling and short yelps. In his mind he saw tearing claws and devouring mouths. He leapt back to his seat.

"What the hell are you keeping in that room, Aarno?"

He was midway through a sip of Merlot. Looked up. Coughed. Wine spluttered out, dripping onto the table and carpet. He dashed to the open-plan kitchen, snatched up a damp cloth and dabbed the stain with furious motions.

"—New carpet," he hissed through clenched teeth.

Erja cast her black-rimmed eyes on him, and he felt the silent censure of her look. Hardening, like ice on the surface of the lake where he skated in winter. But the ice was still patchy and there was danger of falling through.

He had to reach her, before she froze over completely. What wild story would he invent next? He was a filmmaker—he was used to concocting plots. But the wine had slowed his senses. And she was not the kind of woman he could hide something from and get away with it.

He took a deep breath, afraid of her disbelief, her judgment. "What if I told you I found some…creatures," he began.

"Yes…" she urged, grey eyes looking straight into his.

"—and I caught them, and I'm keeping them here—temporarily—"

"What kind of creatures," she asked, pursing her small, rouged lips.

"You're going to find it hard to believe. You might even laugh at me." Aarno's voice wavered with doubt.

Erja leaned forward, resting one arm on her chin. "Tell me."

Aarno took a long sip of Merlot and said, "trolls."

Erja's eyes widened. "I have to see this." She stood up.

Aarno held out an arm. "Wait—they're not used to humans. They might—"

But Erja was already striding to the door, her sock-footed feet sure, her narrow hips swaying.

Aarno had left the key in the door.

He leapt over the sofa, dashed to the door and grasped the handle Erja held. As he touched her hand, a shiver ran through him. He tried to pry off her fingers, but she held tight.

Erja turned the key and tried to pull the door open. Aarno blocked it with his body. The sounds were getting louder: first inquisitive squeaks, then short, sharp bursts of noise, then lower sounds—growling.

She pulled and he pushed. He was stronger than her, determined to defeat her. He wiped a bead of sweat from his brow. She used the moment to yank the door open.

"Wait—stop—" he called out, but it was too late—she had loosed them. Two small compact shapes darted out in a flicker of movement. They were the size of small children, but with short wiry hairs all over their bodies, stumpy legs and flat feet.

"You don't know what they'll do—" Aarno called out, but she was already running after them, silent on sock feet.

The trolls wobbled as they raced, pounding the floor with their wide stubby feet.

Erja watched them, lips parted.

They glanced around with small yellow eyes and sniffed the apartment with long bulbous noses, red as if they'd been playing in the snow.

"The wine glasses—" Aarno bellowed.

But the trolls thundered over the coffee table, knocked the spindly half-drunk glasses onto the carpet and sent the wine bottle flying. Aarno ran forward with a roar but the dark red stains were already blooming. With short rapid breaths and clenched fists he pursued the trolls.

Erja lunged at one of the trolls. It darted away with a kind of cackle, ran into the fireplace, thick with cold ashes, and dashed out again, treading ash all over the carpet. The other troll yanked open the doors of the cupboards, tore out dishes and smashed them onto the floor. The first troll ripped open the fridge and tossed out a carton of yogurt. It burst.

"Hey," Aarno yelled. "Get out of there!"

He chased after the troll but it darted around the island. Aarno slipped on the yogurt and fell to the floor. He cursed.

He pulled himself up. "You take the other side," he called to Erja. "We'll cut them off in the middle." He waved his arm like a military commander.

Erja gave a sharp nod.

They approached from either side of the kitchen island. The first troll was sitting on broken dish shards stuffing grapes into its mouth. It looked up and tried to scramble away as Aarno grabbed it. It thrashed and snarled in his arms but he held tight.

"Why you little—" Aarno said with a similar snarl. He carried the struggling troll to the door of the spare room, slid it in, and slammed the door.

Erja grabbed the other one as it struggled to climb up the counter. It kicked out of her arms and raced back across the floor. She ran after it.

They cornered it in the fireplace. Aarno wrapped his hands around the body, pinning down its small flailing arms.

"You're destroying my house!" He pressed into its neck until its eyes bulged. Its mouth was open, spluttering, choking.

"Stop it!" Erja demanded. "They're like children—they don't know any better."

Aarno eased the pressure and Erja squatted on the floor beside him. The troll wriggled and made a face at her, scrunching up its small button nose and eyes. Aarno felt her proximity as he followed her gaze to the wrinkles on the troll's compact face, its bushy brows and the hair coming out of its nostrils. Erja laughed.

It spat at her.

She recoiled.

Aarno picked up the troll by the scruff of the neck, hauled it into the adjoining room and locked the door. His forehead was beaded with sweat and his brows were drawn together, as if struggling to contain some great suppressed force.

He sank into the sofa, his whole body shaking. Felt a soft hand on his shoulder and flinched. Erja's eyes sought his, concerned. He looked away.

Erja frowned but said nothing.

She leaned against the opposite end of the sofa, stretched out her legs and eyed him through her lashes. "Where did you *find* them?"

"They live in the rocks all around here. Haven't you heard the stories?"

"The stories," she scoffed. "I thought they were just old wives' tales to keep children from wandering off. Or our wild imaginations, giving life to stones. I never took them literally."

"They're real," Aarno said, looking straight ahead. As real as the darkness hiding just below the surface of him.

"There have been disappearances. Especially long ago. Young girls who went walking and never came back. People said the trolls took them. I used to think they just fell down the rocks, got stuck in a crevasse or something. Now I understand there's more to it."

Erja looked away from him. "How awful."

"Yes," Aarno said. He lowered his head.

They were silent a while. In his mind, Aarno saw a young woman, dressed in cream homespun, picking her way across rocks. Her expression of curiosity, lured forward by strange music. The hand that held the poisoned wine, emerging from a dark space, with its dirt-encrusted fingernails. A rough ceramic goblet. The full red lips, sipping. The slow entranced walk into a crevice in the rocks. The passage to an underground chamber. Wilting, growing pale in the dark. Condemned to cook soup for a room full of quarrelsome trolls.

He looked at Erja. She seemed so far away from him, so separate.

Part of him yearned to reach for her hand and squeeze it. The other part wanted to protect her from himself. Could he ever, in good conscience, allow himself to get close to her? His last outburst was like a candle flame compared to his former eruptions. If she ever saw him *really* angry…

"It's probably better if you stay away from me," Aarno said, looking straight ahead at the wall.

"Oh, come on, you're not that bad. Not like—" she shook her head as if shaking out a memory.

"I don't think I can be the man you want. I have…hidden craters. I could explode…"

"Aarno," Erja said in a softer tone. "I accept you for who you are."

You wouldn't if you knew, Aarno thought, but he said nothing.

She traced the long, jagged scar down his forearm. "What happened?"

"Nothing." He pulled his arm away and sat without speaking.

Erja broke the silence. "So what are you going to do with them?"

"Use them in my films."

She gave him a weird look. "They're wild creatures, Aarno."

He looked at her and saw something in her had hardened. He'd missed his chance, again. He felt a stab of self-loathing.

"What will you do then—just *leave* them there, trapped in a room without fresh air or space to roam or—"

"I've blacked out the windows to mimic the cold dark places

of their natural habitat," Aarno said testily. "I'll keep feeding them till they get used to me and start to take food from my hands. Then I'll coax them out. I'll train them in table manners until they can drink tea with me."

Erja laughed a derisive snort. "You think you can tame them? They'll never be tamed. Just like men will never tame women through marriage."

"Woah," Aarno said, sitting back. "What do you have against marriage?"

"It's a mechanism of control. The whole institution should be scrapped."

"How can you say it's so bad? *You've* never been married."

She looked at him through long, mascara-stiff lashes. "Actually, I have."

"*What?*"

She sat very still, looking ahead at the painting of a lighthouse on the wall. "There was a man I loved, once. But marrying him was kind of like lifting a spell—the love wore off and for the first time the ugly contours of his real self came to light."

"That's a harsh thing to say."

"He was actually a horrible person. He would go on manic drinking sprees, become violent, then sink into bouts of depression. He threatened me with an axe once—"

Aarno stiffened. "I'm sorry to hear that. Maybe others have happier marriages…"

"Maybe they do," Erja said in a bleak voice. "But I doubt it."

They sat in silence. Aarno heard the ticking of the clock and stared at the lights of the streetlamps through the window. He wondered if he would become the same monster as her ex-husband. If Erja was doomed to repeat her mistakes.

Without warning, she took his hand in hers. His heart beat faster.

She looked at him, and his instinct was to turn away, to close his tired eyes and bury his face in the cushions, but instead he return-ed her gaze. Saw the facets of her eyes, grey as pigeon wings, and the little clumps of eyelashes where her mascara had stuck together.

Then the gap was closing rapidly between them and her lips were on his—softer than he would have dared to imagine—and he let himself surrender to the kiss.

It softened him. He realized all the hardness he saw in her was also in him. Perhaps he had absorbed it from the rocky lands where the trolls dwelt.

He placed his arm on her back, afraid she would retreat, afraid to hurt her, but she pulled her body closer to him. Where the edges of their bodies met, he felt as if he was melting, like a river flowing into a lake.

Yet if she discovered the dark deed that weighed on his soul...

In reaction, his body jerked backwards.

"What's wrong?" she asked.

His eyes became far away, like the closing inner eyelids of a snake.

He shook his head. "I...nothing."

She kissed him. He let her lips soothe him. Let her kisses take away the doubt that coiled within him like barbed wire. Perhaps she could transform him, like a point of light reaching into a long dark tunnel. Perhaps she could illuminate the vast hollow space within him. But no—he was too dark.

"I've decided," he said when their lips parted and she rested her head on his shoulder.

"Decided what?" she asked, dream-soft.

"To release them."

~ * ~

Aarno rubbed his eyes and returned his hands to the steering wheel. Sleek grey buildings slid past, punctuated by pine forest. He crossed the highway bridge over the Vantaa, flat water turned mono-chrome by a heavy leaden sky.

He gazed out of the window as grey and brown flashes of buildings gave way to the brittle limbs of bare trees and frozen fields. Looked at the hard line of Erja's chin and searched for fissures in her porcelain face. Should he tell her? He was so close to her, but at the same time as far away as the flat line ahead.

Streaks of cloud darkened on the horizon. Rocks stretched, bumpy as a dragon's back, amongst pine trees and swaths of blue water. Erja sat with her head to the side, gazing out the window. Neither spoke. Aarno gazed ahead, fierce eyes on the road. He felt as if he had crossed into a dim, misty land and all sense of direction had vanished. Felt the sobering effect of the sky like slate above them. For all their closeness, her mind remained impenetrable.

Aarno drove to an outcropping of rocks, stopped the car and opened the boot. Inside sat a single cardboard box, wrapped with twine and bulging at the sides. Erja hefted it in her arms and began to walk across the stony, frozen ground.

She cast a glance behind her and smiled into the camera as Aarno filmed. She'd been home since and changed into skintight white trousers and a puffy, pale blue jacket. Her damp hair smelled of mandarins. Now she wore it slicked along her head and pulled high into a thin rope behind her. She looked fresh and he imagined she had slept a few hours. He had tried to, but circles of thoughts, doubts and fears had kept him awake.

It was late afternoon and the sun was waning.

As Aarno followed Erja with the camera, he picked a path over uneven rocks. His breath came in visible puffs.

He pointed to a place between two rocks and they walked there. There was silence, except for the crunch of their boots. The clouds bunched together like a mountain king's eyebrows.

"Here's the place."

"The same place you found them?"

"The same."

"Good." She set down the box and took a knife from her pocket. As she sawed through the coarse twine binding the box, the twine snapped and the flaps sprang open.

A coarse-haired head poked out. Small eyes blinked, adjusting to the steel grey light. The head jerked towards Erja. She sat unmoving, a faint smile frozen to her lips.

The second troll popped up, resting hands with stubby fingers on the rim of the box. It took quick, cautious looks.

The first troll sprang from the box and bounded across the open ground, its hairy flat feet gripping the rocks with surprising agility. The second hesitated. It lifted its head up and produced an inquisitive sound.

The first troll gave a high-pitched response.

The second replied with a burst of noise, like a tinny strange laugh. It leapt out of the box and the other laughed with it. As they scurried across the rocks in short, rapid strides, their grey-brown bodies blended into the landscape and were gone.

Aarno felt a sense of loss, and realized he was enamored with them even as he feared to reveal them. Like his own shadows. But to release them was to gain a liberating lightness.

He panned the camera to Erja, who cast him a smile that spread as slowly as butter dropped into hot porridge.

Aarno turned off the camera.

"Well done," he said.

"Thanks." Erja shrugged. "It wasn't much."

He sat down on a rock beside her. Took her gloved hand in his and squeezed it.

"To me it means a lot."

"It's best like this," Erja said, gazing out at the rocks.

"You're right," Aarno replied.

Aarno could not find words to break the silence. He studied the rocks, afraid to meet Erja's eyes.

He would have to keep his distance from her. Couldn't risk her getting attached, finding out about him. The attacks, the sudden rages. The action he could not forgive.

She moved closer to him, and he felt the nearness of her body through his coat.

"So will you tell me how it happened?"

"How what happened?"

"The scar."

Aarno drew a long, deep breath. The dark memory rose in his throat as if ready to spill out. If it ended his chances with Erja, it was probably for the best. At least he would stop hiding it then. He closed his eyes and began to speak.

"There was a woman in my life once. I loved her. But we had an argument, I don't even remember what it was now but something came out of me—something horrible and vicious and I grabbed a knife and slashed her across the leg but she fought back—"

Behind his eyelids, he saw the terror and shock on her face, heard the screams, the roar as she flew at him, the flash of a knife blade. Saw the blood in a livid red arc against the bright white walls and floor. Heard the door slamming as she ran.

"And she left her mark." He looked down at his arm. Saw himself, fuming in silence and bleeding as he scrubbed. No matter how much he scrubbed, he could never get the stains out so he moved. To a blank slate apartment where he kept everything pristine and the old was replaced by the new.

He pressed a gloved hand to the thick, quilted coat of his right arm. Remembered how he'd clamped his hand on it, but the blood kept flowing, out between his fingers and onto the floor.

"A reminder not to loose the beast within me."

"What happened to the woman?"

"She went somewhere. Far away. I never saw her again. I admitted myself to a hospital. Couldn't trust myself to get close to anyone."

"I understand."

A pause between them.

She placed a hand on his back and he realized he was shaking.

"So now you know. Why aren't you running?"

Erja gave a light laugh. "Because you're just like me. When my marriage first ended, I also held back, afraid of the pain of hurting someone new."

"But how did it end?"

She pulled her bottom lip inward. "With great difficulty. The first time I left, he came after me. We had a terrible fight and I escaped. To hide in the anonymity of Helsinki. To start a new life where I would be safe."

"But where did you live before?"

"Far to the north in a place I cannot speak the name of. The first years I kept to myself. Until the pain faded and I decided to stop denying myself. That love was worth it. I'm willing to take the risk with you."

"Why?"

"Because I believe in you."

Aarno frowned. "But my moods are too volatile—"

"With the right balance, they will stabilize."

Aarno stared at the rocks ahead. "But you can't trust me, I could—"

"Let the small light within you overcome the dark."

Aarno turned to look at her. "You really think so?"

"What happens when you shine light on shadows?"

"They disappear."

"Exactly." Erja smiled. "And in the light they cease to be so terrible. Do you want to close the door on the past? Step into the bright light of a new beginning?"

"I do," Aarno said, realizing as he said it. "More than

anything."

She kissed his cold cheek, and he couldn't help but turn. Felt the hot breath from her mouth before she kissed him. Despite his mind saying *get up, walk away*, he leaned forward.

Light was leaking out of the sky, the landscape returning to darkness. If he could love her, despite his flaws—if she could heal from the scars of her marriage—his lips pressed hers, forming a singular *If*.

As the sky darkened, two silhouettes merged. They erased the lines between them to form a new shape. A single shadow.

~ * ~ * ~

Malina Douglas weaves stories that fuse the fantastic and the real. She explores ruins, caves and jagged rocks that could be the homes of monsters, ghosts or trolls. She was a finalist in the Blackwater Press Contest and her publications include *N is for Nautical* by Red Cape Publishing, *Wyldblood*, *Sanitarium IV*, *Opia*, T*he Periodical Forlorn*, *Parabnormal*, *Flash Fiction Online*, *The Antipodean*, *Metamorphose V2*, *Rhythm & Bone*, *Eye to the Telescope: The Sea*, and the *Land Beyond the World* Magazine. Two highly commended stories were published in the anthologies *When it is Time* and *All Those Things You Thought Never Mattered*. Other anthologies include *Sea Glass Hearts*, *Dragons* by Black Hare Press, *Because That's Where Your Heart Is*, *The Monsters We Forgot Vol. II*, and *Gothic Blue Books Vol 6: A Krampus Carol*. She can be found @iridescentwords or at iridescentwords.com.

Unborn

Katie Kent

12th September 2022

At last, I've done it! I've just invented time travel. I had tears in my eyes when I finally cracked it, and the first time in ages, they were actually happy tears. Tomorrow, I carry out my mission.

"Christopher, dinner's ready!"

I put my pen down, shut my diary and shove it at the bottom of the drawer.

The love in my mom's eyes as she serves up my plate of spaghetti bolognese reminds me of the reason I've devoted so many years of my life to this in the first place. I've wanted to die for much of my life, but I know that my suicide would crush her. I'm all she has left, after my dad walked out on us when I was 10, and her parents died of Covid right at the start of the pandemic. But I'm not willing to keep living, either. It hurts too much.

The thought my torment is almost over brings a smile to my face.

Mom's eyes light up. "You look happy."

She knows I've had mental health problems for most of my life, but she doesn't know the full extent of my depression. I know she feels guilty—Dad used to knock me around, before he left—but it wasn't her fault. He did the same to her. When he hit me, she'd shout at him to stop, but then he'd take it out on her instead. I used to lie under my bed, my hands clamped to my ears as she screamed. Him walking out was a blessing, but those years had affected both of us. I grew up with no confidence, and a constant voice in my head telling me I wasn't good enough.

"Is there a girl?" She winks at me and nudges me with her shoulder.

I roll my eyes. "No, mom. There's no girl." If only she knew the truth. She would probably accept my sexuality, but how can I tell her I'm into boys, when I can't even accept it myself? It's not like I'd be able to talk to a boy, even if I did meet one. My social anxiety sees to that, just like how it stops me having any friends.

"What, then?" she asks.

I just shrug as I twist a strand of spaghetti around my fork. "Can't I just be happy?"

Her smile gets wider. "Of course you can, sweetheart. I just can't remember the last time you told me you were happy. It's nice to see."

"Do you think we could watch a film tonight, Mom?" Even though I'm happy to have found a way out of this pain, there's still a lump in my throat when I think about this being our last night together.

"That would be lovely." She won't remember all this, of course —how can she remember a son who was never born? —but for a moment, a stab of guilt hits me right in the stomach. I dismiss it straight away. I'm doing this for her as much as I am for me. I know she would have had a happier life if she hadn't met *him*.

13th September 2022

Today is the day. It's finally arrived. When my alarm went off this morning, a feeling of relief hit me. I can't remember the last time I didn't feel that pit of emptiness when I opened my eyes.

"See you later, darling." Mom bends forward and kisses me on the cheek.

"Love you," I say.

She smiles again. "I love you, too." Mom puts a brave face on things, but I know she's just as unhappy as I am. I know my mental health problems stress her out. I heard her on the phone to her friend a few months ago. "I just don't know how to help him," she'd said. "He just seems so down. The doctor put him on medication, but it doesn't seem to be doing anything. I know I've failed him."

Her words just made me more determined to find the solution. I've always been smart—the one positive thing I got from my dad. In one of his more lucid moments, when he was sober, he'd said he believed time travel would actually be invented one day —that it wasn't just science fiction. I'd forgotten all about that, until I stumbled upon his scribbled notes hidden in the basement when I was 13 years old. I'd dropped the notebook in shock when I'd realized it was rough plans for a time machine. I almost took them straight to Mom; but then it dawned on me they could be the answer to my prayers.

When she's left for her evening class, I get up from the sofa immediately, then descend the stairs to the basement. Luckily, Mom never comes in here anymore—she'd found Dad in here with another woman one day, and now it just brings back bad memories. It's meant I've been able to work on the time machine without fear of her discovering it. Every Tuesday night since I was 13, and weekends when she goes out with friends. It's been painstaking work, but as I gaze at the handheld machine on top of the bookcase, I know the 4 years of hard work have been worth it.

I already know the machine works; obviously, I had to test it. Mom doesn't know but I skipped school yesterday, putting the finishing touches to the machine so I'd be ready this evening. I went back by 10 minutes, hiding behind the pile of boxes and watching myself picking up the machine and programming the time coordinates in. Checking my watch, I verified it was exactly 10 minutes before I'd left. A thrill had gone through me and I could hardly wait to get started on my mission, but I knew I'd regret it if I didn't have one last night with Mom.

Now, the moment is finally here. I wipe my sweaty palms on my jeans. This is the right thing to do, I'm sure of it. No more pain and torture. No more sadness in Mom's eyes. But that doesn't make it easy.

Luckily, my dad had told me the story of how he'd met Mom several times. I would watch as she flinched, but at least it meant I knew exactly when to travel to. June 14, 2002 at 9am. He'd been coming out of a café, rushing as he was late for work. She'd been walking past and whilst he was checking his watch he hadn't seen her, and had banged right into her, knocking her bag to the floor. "It was love at first sight," he'd said, each time he told the story. "Isn't that right, Anne?" She'd just smiled and nodded, touching her fingers to the bruises on her face.

I take a deep breath. Soon, all that will be erased. Soon, I will be erased. Soon, Mom will have a new life. I stop for a few seconds to imagine it. Maybe she'll have a better husband, one who treats her the way she deserves. Maybe she'll have a better job, one that is more rewarding than stacking shelves at a supermarket. Maybe she'll have a better kid, one who doesn't constantly wish he was dead and struggle to speak to anyone. Hopefully, she'll be happy. I program the date and location into the panel on the side of the time machine, then press the big, green button, and shut my eyes. Seconds later the machine powers down, and I know I've arrived. I drop to my knees, waiting for the nausea to pass, then straighten myself back up and look around.

The bright sunlight makes my eyes sting. I'm in a field and, as I hoped, no one is around to witness me appearing out of thin air, other than a couple of cows. One of them moos as I rub my eyes. Gripping the machine in my hand like I'm carrying a torch—I was glad I'd figured out a way of putting the technology into a handheld device rather than having to hide a big machine—I start the walk into town.

My watch tells me it's 8:45am as the sign above the café comes into view. Perfect timing—I didn't want to arrive right at the last minute. I park myself on the corner, but curiosity gets the better of me, and I find myself pushing the door open and entering the café.

I see him immediately, sitting alone at a table near the door. He flicks through a newspaper, and sips from a cup of coffee. He's wearing a suit and looks much more put-together than I remember him, in the future. I can see why Mom fell for him.

"You want something?" he asks, as he looks up.

"N…no, thanks," I stutter.

He nods. "Quit staring at me, then."

Feeling myself blush, I rush back out through the door and stand at the corner once more, checking my watch again. It's 8:50am. I scan the streets with my eyes, looking for any sign of Mom. I don't know which side she'll appear from.

"I can't let you do this, Chris."

I jump, shielding my eyes from the sun as I look up into the face of the speaker.

I sigh. "L…leave me alone, Chris." I recognize myself immediately. I have more wrinkles, there's a tinge of grey to my hair and I've grown a beard, but there's no mistaking that face. It's the one I've cursed so many times in the mirror over the years. The one I've wished was never born.

He shakes his head. "Uh-uh. You know what this means, right? Me being here?"

"I…I make it. I don't die." A pit of despair opens up inside me, and I clench my fists.

His expression becomes more sympathetic. "I know how that makes you feel. But you were never going to die. You just would have faded out of existence."

"You know that's all I've ever wanted." My breathing becomes shallow. "For them not to have met. For me not to have been born. I've devoted four years of my life to this."

"I know." He puts his hand on my arm. "Don't forget I was you, once. I was sure this was what I wanted. But someone made me see the error of my ways. And one day you'll stand here in my place, preventing the past you from making this mistake."

"Y…you can't stop me from doing this." My hands shake. "I have free will. I can make my own decisions."

"That's all true. But I know you won't do it."

I want to slap his face as he stands there in front of me, arms crossed casually, smiling at me. I can't ever imagine being this confident guy. "How old are you?" I ask.

"I just turned forty."

"I bet you're going to tell me that cliché now about how life begins at forty." I look around him for any sign of Mom—there's still time to stop this.

"I wouldn't dare. I know how much that would have pissed me off," he says.

"What, then? How do you think you're going to talk me out of something I've planned for years?"

He looks me up and down. I wonder if I bring back bad memories. It's hard to believe he used to be me. "I can't pretend to have it all figured out, Chris. All I can say is: I love life these days. Wouldn't you like to be able to say that, one day?"

"Sure." It's what I want, more than anything. "But I've tried. It never gets any better."

"*Have* you tried, though?" His eyes pierce mine. "Have you really? Have you tried therapy, for example?"

"You know I can't." My hands start to shake. "I…I can't talk to a stranger."

He shrugs. "You're talking to me, aren't you?"

I huff. "You're hardly a stranger." I like how he doesn't bring up my stuttering.

"Why don't you try talking to me, then? I mean, really *talking*. About the things you're too afraid to tell anyone else."

I look at my watch, feeling my stomach tighten. It's 8:55am.

"You can spare a few minutes." He leans back against the wall, watching me.

I press my fingers to my forehead. "I don't know where to start."

"How about you tell me what's led you to make this decision, then?"

I look down at the ground, scuffing the pavement with my trainer. "I hate myself."

"Why?"

I look into his eyes. "You know why."

"Humor me."

I take a deep breath. "Dad hit me. I have no friends, and I find it hard to talk to people." I feel my cheeks turn red. "And I... I..."

"Say it," he urges.

I take a deep breath. "I'm...I'm gay." My voice is little more than a whisper.

He gives me a reassuring smile. "Well done, Chris."

I train my eyes upon the door of the café. I'm so close to achieving my plan. "I've got nothing to live for. Only Mom, and you know she'd be better off if none of this had happened."

"Well, how about you live for me?"

"You?" I scoff.

"Yes, me." His eyes don't leave my face. "I know no one would know if I suddenly faded out of existence. My husband would never have met me, and my kids would never have been born. But that doesn't make it any better."

I gawp at him. "Husband?" I whisper. "Kids?"

"Yes, Chris." He smiles. "It turns out we're not unlovable after all. It turns out we're capable of forming a relationship with someone."

"Are you playing with me?" I ask. "Is this just some lie to talk me out of my plan?"

"It's the truth." He pulls his phone out of his back pocket and shows me a photo. The phone is so thin I can barely see it, but the photo hovers over the surface. There's the older me, and next to him is another guy. He's handsome—clean shaven, with blond hair and blue eyes. We are smiling at each other tenderly, our arms around each other, and in front of us stand a little boy and a slightly older girl. They are unmistakably our children—with my dark hair and his eyes.

I hand the phone back with tears in my eyes. "How can this be possible?" The idea this could be mine one day—it's almost too much to hope.

"I told you," he says, kindly. "I'm not saying it's going to be easy. But we survive. More than that—we thrive." He puts his hands on my shoulders and looks into my eyes. "You've got this."

I turn as a young woman with dark hair walks past in a yellow cardigan and white skirt. *Mom.* She looks more carefree than I've ever seen her, the pain I'm so used to seeing in her eyes missing. It takes everything in me not to reach out and grab her arm, stop her meeting Dad, like I've dreamt about doing for years.

"How can I put her through all that?" I ask older Chris.

He sighs. "I used to ask myself that all the time. Could I have intervened some other way? But you know the answer to that. She's our mom, and he's our dad, whether we like it or not. Any attempt to change the path of their relationship would endanger our existence. It would endanger the existence of *our* children. We have to let it play out naturally."

"But she's so unhappy." I can almost hear her screams in my ears. I haven't told her I hear her at night, just like I never tell her about the nightmares that plague my own sleep. We skirt around each other, neither one of us willing to admit the depth of our pain to the other.

"We're not responsible for his behavior," he says. "But you might want to start by being honest with her. Maybe suggest some family counselling." He shrugs. "Just an idea."

The clock tower starts to chime, and I almost hold my breath, counting up to nine in my head. As the clock falls silent we both watch Dad walk out of the café, his eyes glued to his watch. We see him bang into Mom, and stop to apologize. Then they stare into each other's eyes. He reaches out for her hand, brings it to his mouth and kisses it. She giggles.

Older Chris turns away. "It's not any easier to watch the second time around. When I think about what he's going to put her through…what he's going to put us through." His mouth is set in a tight line. "But there are good things in store, for both of you. I hope that will keep you going."

~ * ~

Back in my basement, I put the time machine away in a drawer. I have no intention of using it again any time soon, but I know I'll need it when I'm 40. My whole existence depends on it. If any of us mess up… I shake my head. The future lies ahead. For now, I just need to get through the next few years, one day at a time.

"You're up late, sweetie." It's 11pm when Mom walks through the door. "Everything okay?"

I look at her, remembering the past version of her, the one with the happy smile. I look forward to seeing that version of her again some day. And not just her—me, too. It would be nice to see my face in the mirror without that haunted look.

"Mom." I reach across for her hand, blinking away tears. "We need to talk."

~ * ~ * ~

Katie Kent is a writer of fiction and non-fiction living in the UK with her wife, cat and dog. She likes to write stories, mostly for a YA audience, particularly about LGTBQ characters, mental illness, time travel and the future—sometimes all in the same story! Her stories have been published in *Youth Imagination, Limeoncello, Breath and Shadow* and *Northern Gravy*, amongst others, and in a handful of anthologies including *The Trouble with Time Travel, Summer of Speculation: Catastrophe, Growth* and *My Heart to Yours*. Her non-fiction, mostly mental health-related, can be found in publications including *The Mighty, You & Me Magazine, Ailment, OC87 Recovery Diaries* and *Feels Zine*.

You can visit her website at katiekentwriter.com/.

This Man Paul

RF Thomas

Every man has a breaking point and this man Paul was within an inch of that dark and razor-thin line. He wasn't near a tearful collapse, or the so-called nervous breakdown, but right at the actual edge of giving up. For real and for keeps.

Just now he stood in front of a hallway mirror, a body-length one with good lighting that he always preferred because it made him look a little slimmer than he knew he really was. A frowning face of disapproval reflected back, for all he could see was ugly and wrong. A balding head atop a body turning to early middle-age softness.

"You have no friends. No job. No prospects." He watched the man in the mirror tick off these points on his fingers. The face scowled. "And you are almost two hundred thousand dollars in debt." His wife had finally lost her long battle with cancer, and he dreaded the years ahead of climbing from the pit of medical debt. The thought was nearly unbearable. His scowl grew into a glower of abnegation. "You are alone and without help."

Paul was very near a final decision. He took a deep breath, turned sharply and went to the telephone.

"Barb? Paul. I know it's short notice but I was wondering if you wouldn't mind having JoJo for the night. I just had a call from an old buddy whose wife is in the hospital. Up near Milwaukee. I'd like to drive up there this afternoon, probably be back tomorrow before dark." The lie came easily, out of nowhere. He suddenly felt confident and inspired.

His mother-in-law said of course she wouldn't mind, as he knew she would. Barb jumped at any chance to spend time with her only granddaughter.

Josephine was six and had Down syndrome. Everyone called her JoJo. She was blonde, roly-poly, and her innocent, slightly drooly smile was contagious everywhere it shined.

Paul drove blankly through the busy afternoon traffic, his daughter buckled safely into the back. He didn't have to check the mirror to know she was staring out at the early December drizzle with cheerful interest. He was keeping a tight grip on his thoughts, not allowing himself to go in any direction very far. Keeping it very superficial. I will think it out after I drop JoJo off, he promised himself. But he was beginning to feel very grim indeed. Is this the last time you will ever see your daughter? Of course not! But what if it is? No. But it could be. No.

It was a strain maintaining normal appearances during his goodbyes—Paul felt like an unconvincing actor in a bad play. He drove south after leaving JoJo at her grandmother's and headed towards the Skyway and its High Bridge. It was the tallest bridge around, and even though he wasn't having any sort of clear inner dialogue, his vague notions were taking form. He began muttering to himself. "Has to be maybe ten stories high. High enough." He drove faster, sensing the approach of something that would matter. Heading towards some sort of resolution, maybe even some sort of relief.

Lost within himself, he not only failed to notice the thickening drizzle on his windshield turning to ice, he was also late seeing the red light. He hit the brakes much too hard, causing the car to slew around. That's the moment everything changed for this man Paul, because his slide carried him into the intersection, where a garbage truck traveling at nearly 40 mph slammed his car into a violent, spinning, glass-shattering stop.

Sirens, flashing lights, an ambulance, chaos in the emergency room, phone calls, the waiting, the worrying, the confusion. And finally, the conversation. Broken ribs, broken arm, internal bruising, concussion, possibly severe. Worst of all: unconscious and unresponsive.

~ * ~

This man Paul stood at the side of a road that descended into a long, green valley. He had no memory of how he had come to be here, nor did it seem strange. The valley went on as far as he could see and the road ran straight along its bottom. Looking down, he noticed an ancient, weathered road marker with faded chiseled letters. He bent for a closer look.

"Damascus?" His voice was a dry whisper. Feeling self-conscious, as if he were being watched, he said in a louder, stronger voice, "What is this place?"

He didn't expect an answer of course and so when a voice

spoke from behind, he jerked around in surprise.

"This is a place to lay down one's burdens." The voice belonged to a tall man with long, dark hair, a brilliant white smile, and sparkling eyes. He exuded a confidence that was almost otherworldly. Paul felt the absurd urge to bow, but resisted it.

The tall man gestured to the thick grass at the side of the road. "Why not lay aside your burdens and rest awhile?"

Paul nodded, it sounded like a wonderful idea. He became aware of a balmy breeze, and insects buzzing, and the sun was warm and it felt like a lazy spring day. Why not rest here? His limbs were heavy and so he took a step into the grass, then another, and lay down and closed his eyes.

When he woke, he was without a sense of time or place, but then he remembered the tall man. He stood up and saw the road and felt drawn to it.

Almost against his will, he went to the road and began walking. The going was downhill and easy at first. But he noticed a peculiar thing as he went. The sky darkened from blue to gray, and the air grew thick, and it became hard to breathe. Paul soon became weary.

He stopped, and stood dumbly. What was he even doing here? And then he heard a tiny, almost imagined whisper that seemed to come from inside his mind. *You must go on.* It sounded stern, that tiny whisper.

But it was too hard. He didn't want to walk anymore. He didn't even want to think. He stumbled off the road and was grateful once again for the thick, soft grass. He went down into it and slumber took him.

~ * ~

Paul's first day in the hospital came to an end. Nothing had changed. Vital signs stabilized. Unconscious, inert, tubes and monitors, clean sheets and bandages and a hospital bed.

~ * ~

Paul woke up to another sunny day, and wasn't surprised to see the tall man standing nearby, watching him intently. Then the man smiled his confident smile. "Stay here Paul. No more worries, no more weariness. It's your choice."

Paul didn't answer. He went to the road and began walking.

He didn't know why. He didn't particularly want to walk it. He wanted to just curl up and forget. Yet something pulled him along, just enough to put one step in front of the last.

He was on the valley floor, flat and level. And as before, the sky darkened as he went. But now the valley narrowed and closed in around him. The ground grew rocky and he stumbled often. His limbs were heavy and his breathing labored. What was the point? Why go on at all?

Then the stern whisper again, a little louder this time. *You must go on. Soon it will be time to make your choice.*

His world had shrunken to a dim, grey place. Just the rocky road and him. Sweat rolled down his face, his legs burned, his heart was heavy, and he just wanted to close his eyes and forget.

Paul shook his head in denial. "I don't have to do anything." He staggered to the edge of the road and there was the thick, soft grass waiting. He closed his eyes and forgetfulness washed over him.

~ * ~

The end of Paul's second day in the hospital saw no change. His mother-in-law wanted to bring JoJo to visit. She told the doctors it might make a difference and help Paul recover. The doctors didn't think it was a good idea yet.

~ * ~

Paul opened his eyes to the blue sky above. He rose from the grass and saw he was almost across the valley now. In the distance the road rose sharply and disappeared over the top. The tall man was there of course, smiling and confident.

"Have you had enough yet Paul? Ready to give in?"

Paul felt troubled. It was difficult to look the tall man in the face, and so he dropped his eyes and for a split second he caught something wrong with the man's feet. Paul blinked, and saw only normal feet again. He shook his head, but did not answer the man. Fear descended over him.

"Why not decide just this once to do what you want? Do what is good for you. Why go on, when there is only suffering ahead?"

Before he could stop himself, Paul blurted a question, even as he feared the answer. "Who are you?"

The tall man's smile grew. It went from *you can trust me* to *you finally caught me.*

"In this place my name is The Morning Star."

An appalling rush of confirmation surged through Paul's mind. He tried to raise his eyes but was unable to. "You're the Devil, aren't you?"

And then everything changed. The figure next to him shimmered and darkened and grew in stature. Terrified, Paul dropped to his knees and as the thing next to him faded away, Paul's last image was of two feet blurring and becoming enormous cloven hooves.

A horror grew in Paul, threatening to overwhelm his senses. But then all thought was completely swept away because all around him the valley and the grass and the breeze and the sunlight disappeared. The truth was revealed now, and behind him a vast plain stretched to infinity. All around were countless figures, pathetic, cringing, anguished, on their knees, or crawling, or lying sobbing. The road was still there ahead of him, a short, steep section. The darkness grew.

~ * ~

Barb brought JoJo with her on day three, convinced the staff to allow her to bring the child into her father's room. At first JoJo was subdued, her eyes big and solemn. She didn't know what to think when she saw her father in his hospital bed. But Barb encouraged JoJo to talk to Daddy, to hold his hand and just talk to him.

~ * ~

Paul stood paralyzed, numb, afraid to move and be noticed and become a permanent part of this place. Then the stern voice came, and filled his mind.

"It is time to make your choice Paul. Choose for yourself, or for another."

Paul swallowed. "Another?"

"The child."

"The child? What child?"

"You have a daughter Paul. And she is very special."

Paul was dumbfounded. Amazed, "Special. How?"

"All children are special."

Paul squeezed his eyes shut, closing out the terrible landscape. He knew who the speaker was now. And so he asked the question all of humanity would have asked, had they been there.

"What does it all mean? What am I to do?"

"There are no hidden secrets. Love one another. Help others before yourself."

This man Paul, with a tremendous effort, took one step, then another, and then he was running. He lurched up the slope atop legs that felt like wooden stilts, each step sending shards of pain. He could not breathe, his vision was dimming, he could feel the powerful and growing hold the place had on him.

And then he was at the top. He stopped, hands on knees, gasping, retching. The road ended in a narrow door-like arch. An arch that was filled with light.

Beside it stood the outline of a man, and he knew it was the owner of the stern whisper. Paul lowered his eyes and could not speak nor move.

"Well done, Paul. You have been given another chance."

~ * ~

On the third day, Paul awoke, changed. He had only a fleeting, shadowy memory of the valley. But there was something new in him. A growing sense of deep resolve.

He opened his eyes and turned his head. There by his side sat his daughter and the girl's grandmother. They both reacted to his movement, looking up with wide, red eyes. Then JoJo smiled and threw herself across Paul's chest in a ferocious hug.

"I knew the bad man wouldn't keep you, daddy! Knew you'd come back!"

~ * ~

Paul and JoJo were going to Whizzer's for dinner. Whizzer's was JoJo's favorite place. They hadn't often been able to afford nights out, but when they did, it was Whizzer's pizza. Whizzer's gave customers a free oversized cupcake on their birthdays and sang a hyped-up version of Happy Birthday. Because the manager was a nice man, JoJo got the special treatment every time they went, birthday or no.

Now, a week after finally coming home from the hospital, they were going to dinner. Christmas was coming soon and there would not be many presents, so Paul wanted to give his daughter a treat.

She had been so excited all day she hadn't even asked where mom was. Not even once.

~ * ~

Kylie was 17, self-absorbed, and had tired, sore feet. This was her first full week as a waitress at Whizzer's and she just wanted to make it to the end of her shift. She hated having to come to work five nights a week after school and she hated her friends knowing she had a job even more. Tomorrow was her first day off and at least she could hang out at the mall and not deal with all these stupid people with their loud, stupid kids.

The worst was table 5. She knew already from experience there was no tip coming from table 5. The man had one arm in a sling, was dressed in cheap, worn clothes and the little girl not dressed much better. The man looked frail and sickly and had a homemade haircut. Plus he had what looked like food stains on his shirt. No watch, no jewelry, and now to make things worse, her manager was gathering a few of them to sing their version of Happy Birthday to the little girl and Kylie figured it probably wasn't really her birthday.

So they brought the little special needs girl her chocolate cupcake and sang their song and everyone thought it was the best thing ever. Except Kylie. She walked back to the counter on the edges of her feet, gingerly trying to avoid the painful spots on her heels. She rolled her eyes at her manager when she heard him say, "They look so happy."

Whatever. Except he was serious. "No, really. Just look at them and tell me they aren't happy." Her manager was a huge softie. But dutifully Kylie turned around and looked. And then something happened. For the first time all week, maybe the first time ever, she really saw people as persons. All the distractions of learning a new job, all her complaints and worries and problems fell away in an instant and the good part of Kylie, the part deep inside that her mother and perhaps one or two friends knew about, really saw the two at the table for who they were.

And her manager was right. They were happy. There was something very moving about their faces, now that she took notice. Kylie stood there and forgot about her feet and just stared. Two people obviously not well off, and one of them with special needs, sitting in a cheap pizza place a few days before Christmas, and they had on their faces the purest expressions of peace and happiness she had ever seen. Their faces shone with it. Beyond what her young life had ever experienced. And her heart was changed.

Ripple.

Frank came home from work tired and hungry as usual. And with a hundred things on his mind, things that needed done at work before the holiday break. He was starting to feel stressed even more than usual. At least they had gotten their Christmas bonus checks today.

He smelled dinner as soon as he came in the house and by the time he hung up his coat and took off his shoes, his stomach was rumbling. Into the kitchen, kiss the wife, noticed the empty chair.

"Where's Kylie?"

His wife smiled and her eyes twinkled. "She ate already. She is spending a few hours volunteering at the soup kitchen."

Frank just stared.

"The one off of Delaware." As if that clarified anything.

Frank shook his head. "Our Kylie?"

"Yes dear. Our Kylie."

"Volunteering. At a soup kitchen."

"She said she saw some poor people at work today that inspired her."

Frank sat down at the table and his wife went to the stove to dish out dinner. He cocked his head and turned to look at her. "Huh."

Later that night, lying in bed, Frank and his wife discussed Christmas, gifts to buy, and how to spend his bonus. They also discussed Kylie.

The next day at lunch, Frank went to the bank and withdrew three one-hundred-dollar bills and then drove to the nearest Mega Box store.

He hung out near the cash registers, pressed in the crush of the Christmas crowd, holding a single pack of gum, looking for a target. And then he spotted one coming. A cart full of toys and clothes, pushed by a harried young woman with two small kids trailing her. She was dressed in cheap clothes and so were the kids. They all looked thin, but the children were smiling and excited.

Frank pushed his way towards her and just as she got in one of the long lines to check out, he put a hand on her shoulder.

"Excuse me, mind if I cut in quick?" He held up his pack of gum, and looked down at her cart, packed full and over the top.

The woman nodded and Frank murmured his thanks. After a long wait, he got to the cashier and as he paid for his gum, he leaned in close and whispered, "This is for the lady behind me. I want to pay for her cart. Put whatever is left over in the charity bucket outside." He slid the three one-hundred-dollar bills into the startled clerk's hand.

Ripple.

Angie was tired. And stressed. And to be honest, kind of depressed. She knew there were a ton of single moms out there just like her, scrimping to make ends meet and somehow come up with Christmas gifts for the kids. She had gone over her list as she shopped; mostly buying things they needed, clothes and such, and was sure she would be cutting it very close. She had no credit card and knew to the penny what was in her debit account. And had the electric bill to pay before her next check too.

When the big burly man asked to cut in front, she just nodded with weariness. One more thing. She was used to not mattering. No one cared about anyone else's problems. The man had something to say to the clerk, but Angie didn't pay any attention. She was mentally adding up the total again as she laid each item on the checkout conveyor belt.

She watched the digital numbers rise and climb and sighed with relief when the total was just under what she had calculated. And then her mouth dropped open as she reached out her debit card because the smiling clerk said, "Put that away, the man in front of you already paid for it."

Ripple.

Another twelve-hour shift standing at the cash register. This time of year was a killer. But there were good moments too, even during the mad holiday rush. Mariah saw a lot of greed and impatience and intolerance and outright ugliness from the never-ending line of customers. But she also was witness to bright moments of human kindness. Today, right before her shift ended, a man had paid $300 for a complete stranger's cart of gifts for her kids. And if Mariah was any judge, the woman needed all the help she could get.

She handed the register off to the next shift and with the leftover money in her hand, started towards the doors and the bell ringers outside. But then she paused. One act of kindness from a complete stranger had started an idea in her head. With what she held, and her employee discount, she figured she could buy three of those heavy winter coats on sale in the children's section. She turned around and went towards the apparel aisle. Her church was putting on a coats for kids drive and she could drop them off in the morning on the way to work.

Ripple.

Now that Mrs. Hamilton was retired, she tried to find things to keep herself busy, things that mattered. Her husband worked in a downtown office and she was on her own much of the day. She loved Christmas because there were all sorts of things to do. Just now, she was boxing up cookies to take to the church bake sale. She felt good about helping out in this small way. The Hamiltons didn't go to church often, but this time of year they liked to put in an appearance.

The church was walking distance, and as she approached the parking lot she saw a woman she recognized getting out of an old, somewhat beat up car and go around to the trunk.

Coming closer, Mrs. Hamilton recognized the girl as a member of the church. She couldn't remember her name but thought she was a cashier and not very well off at all. The girl took a handful of coats from the trunk and turned to carry them inside.

The coats reminded Mrs. Hamilton there was a drive for children in need. Suddenly the plate of cookies in her hand didn't feel very important. Then, she had an idea. Something to talk about with her husband tonight.

Ripple.

Pastor Tom sat in his office, wondering what the Hamiltons wanted on such short notice. It was the busiest time of year and he had several irons in the fire, but the phone call had sounded urgent and so he agreed to meet them right away.

"I won't waste your time, Pastor Tom." Mr. Hamilton leaned forward in his chair, gold watch prominent on his tanned wrist. He was handsome and still dressed in his business suit from the workday. His wife was well-dressed as always and expensively coiffured. Pastor Tom suppressed a sad smile to think of the contrast between these two and the bulk of his parishioners. The less fortunate, the poor, the sick, so many who had so little.

"We usually take a week and go to Hawaii in January," Mr. Hamilton said. "Chicago winter and all that. But we've been thinking. Maybe this year we'll stay home. Pastor, do you have any big money needs? Any projects you just don't know how to fund?"

Pastor Tom didn't hesitate. "Actually yes. Just yesterday it came to my attention Mrs. Morningdale had a tree fall on her roof during that last ice storm. From what I can tell, the house is actually open to the elements in one corner. I don't know if you know her, but she is, oh I would say going on eighty, and living on a fixed income. Poverty level would be my guess."

"Now isn't that something. And what kind of cost would that be?"

"Her neighbor dropped some coats off yesterday and was telling me about it. She said some men quoted her a fix for about five thousand dollars."

The Hamiltons shared a look. They smiled at each other and then Mr. Hamilton laughed out loud. "Well I don't know if you believe me Pastor Tom, but that is exactly what we budget for our trip every year."

Mr. Hamilton reached inside his coat and as he pulled out a leather checkbook, Pastor Tom was filled with a warm glow. He decided to scrap his upcoming sermon for a new one. He had just enough time to write one about the power of charity and the far-reaching effect of human kindness.

~ * ~ * ~

RF Thomas once studied journalism at Eastern Illinois University and now after more than 20 years in the manufacturing industry is chasing his American dream of becoming a full-time novelist. His published works are listed at rf-thomas.com. With lifelong roots in the Midwest, he currently calls Central Illinois home.

More Great Anthologies from WolfSinger Publications

Never Cheat a Witch – edited by Carol Hightshoe

Magical curses. Arcane revenge. Being transformed into a frog. Things evil witches do to mere mortals who cross their path. But, what if there is more to the story…

Deals made with a witch are magically binding and can bring dire consequences to those who even think about breaking them.

Whether they are seeking revenge for wrongs done to them, helping others or simply trying to live their lives—it is NEVER wise to try and cheat a witch.

Open your spell book and join our authors as they relate tales of witches and mortals. From classic fantasy witches to modern day witches and even the legendary Baba Yaga. Good and Evil as well as every shade of gray in between. And, yes—there is a prince who is turned into a frog.

Time Capsules – edited by Carol Hightshoe

Time Capsules–history and mystery–a gift or a message from the past to the future. Messages that can easily be misunderstood.

What were the reasons for passing along a pair of pink, fuzzy handcuffs?

A glass vial containing a perfect dandelion puff?

A Japanese Katana?

A red and blue scarf?

A wooden spoon?

What magic do these items contain? What stories do they tell?

From the past to the future. Mysteries and meanings abound within these pages, as well as reminders of the things people find precious. What will you find?

US/THEM – edited by Carol Hightshoe

US/THEM – THEM/US

Fear of the *Other* breeds hatred of the *Other*

They aren't like us—so they must be bad…inferior…dangerous…

Humans are by nature social animals, but we tend to bond with other humans with whom we have something in common: beliefs, experiences, likes and dislikes, etc.

With the expansion of humans across the planet, it seems that, even as our numbers grow, we find ways to whittle our groups into ever narrower, specialized, and exclusive blocks. We target the *Other* for the most minor differences and interpret everything from *THEM* as an insult or an attack.

Within these pages you will witness hatred, intolerance and fanaticism as well as love, understanding and acceptance. Most of all, I, and the authors, hope you discover stories that will cause you to pause and think before condemning someone as being *THEM* and not *US*.

Crunchy with Ketchup – edited by Carol Hightshoe

It has been said that one should never meddle in the affairs of dragons—for you are crunchy and taste good with ketchup.

Come enter the dragon's lair.

Take your chances with other would-be heroes and heroines who decide to face off against one of the biggest, baddest predators ever.

Witness a dragon civil war.

Hear the true story of the Battle of New Orleans.

Find out what it's like in the belly of a dragon.

Discover why cats can spell disaster when stealing a dragon's egg.

Meet a group of dragon riders who protect us from nuclear devastation.

Follow legends of modern dragons, only to find something very unexpected.

And more…

Crunchy with Chocolate – edited by Carol Hightshoe

It has been said that one should never meddle in the affairs of dragons—for you are crunchy and taste good with chocolate.

Come enter the dragon's lair and roll the dice. Within these pages you will still meet some of the biggest, baddest predators ever—but if you are lucky, you will also discover some that have a sweeter side.

Meet a dragon with a soft spot for hard luck cases and another who is a hopeless romantic.

Enjoy a musical battle between a dragon and the specter of one of the greatest guitarists to ever play.

Meet a dragon in trouble with other magical creatures because he enjoys hanging out with human children.

Join a mother and daughter and their teams of dragons on a dangerous cross-country race.

Reconnect with an imaginary friend – who is not so imaginary and escape the isolation of the pandemic.

And more…

So enter in BUT tread carefully—remember you are crunchy and taste good with chocolate.

Cat Tails: War Zone – edited by Rebecca McFarland Kyle and Dana Bell

Cats have been our companions since long before they graced the temples of Ancient Egypt. In addition to being members of our families, they have also stood with us through difficult times. From keeping pests and vermin away from our food stores to providing a comforting paw when we have been wounded; cats have been our sidekicks and friends in many different battles.

Cat Tails—War Zone contains twenty-five stories from Ancient Egypt to the far-flung future, about some amazing cats who have served as compatriots during war times. But beware, for they can also be tricksters sent to teach lessons.

The real heroes are the volunteers of SHADOW CATS, an Austin, Texas-based rescue that has saved the lives of 9,000-plus cats since 1997. Trappers, veterinarians, nurses, and adoption social workers volunteer to trap, neuter and return ferals, provide care for ill, injured and behaviorally-challenged cats, find perfect adoptive parents, educate on proper feline care, and advocate for real change in communities.

Proceeds from this book will continue their efforts.

Tales From the Fluffy Bunny – edited by Carol Hightshoe

Welcome to the Fluffy Bunny

We welcome everyone—especially those with a story to tell. Adventurers, mercenaries, guardsmen, merchants, noble and peasant. Whoever. If you have a tale to share, then come in and have a seat. First drink and a hot meal are on the house.

What's a tale without an audience to appreciate it? So, even if you don't have a tale to share, come in, pull up a seat and enjoy these 17 tales of how a warrior or their weapon earned their name.

Visit us at www.wolfsingerpubs.com for more information

www.ingramcontent.com/pod-product-compliance
Lightning Source LLC
Chambersburg PA
CBHW051507260626
47162CB00008B/2858